Too Little, Too Late?

LIFE AND LOVE:
A Lesbian Medical
Romance Series

M.T. CASSEN

CHAPTER ONE

RACING HEART

Pounding, *pounding, pounding.* The echo of Maddie's heartbeat continued to pound loudly in her ears. She was almost there. She could make it. Her breath came in quick bursts as she tried to relish each inhale. Even in the Spring, the bitter Chicago wind stung her face. Her legs ached as she listened to the wind whistle and the steady pounding of her heartbeat. *You've got this. Don't give up now.* She'd raised over $2,000 via sponsorships for this race, surpassing her initial goal by almost $500. Now all she had to do was finish the damn thing. Tears stung the back of her eyes as she stared forward and tried to drown out the sound of her breathing. *You've got this!*

Maddie Anderson knew she had no choice. Despite all the pain and agony, she had this. If she could trust those voices in her head, she could crumble. *Don't think that way. You've got this!*

Pounding, pounding, pounding.

With every race Maddie ran, she refused to listen to the doubt inside her. Yes, she was sore. She was on the verge of collapse. Yet, she had one person she had to do this for. He counted on her, and most importantly, he believed in her.

"Just a little while longer, Maddie. Don't stop now." From her peripheral vision, she saw the people standing on the side-lines. Many of them were friends who she had met through various charity races. They bonded over their love of runner's highs and their shared commitment to the American Heart Foundation. Many of her friends ran to raise money in memory of the loved ones that they had lost to heart disease. Maddie knew she could count on her friends at the foundation to counsel her through the highs and the lows. They weren't just friends; they were practically family. Some of them even drove out from the suburbs to watch her today. *That* was worth fighting for. The aching in her body wouldn't even allow her to stop that fight. She couldn't give up on the American Heart Foundation. She wasn't about to give up on herself. She could see the edge of the banner flapping in the wind signaling the finish line. She took in a deep breath and grinned. *Just a few more steps, and I'll be there. Her whole body buzzed with the thrill of success as she crashed through the banner noting the finish line.*

Her head came forward. She was panting. Her hands dropped to her knees. Eventually, she smiled. Just like the voices encouraged Maddie to continue, she didn't allow anything to get in the way. She did this, and she was proud that she succeeded.

Maddie fished her phone out of her pocket, sweat dripping from her face. She needed to mark this occasion. She pulled up Instagram and took a selfie. Her green eyes squinted in the sun, and her long, blonde ponytail was slick with sweat. She wore a pink nylon running top with her race number pinned squarely on the center of her chest, black running shorts, and her trusted Nike running shoes. She zoomed out and angled her camera so she could fit most of her outfit in the frame. Thankfully, Maddie never had to worry about the perils of running with large boobs. She was 5'3, and surprisingly muscular. In the photo, Maddie looked exhausted but happy. Satisfied with her selfie, she got to work perfecting the caption. She typed: Another ½ *Marathon for American Heart Foundation. Mission Accomplished.* "And send," she mumbled.

"Young'uns, nowadays, they're so self-absorbed. Why don't you look up from your phone for once and live a little?"

She looked up to see an older man shaking his head. He glared at her, and Maddie fought hard not to frown. He spun on his heel and started walking away, grabbing hold of the hand of a young boy.

"Sir, I don't see you running a half marathon!" Maddie yelled out.

The man never once stopped to acknowledge her remark as the boy beside him scrambled to keep up. Based on the age gap, she deduced it to be his grandson. The man moved faster, never once turning around to acknowledge her words.

Some people didn't understand the power of fighting for a cause with a tangible goal. She turned from the man and toddler, nearly bumping into a woman who approached her, towel in hand.

The woman held it up with a smile. "Thank you!" Maddie dabbed off the beads of sweat and wrapped the towel around her neck.

"Good race," the woman said. She smiled, but she left before Maddie could thank her.

Maddie headed off towards the cooling tent. The minute she entered it, she released a sigh. Now that's what was truly needed. She took a sip of her water and scanned the crowd. Her eyes landed on her father—the man behind her mission.

Her junior year of high school came rushing back to her. The memory was as vivid today as it was back then. A call that nearly changed the trajectory of her whole life. *Your father had a heart attack and is in ICU.* To Maddie, he seemed the spitting image of health. Little did she know that just because one doesn't get sick often doesn't mean they're the picture of health. He was always the strong one in the family, but a fried food and beer diet wasn't going to cut it. Knowing that she could lose him practically killed her. Luckily, he survived, and two weeks later, he was home.

She opened her eyes and stared back at him. He knew then that he had to live a healthier lifestyle, and Maddie ensured he never forgot that. Now in his mid-'60s, Dave Anderson's once thick, curly hair had thinned, and his beer gut had slimmed to a fatherly paunch. But, even though his round face had a couple more wrinkles, he had the same bright blue eyes that sparked whenever he heard anything interesting or caught a World War II documentary on T.V. He was Maddie's best friend. Maddie was with him every step of the way. Together they worked to incorporate healthy foods into his diet, and much to his chagrin, he even accompanied Maddie on the occasional run.

If she lost him, her world would never be the same. Her father was her one true rock, and doing what she could to ensure she was always there by his side was necessary.

When she drew closer, he looked up from his phone and grinned, slipping his phone into the pocket of his navy vest, which he wore over a white T-shirt emblazoned with the American Heart Foundation logo. "You did great out there, sweetheart."

He kissed her cheek.

"Thanks, Dad. Hope I made you proud."

"Always and forever." He held up his phone, and your fans seemed to agree. A twinge settled in her stomach, and Maddie clenched her gut. "Everything all right?" He arched an eyebrow and instinctively wrapped his arm around her shoulder.

Maddie quickly straightened up. "Of course."

Maddie forced a smile, despite the earlier tug that startled her. "I'm starving. I only had a couple of eggs and a smoothie before this." She got through the race thanks to a double shot of espresso and willpower. She released a slow breath, and her stomach lurched. She told herself that she was just hungry. It'd been a long morning. Her dad's smile returned, relieving Maddie.

"Let's go get something to eat," he said, keeping his arm around her.

Maddie grinned. That was what she needed— quality time with her dad and a good hot meal.

CHAPTER TWO

FRESH REVELATIONS

Maddie stifled a yawn. How could she be so tired when the day was barely beginning? She shook her head, "Focus, Maddie. Focus." She blinked a few times, shook her head, and then returned to the chart. The half-marathon over the weekend was still catching up to her. Why wouldn't she be exhausted? Her body was begging for rest.

"Not now. You have seven hours left in your shift," Maddie reprimanded herself.

Maddie glanced over the chart. Her next patient, Mike Bishop, was a regular. It wouldn't take her long to finish his session, and she could be onto her next patient. She heard a slight murmur and turned to see Lourdes Russo. Her cheeks flushed when she saw Lourdes staring at her. Lourdes was a cardiac nurse practitioner. She was higher up on the chain of command, compared to Maddie, who was just a nurse. Lourdes arched an eyebrow, then snickered.

"Talking to yourself?" Lourdes glanced around the empty nurse's station and winked, and Maddie felt a blush creeping up her cheeks. Why could she always get caught in the most awkward of situations?

"Are you sure you didn't see them? You just missed 'em," Lourdes grinned. Her face lit up most beautifully. Lourdes Russo was downright gorgeous. She had luminous brown eyes framed by ink-dark lashes and an olive-toned heart-shaped face; Maddie could barely force herself to look her in the eye. Lourdes wore her curly, dark hair in effortless waves that cascaded down her back. She was the only person Maddie knew who made scrubs look sexy. Maddie could see the outline of her curves beneath the cotton fabric of her scrubs. She couldn't help herself as she noted Lourdes' ample breasts straining beneath her top. Lourdes was a Mediterranean goddess. She looked like she should be sunning in Mykonos, not fielding patient concerns. She made Maddie look like a middle-school boy in comparison. While Lourdes was all soft lines and curves, moving through the hospital with ease and leaving behind a jasmine-scented cloud of her perfume, Maddie was flat as a board and practically tripped over her feet.

Maddie's heart clenched as she forced herself to look away and focus on Mike's chart. Besides, she consoled herself it had been years since she had been in a relationship or even gone on a date. Her last serious relationship ended after she graduated nursing school three years ago. Even though it was painful, Maddie and her ex Allison kept in touch, liking each other's Instagram posts now and again. Sure, it got lonely sometimes, but once work took over, she didn't even have time to focus on her broken heart. Nor did she have the time to plan elaborate dates for gorgeous Mediterranean women. Not that she ever thought about going out with Lourdes.

If she didn't look up, Lourdes was bound to leave. She heard a couple of pops and looked up to find Lourdes cracking her neck. Maddie's mouth was agape, and she stared. Lourdes' olive skin glowed, and her high-rise cheekbones shone below her light ruby blush. Lourdes shifted her neck, and a couple more pops sounded.

"Rough day?" Maddie asked.

"You could say that," Lourdes mumbled. She put on a bright smile.

"But hey, I didn't stop by to discuss my day. I wanted to talk to you."

Maddie tried not to frown," Oh yeah?"

What could Lourdes possibly have to discuss with her? Lourdes probably wanted to remind her of how green and inexperienced she was, unlike Lourdes.

"Patient concern?"

"Russo to room 124. Russo to room 124."

Lourdes turned from Maddie. Lourdes groaned and darted her gaze over to the room. "Hold that thought. We'll catch up later." She tossed a wave over her shoulder and rushed off. Lourdes disappeared into a room. Still, Maddie tried to hold her gaze.

Now she'd have to wait for however long to see what Lourdes needed to discuss with her. Surely, it had to do with work. What else could it be? Lourdes had only been with the department for three months. Before that, she worked in the ER for less than a year. They couldn't exactly be considered friends. Yet, acquaintances seemed harsh. She liked Lourdes, even though she didn't know much about her. But everything she did know seemed to point to the fact that Lourdes and her could get along outside the walls of CAPMED. Assuming Maddie's introverted nature wouldn't turn Lourdes away.

Someone cleared their throat behind her. She jerked and turned to see her best friend, Eric, a fellow nurse. Eric was stocky and jovial, with dirty blonde hair and brown eyes. Round dimples appeared on his cheeks whenever he smiled, which was often. He was only 5'9 but made up for it with his larger-than-life personality.

Eric chuckled, "What's with the thousand-yard stare?"

Maddie rolled her eyes. "I don't. Just thinking. Why do you always read too much into a situation?" She looked back down at the chart and then checked her watch. She still had some time before she had to grab her patient. "Has it been a long morning? Or is it just me?"

"I don't think it's been too bad. I'd say it's moving along rather nicely," Eric shrugged, and Maddie arched an eyebrow. It would have been nice if Eric had just nodded and agreed, but Eric was grinning, which caused Maddie to snicker.

"Then I guess it's just me."

The grin continued on Eric's face. "But seriously, though. Were you staring at Lourdes?" He wiggled his eyebrows when Maddie looked up to meet his gaze.

"What?" Maddie hissed. "You weren't just reading too much into a situation. You're downright foolish. Besides, why does it matter even if I was looking at Lourdes? Am I not allowed to look at a co-worker? Perhaps I should be forbidden to look at or even talk to another person besides you. Is that what you're saying? People can look at other people!"

Eric tilted his head. "Too much caffeine?"

"You started it," Maddie mumbled. She cringed. Why the sudden urge to go off on Eric? She grimaced and looked down at her patient's chart.

"You had a busy weekend. I saw your post on the 'gram. Your dad must be very proud. I know I was."

"Thanks, Eric." She forced a smile after rambling a few minutes earlier.

"I like to think I made him proud," she replied. "I raised another $500 once I posted the selfie at the finish line." Sometimes hiding behind the phone helped ease Maddie's nerves. While the thought of public speaking made her want to barf, social media allowed her to share her story without the added pressure of face-to-face interaction.

"I saw that pic, too."

Maddie looked up when another voice joined the conversation. Shannon, a fellow nurse, came into the station. She picked up a bottle of water hidden by the phone and took a swig. "I was there, too," she added.

"I thought I saw you before the race started," Maddie replied. "Great job to you, as well."

Shannon nodded. "You were ahead of me, but it was still exhilarating to be able to run."

"Exactly," Maddie said. "Not about who's ahead, just who participates. No one gets ahead by sitting on the bench."

Eric arched an eyebrow. "You're making me feel like a complete dud," Eric replied. He offered a teasing grin.

Maddie laughed. "You had an excuse. Someone had to work."

"Best get back to work. See ya around." Shannon waved and left the station.

"Weird," Eric mumbled. "That's the most she's ever really talked." While it was true, Maddie didn't think much about it. "But as you can see…everyone thought you did great."

Maddie smiled, brimming with pride. She released a yawn and covered her mouth. "Now, if this day would just speed up a little, I can go home, have a long bath, and get some rest. But, enough about me. How's James?"

Eric's grin grew wider. "As gorgeous as ever."

Maddie giggled, grabbing Mike's chart. "I swear, the two of you make the cutest couple."

Eric sighed. "Don't stop. Tell me more. Tell me more."

Maddie playfully slapped his shoulder with the chart. "Give James a kiss for me," Maddie said, winking.

"My patient awaits." She held up the chart.

"Talk to you soon." Maddie barely survived Eric's teasing. Her heart hadn't stopped racing since Lourdes disappeared into the patient's room.

"Looking forward to it," Eric called out, sitting behind the computer. Maddie's thoughts shifted to the other woman, and she couldn't help but smile. Suddenly, Maddie wasn't so tired after all. Still, she wondered what Lourdes could ever want from her.

CHAPTER THREE

A FLUTTERING HEART

"Hey, Mike! How are you doing today?" Maddie called as she entered his room. The rapport she developed with patients was one of her favorite parts of her job. She got to know the patients almost as well as her family and friends.

Mike smirked and gave a slight grunt. "Same ol' same ol', you could say." Maddie helped guide him through the triage area, nodding at other familiar faces as they trudged down the hall. He didn't walk as quickly as Maddie would have liked to report. His breathing seemed a bit raspy after just a few words. He shrugged, "I've had worse days, I suppose."

Maddie smiled, letting Mike lead them into the room where the rest of the session would occur. "Before you know it, you'll have some of your best days." She winked, and he grinned in response.

"I'll hold you to that."

Maddie motioned for the chair, but Mike had already started to take his seat. Most of these therapy sessions consisted of a routine built over time. Maddie was confident that many of her patients would rather be anywhere but here. Some would choose a root canal over the pain therapy brought them. Yet, it was Maddie's job to maintain the comfort they received. It was how she wished her father had been treated when he was in the same position. Sadly, she was aware that when he was in the hospital under emergent care, most times, he was a number. The staff appeared overworked and rushed, sometimes coming across as bothered. From that moment on, she vowed that once she became a nurse, she would always do her best to make her patients valued and welcomed. But nursing didn't come as naturally to her as she had hoped during her days at school. Some days, she felt a panicked ache in her chest the moment she walked through the doors of CapMed. Even so, every day she walked into work, she made good on that promise to herself, her father, and her patients.

"So, it's been a week since you were last here. Have you noticed an increase in stamina and endurance?" She tossed his file down on the counter and moved over to him. She grabbed the blood pressure cart and wheeled it over to him. As she put on the cuff, he shrugged.

"Not particularly." He quickly looked away from her, glancing at the corny painting of Lake Michigan that hung on the back wall beside the clock. Maddie heard his labored breathing.

She documented his pulse and grabbed his blood pressure as the machine beeped. "It's a little high today. Are you sure you're not exerting yourself more than usual?"

He shook his head, but his face fell. "Guess I forgot to take my meds the past couple of days."

Maddie groaned. "Just a couple?"

Again, he shrugged. "Maybe a few."

"That's not a good sign. The meds are needed to make sure your BP stays regulated. Long periods of hypertension increase the risk of heart attacks. That's not good for you or your loved ones," Maddie admonished.

"Geez, doctor. I'll do better." He added a teasing smile, but Maddie wanted him to take it more seriously. When things got intense, Mike tended to overcompensate with the jokes, and Maddie feared he didn't truly realize how important his health was. She felt her palms start to sweat. A tinge of pain tugged at her heart, and she released a shaky breath.

"At least try, Mike. You owe it to yourself and that son of yours."

"I know. You're right." The earnest look on his face relieved Maddie slightly. "But I guess I'm just getting frustrated. I keep telling myself that we haven't been doing this for that long and that I have to be patient and have faith that things will be back to normal one day."

Maddie removed the cuff from him, pushed the machine to the side, then sat on the stool and continued watching him. His lips curved downward, and he shifted his eyes to the floor.

"It hasn't been that long. But I have to ask...." Maddie smirked slightly. "After all, it's in my contract and how I get paid." Mike snickered but never spoke out of turn.

"Besides the not taking your medicine part, are you going by the doctor's orders? Have you been doing your breathing exercises? Have you been gradually working on your cardio?"

"Of course," he quickly responded. His eyes dropped the minute he met Maddie's gaze. "Mostly."

Maddie groaned. She was so close. "I see." She jotted down a note. He wasn't the most responsible patient, but being a single father, she knew he took pride in being there for his son. "How's Myles doing? He's getting ready to try out for the little league, right?"

He nodded. " He wants to be a pitcher." Mike proudly sat up in his chair, a huge grin crossing his lips.

"If memory serves me, you were a pitcher in college, right?" Maddie inquired.

"Until a shoulder injury took me out. I don't want Myles to have to deal with the same suffering I had to. Once that happened, I felt like I had lost my way. I'll be damned...." He snapped his mouth shut. "Pardon the language."

Maddie smiled. "No need to apologize."

"I just want to ensure he's ready and prepared for what life is about to throw him."

"So, have you been helping him? Probably doing some conditioning on the field?" Maddie arched an eyebrow.

He smirked. "Hey, you said cardio, right?"

"Well, there is such a thing as too *much* cardio. Whatever you do, don't overdo it." He opened his mouth to argue, but Maddie held up her hand. "Myles is everything to you. You want the best for him. I get it. Just don't overdo it."

"Aw shucks, Maddie. Keep that up, and people will start to believe you care." He gave her a wink.

Maddie shook her head. "And you, kind sir, are just trying to change the subject."

"Did it work?" he teased.

Maddie laughed and nodded. "You know the drill. Follow me."

Maddie led him out of the room and down the long corridor to the physical therapy room. "Noelle will be right with you." She put her hand on his right shoulder and squeezed slightly. "Take care of yourself. I'll be seeing you next week."

"See ya, Maddie."

She closed the door behind him and returned to the nurse's station. She wouldn't be doing this job, living the stress that came with it, if she didn't care. She hoped all patients realized how much she truly cared for each of them.

When she got back to the station, she glanced at her watch. "You still here?" she teased. "Don't you have patients to take care of?"

Eric glanced up from the screen. "I've been gone and back. What took you so long?"

Maddie shrugged. "Guess I provide a little more TLC than the next person." Maddie glanced over her shoulder, and he scowled. It was all good fun, as Eric could dish it out as much as the next person. Turning back to her computer screen, she spotted Lourdes and gave her a slight nod before returning to her documentation.

"It's been one hectic morning," Lourdes said, sighing as she entered the work area. " I've been trying to eat this freaking apple since 9:00 A.M. That's how bad it's been. No downtime. Nothing. Guess the good part is that the day is zooming by."

Lourdes snuck over to the nurse's station and fished an apple from her canvas tote bag, which she had stashed under the desk.

The apple crunched loudly. Lourdes chewed and swallowed before glancing up at Maddie and giving her a friendly smile. Maddie returned the smile, then tried to look back at her computer. "Definitely a busy one. I don't know where the day's gone."

Eric shot a confused glance in her direction, "Well, you know what they say, time flies when you're having fun. And with gorgeous co-workers such as yours truly, not to mention L—."

Maddie kicked his shin, and he shot her a look, then grinned and looked away from her. "You were saying?" Lourdes asked.

Eric shrugged, "Never mind."

"It certainly has been a crazy day," Maddie said, staring at her computer. She could see Eric smirking out of the corner of her eye.

"Not always a bad thing, I suppose. But sometimes, these patients are enough to drive anyone up the wall," Lourdes exclaimed.

Maddie looked up, suddenly intrigued by the conversation.

Lourdes continued, "Take room 124. I'm getting called every thirty seconds because her oxygen is slipping." She rolled her eyes. "It's not. She's just a hypochondriac, and everything goes wrong in her eyes." Lourdes heaved a sigh. "But I don't have to tell you about troublesome patients. You both experience that, in many ways, more than I do." Lourdes took another bite of her apple.

Maddie looked back to her computer and quickly finished the notes, ensuring that Mike's physical therapist, Noelle, had everything she needed in Mike's chart. Another crunch of the apple and Maddie turned to Lourdes.

"Yeah, sure, we all have those patients."

Lourdes smiled and tossed her half-eaten apple into the trash can. "Enough about that, though. Seeing I have about five minutes, I was going to talk to you, Maddie."

"Oh yeah. That's right." Maddie was glad Lourdes had brought it up again. She didn't want to appear eager to hear what she had to tell her.

"I saw your Instagram post after the race. Kudos to you for raising so much money. I heard that you raised over two grand. That's amazing! Good job."

"Yeah, I raised over my goal, so that was pretty cool," Maddie said.

Maddie's cheeks burned once again. How exactly did she hear this? To her knowledge, Lourdes didn't follow her. Right? Perhaps she heard others talking and just happened to glance at the post. Either way, Lourdes acknowledged it. Maddie didn't do charity runs for recognition or to give people an excuse to pat her on the back. But sometimes, running these races felt thankless, even isolating as she dipped out on plans with Eric to train. While it was the last thing Maddie expected, it felt great that someone like Lourdes acknowledged her hard work.

"Wow, thank you. That's nice of you to say. I was just happy to do my part."

Lourdes glanced at her watch. "Keep up the great work. Back to work, I go." She waved, then rushed away from the station. Maddie's gaze followed after her. Lourdes' ponytail swung behind her, exposing her elegant neck. Lourdes moved through the world with a dancer's grace. Her back muscles rippled in her scrubs as she walked. For a moment, Maddie wondered how holding her close and kissing her would feel. She thought about how it would feel to have those strong arms hold her and finally muster up the courage to press her lips to hers. Maddie bit down on her lower lip and couldn't tear her eyes away.

Eric laughed. "So, apparently, James and I will have to duke it out with you and Lourdes to see who's the cutest couple in this hospital."

Maddie twirled around. "Huh? What? Excuse me?"

Eric grinned. He cupped his hands together and swayed back and forth, cooing like a love-sick teenager. Maddie's jaw dropped as Eric continued to smile.

"You ladies would be on fire." He shook his hand. "Sizzling hot. Like, grab the hose and water you down, hot."

Maddie rolled her eyes. "In your dreams."

He laughed. "I mean it. I saw the way you looked at her. You looked like you were in heat or something."

"Are you serious?"

She cupped her hand against his mouth. "Shut up! You're making me sound like an absolute horn dog. Besides, I don't even sound like that. I was strictly having a simple conversation with another employee. Or am I not allowed to converse with other co-workers either?" He laughed, and she slowly pulled her hand away. She playfully slapped his wrist.

"And what do you think you were doing? You were out here trying to make me sound like a whiny fool. Some friend!"

His jaw dropped, "Why do you even care? I mean, if she's just a co-worker and all."

Maddie rolled her eyes. "Just because I don't want my co-worker to think I'm lazy doesn't mean I have a crush on them. I just don't want to look like a slacker. Besides, Lourdes is a mature woman. Even if I were the least bit intrigued, it wouldn't happen."

Eric scoffed. "Maddie, give yourself some credit! You're smart, you're funny, and you're an absolute catch! Perhaps if Lourdes knew you were interested, things would move right along." He winked as Maddie looked away from him. Her eyes landed on Lourdes, who was now talking to another woman, someone Maddie didn't recognize.

"You're relentless," Maddie mumbled. She could see her silhouette as she laughed and spoke with the stranger. Her smile was gorgeous. Her eyes seemed to dance with every movement she made. Anyone would have to be blind not to notice how beautiful it was inside and out. "We're so different." Maddie turned back to him. He was smiling so big that the skin around his eyes was crinkled.

"You heard the way she talked about her patient. It's like she doesn't even care or have empathy."

"Maddie, girl, stop making excuses! Lourdes has plenty of empathy. She's just a little more cynical than you. You might be the woman that can break through that rough exterior." Without another word, he left her, and she glanced at Lourdes. At that exact moment, Lourdes turned and caught her staring. Lourdes smiled slightly, catching Maddie off guard. Lourdes turned back to the other woman. She didn't misread that, did she? Lourdes genuinely smiled, almost like she could read Maddie's mind. Maddie spun on her heel, swallowing the lump in her throat. Her cheeks were on fire again. It was ridiculous even to consider.

Even if, at that moment, her knees were about to buckle and her heart was aflutter.

CHAPTER FOUR

GROWING INFATUATION

An intercom screeched to life as Maddie walked towards the break room.

"Just five minutes," she whispered, practically willing the loudspeaker to call another name. She waited, then waited a few more seconds. How long has it been? She glanced at her watch like she wanted to count the minutes. All she heard was the sound of fuzziness and soft chatter. Perhaps a mistake. Then the intercom went dead. She sighed, and a smile crept to her lips. She might get those five minutes after all.

She pushed into the break room and grabbed the seat furthest from the door, feeling her body sigh with relief. Today was a mad-house. Three patients came in on an incorrect day and had to be worked into the schedule. Two other patients were nearly twenty minutes late for their appointment. It seemed as if the minute she felt caught up, another bevy of problems appeared, vying for her attention. Maddie yawned just as a notification vibrated on her phone.

She slid the phone out of her pocket and pulled up Instagram, smiling when she spotted her dad's name. He liked her latest post on eating healthy when you're addicted to carbs. *Everything is necessary for a heart-healthy lifestyle.*

"Thank you, Dad," she mumbled.

He had come a long way when it came to social media. Maddie never thought she'd see the day when her dad liked her posts and followed everything she had to say. But sometimes, people have a way of changing, even when kicking and screaming.

She scrolled through her posts; each one garnered more and more likes. It was all about getting noticed, which would ensure people were talking. That's when you get awareness out there, and that's when you make a difference. She smiled. It worked.

The door to the break room swung open, and Maddie looked up to catch Lourdes' gaze as she entered. Lourdes smiled widely. "Hey there!"

"Hey!" Maddie warbled. She swallowed. Why was she suddenly so nervous?

"Mind if I sit down?" Lourdes motioned to the seat across from her.

"Of course not." Maddie quickly slid her phone back into her pocket.

Lourdes took a long swig of her water, and Maddie couldn't look away. Her skin glistened with beads of sweat as if she had just been outside in the blazing sun. As Lourdes smiled at Maddie as she put down her water. Maddie looked away quickly.

She had been gawking long enough. She needed to control herself. In the space of one week, her crush on Lourdes became an infatuation. Whenever she thought of Lourdes, her heart quickened and her breath grew ragged.

"It's a hot one on the floor. I sometimes think administration thinks when it's colder outside, they need to bump the heat up to 100." Lourdes laughed. It was like the sound of music moving through the air. Maddie could listen to Lourdes laugh for hours. Unfortunately, it died way too soon.

"Don't ya think?" Maddie met her gaze, realizing she probably had been gawking at Lourdes. "Yeah, absolutely. They can never seem to regulate the temperature correctly."

"Another busy day. At least I can grab a few minutes to sit down."

"Agreed." Lourdes' foot briefly brushed over hers. Maddie jerked but tried not to dwell on the simple movement. Lourdes didn't seem to notice as she took a long drink of her water.

"But hey, I was gonna talk to you more about the half-marathon."

Maddie quickly jolted back to attention, moving her gaze to Lourdes'. "Oh yeah?" Maddie assumed they had all the conversation they needed to regarding the race. It'd been five days since they first discussed it. She hadn't anticipated a replay of that conversation. Yet, at that moment, she would have talked to Lourdes about the break room's new carpet if it meant getting a few more minutes with her. "What's that?"

"The truth is," Lourdes started, taking another sip of her water. "I was supposed to be there, too."

"Really?"

Lourdes shrugged. "Got called into work early. Not much

you can do when they're down a practitioner. But, as for you, I see you're continuing to gain the pledges. Even a week after the race is over. Truth be known, I pledged under your campaign. Don't tell the other staff members." She winked, and Maddie got lost in those eyes of hers. When Lourdes quirked up her lips into a smile, Maddie blushed.

She wished she had her bottle of water to hide behind. She didn't even have a chance to grab her phone.

"Thank you, Lourdes. Won't say a word." She crossed her ankles and accidentally kicked Lourdes. "Oh, sorry," Maddie mumbled.

"No worries." Lourdes took another sip, and Maddie stood up from the table. As she walked over to the vending machine, she was mindful of the sound of her feet tapping against the linoleum. "Well, now that you mentioned, I'm surprised you're into social media and all that stuff." I'm *especially surprised that you follow me.* Maddie bit her tongue so that she wouldn't word-vomit all over Lourdes. She got herself a bottle of water and turned to face the table. Lourdes had her eyes fixated on Maddie.

"Are you kidding me? The hospital is abuzz with the star athlete. I have no choice but to check it out." She winked again. Maddie's toes curled. She looked down, so Lourdes wouldn't notice how one moment had turned Maddie into mush. Maddie opened the water and chugged it before returning to the table. "It's impressive, Maddie. You should be very proud of yourself." Lourdes grinned. "I'm embarrassing you."

"No, you're not," Maddie quickly blurted, staring Lourdes square in the eye. Lourdes nodded, giving a knowing smile.

"You should be used to people gushing. After all, the way

you get likes and comments on your Instagram, you're very popular."

"I wouldn't go that far," Maddie softly stated. "Besides, I did this for my Dad."

Lourdes arched an eyebrow, and the table was silent. Maddie didn't know how much she wanted to dive into more information. She had already said way more than she expected. Lourdes didn't waver from the staring match that had ensued.

"It's a long story," Maddie continued.

"I see." Lourdes took a long swig of water, finishing off the bottle. "Perhaps you'll tell me about it sometime. Maybe even over coffee?"

"Maybe," Maddie whispered.

Lourdes stood up from the table and tossed the bottle into the trash can, making a perfect score, then glancing back at Maddie momentarily. Maddie swallowed another lump that was lodged deep in her throat.

"How about tomorrow?" Lourdes asked.

Maddie's jaw dropped slightly. Was she asking her out on a date? Or was this strictly platonic? *Breathe, Maddie. Breathe.*

"I've made you uncomfortable," Lourdes replied. "It's just an idea. Forget I ever said anything." She turned around. "I'll be seeing ya."

"Yes," she blurted out before Lourdes could reach the door. "I'd love to grab a coffee with you. That sounds nice. Have you ever been to Jolt?" Jolt was a trendy coffee shop located a couple of blocks from CapMed that served artisanal lattes made with house-made syrups that were small-batch, healthy alternatives to the store-bought syrups that Starbucks shilled. Maddie liked to buy their beans in bulk. Whenever she felt down, one sip of their cardamom rose latte never failed to brighten her day. She suspected Lourdes would enjoy it if she weren't already a regular. Lourdes looked over her shoulder, grinning in a way that made Maddie's stomach drop. "I love Jolt! It's one of my favorite spots in the city. Let's plan on it! I'll see you tomorrow, yeah?"

Lourdes left the break room, and Maddie sank back into her chair. She couldn't wait. The next day could be one of the best days of her life as long as she didn't get in her own way. She tried to tamp down the burgeoning hope that was bubbling in her stomach, but she couldn't stop smiling.

CHAPTER FIVE

COFFEE FOR TWO

Maddie spotted Lourdes as soon as she walked into Jolt. She wore a ribbed forest green crop top paired with dark-wash high-waisted jeans and beat-up Converse sneakers. Lourdes gathered her long, dark hair into a ponytail at the nape of her neck. She looked gorgeous, as always, sun-kissed and undeniably alive. Maddie yanked at the hem of her favorite flannel, wondering if she'd dressed too casually. After an hour-long pep talk from Eric last night where he urged her to "just be yourself," she'd picked her favorite flannel and perfectly worn Wrangler jeans. It was early Spring, and the sun was starting to shine more, but it was still chilly during the day. She paired the flannel with a black short-sleeved T-shirt. She'd had this flannel since she was twenty. The red and black buffalo check pattern had faded, and the fabric was soft. It felt like a hug. It made her feel confident, and she figured she could use all the extra confidence she could get. She'd stuffed her wallet and phone into a beat-up tote bag and practically shoved herself out the door before she could devise an excuse. Except now, standing next to Lourdes in a hip coffee shop decorated with hanging Edison bulbs and a mural made out of dried flowers, she felt like a lumberjack who stumbled into the wrong place.

Lourdes smiled when she saw her, "Hey! I was just looking at their new Spring specials. Do you have a favorite?" she asked.

Maddie walked over to her, and to her surprise, Lourdes enveloped her in a hug. Her shampoo smelled like lavender and thyme, earthy yet feminine.

"I, uh, the, uh, rose cardamom latte is really good," she stuttered.

Lourdes beamed, "That's what I was looking at!" She turned to the barista, an artfully tattooed hipster in their mid-twenties, "Two rose cardamom lattes, and," she glanced at Maddie, "Do you want any snacks?"

"Their vegan breakfast bars are great," Maddie said. Her stomach growled. She had been too nervous to eat before she met up with Lourdes.

"And two vegan breakfast bars," Lourdes added. Maddie dug around her tote for her wallet, but Lourdes grabbed her wrist and stopped her.

"I've got it," she grinned, handing over her card before Maddie could protest.

After a couple of cursory laps around the shop, Maddie and Lourdes found an open table. Lourdes grabbed their drinks from the bar and passed Maddie a steaming mug and a breakfast bar.

Maddie nibbled the edge, trying to find comfort in the familiar sweetness of carob chips and maple syrup and the crunch of oats and pepitas.

Maddie glanced at Lourdes over her coffee cup; her breath caught again. Why was it she was suddenly feeling like a princess in a fairy tale, and Lourdes was the woman there to whisk her away? She cleared her throat and took a quick drink. Lourdes' eyes latched onto her, and a hint of a smile sparked on her lips.

"I have to tell you something, Maddie." Lourdes put her cup down, her eyes steady.

"I didn't think you would say yes."

Maddie smirked, staring down at her coffee, then looked up, hoping her eyes were filled with flirtatious curiosity even though she felt so timid.

"I'll admit I wasn't sure I should." *Or whether this was even classified as a date.* The flirtatious smirks and lust-filled glances Lourdes tossed her way slowly reassured Maddie that nothing about this was platonic.

Maddie situated herself in her seat, hoping to straighten her posture and project an aura of maturity and confidence. Lourdes didn't need to know that she was a total introvert just yet; that was a third-date problem. Maddie slid a finger around a strand of her dirty blonde hair and pushed it behind her ear. She was glad she had let her hair down from her usual ponytail at work. It helped to make her into the strong woman she hoped she could be.

"I'm glad you did." Lourdes took a sip of her coffee, then grinned wider. "I don't know a ton of people in the department. Since I've been there for a few months, it's hard to know who I can trust and count on. It's lonely when you don't feel like you have a confidante."

"For sure," Maddie shifted again in her seat.

"So, I need to know what's up with the staff. Who can I trust? Who should I avoid? I need a tour guide. I need someone who can give me the lay of the land." That's what this was. Maybe all the flirtation was so that Lourdes could use Maddie. Was that all?

Disheartened, Maddie continued, "Well, I can tell you that everyone in our department is great. You can pretty much count on them to do anything for you."

She reached for her cup of coffee. "But, I imagine it's probably similar to the ER." She drank from her mug, forgetting it was fresh and piping hot. She gasped, choking, nearly dropping the mug on the table.

"Are you alright?" Lourdes jumped up and hurried over to Maddie's side, quickly patting her on the back as Maddie attempted to catch her breath.

"I'm fine. Good." She coughed loudly and shook her head. She wasn't fine. She practically choked to death in front of the woman she was romantically interested in. What had gotten into her? This wasn't like her. She didn't go outside of her comfort zone. Where did it leave her? Choking and red-faced, looking like a complete dweeb.

"Hang on a second," Lourdes' returned a few seconds later. She forced a glass of water to Maddie's lips.

Maddie grabbed the glass. "Thank you!" she muttered, taking a sip of ice water, desperate to soothe her burnt throat. "All better." She choked, forcing a smile, but Lourdes knelt before her. Lourdes' brows furrowed. "I mean it; I'm fine. It just went down the wrong pipe. No need to be concerned."

Lourdes tilted her head but then backed up to her chair and sat down. "I know CPR and the Heimlich maneuver if you would have needed either one." She winked, which caused Maddie to drop her gaze to her water. Why was Lourdes flirting with her if Maddie was just a work friend? Why the mixed signals at all? She took a drink of her water.

"So, as I was saying…." She tried to calm her breathing with a couple of short breaths.

"Our department probably isn't much different than the ER. I'm sure you made friends and such there. You were there for a year, right?"

"Ten months," Lourdes replied.

"And I suppose, but there really wasn't anyone I hit it off with. I mostly came to work, did my job, went home, and that was it. Sure, I know people, but what does it really matter when you have no true outside connections? You know what I mean?"

Maddie nodded slowly, quite surprised by Lourdes' response. Lourdes seemed talkative. She was personable and always in good spirits. Maddie couldn't fathom that Lourdes didn't make friends everywhere she went. She sipped on her water, her throat slowly getting its sensation back.

"Plus, I've never really vibed with anyone to the point where I wanted to really get to know them."

"Well, I can assure you that if you need anything, you can come to any of us."

"That's always great to hear," Lourdes replied. "But since you're here, I want to know more about you."

"I'm not going anywhere," Maddie laughed, taking another

sip of water, then pushing it out of the way to get back to her coffee. Slowly her embarrassment dissipated. They were there. She would sit back and see what Lourdes' agenda was.

"You're pretty athletic, aren't you? You did the half-marathon. You've got those runner thighs of steel. .."

Maddie's cheeks burned from the compliment. "I do my best. I enjoy jogging whenever I get the chance. Eating a healthy diet is also very important to me."

"Same here," Lourdes replied.

"I choose to stay mostly vegetarian. Once I went that route, I felt much better. I used to be constantly exhausted. Ever since I started eating organic, I've felt like I could run a marathon. I'm not a star athlete like you, of course."

Maddie felt herself blushing again.

"That's amazing." Maddie leaned into the conversation, putting her choking fiasco behind her.

"I had a friend in high school who had chronic fatigue. She had to see all these specialists, but maybe she should have gone that route."

Lourdes smiled, "It isn't for everyone, but I can't imagine my life any other way." Maddie watched as Lourdes sipped her coffee. Her olive complexion continued to glow behind the coffee cup. Maddie's heart did a flip-flop. When Lourdes met her gaze, Maddie diverted her gaze and reached for her coffee cup. This wasn't a date, not in Lourdes' eyes. Now that she knew that, she had to force herself not to get lost in every word Lourdes spoke.

"What do you want out of life, Maddie?" The question surprised Maddie; she feared she would start choking again. Maddie tried to avoid ever pondering those sorts of questions her whole life. She always believed that nothing else mattered as long as she was with her father, a belief that only intensified after his health scare. Why dream? Why have goals? Why not just live in the moment, and whatever happens, happens?"

"I guess I never really considered it," Maddie admitted.

Lourdes sat back. Her mouth hung open.

"You never drew out a road map to your life? You've never wondered where you would be in five years or ten? You never desired something so intensely that if you didn't have that one thing in your life, you would break?"

Maddie giggled. Yet, Lourdes didn't shake her attention." I…" She closed her mouth, then shrugged.

"Tell me about your dad."

Maddie frowned. "Huh?"

"Well, you said that you did the half-marathon because of him. Right?" Maddie nodded.

"Tell me about him because I'll tell you that you were glowing in that picture from the race. I saw passion there and a desire to help others. So, share that with me. Please?"

Did she see all that from a single picture? Maddie began to tell her everything, from how she nearly lost him to the moment she realized she had to be the one to change his lifestyle. If she didn't, who would? Maddie shared how she hated seeing the nursing staff treat her dad and how that inspired her to become a nurse. She told her more than she had ever confided in another human, and Lourdes followed every word.

Maddie blushed. "You ask, and you shall receive. I tend to overshare.."

"That's why you do what you do. That's who you are, and if that isn't passion, then I don't know what is," Lourdes said. She reached across the table and placed her palm on Maddie's hand. Maddie didn't move away.

Instead, Maddie met her gaze again, "So, now that you know my life story, what about you? What makes Lourdes, well, Lourdes?"

Lourdes leaned back into her chair, "I knew from a young age," Lourdes began, "that I wanted to see the world. I have traveled close and far, helping others, volunteering where needed."

She smiled and grabbed her phone. Maddie watched as she swiped through several images before showing Maddie the picture, "Here I am at the Pyramids in Egypt."

"Wow!" Maddie exclaimed.

"That's amazing."

"I can't imagine not traveling. And I can't imagine not helping others." She grabbed her phone back and slipped it back into her pocket.

"You and I are alike in so many ways. We go all in for things that are important to us. We both like to exercise. We try our best to eat healthily," Lourdes continued to tick off things. Maddie nodded after each one. Maddie was exhilarated by what they did have in common. It made their differences seem so trivial.

"We do have a lot in common. More than I even realized. It's just …" Her words trailed off, and she sipped her coffee. She couldn't stop the burning question that played in her mind.

"I guess I'm a little confused about what this is. You know, us together in this coffee shop," Maddie confessed.

Lourdes tilted her head, a sparkle in her eye. "What do you think it is?"

"I'm not sure," Maddie cautiously admitted, laughing. "That's why I ask."

When Lourdes didn't attempt to move, Maddie proceeded. "I mean, I guess there was a part of me that thought maybe it was a date." She choked out the last word, leaving a bad taste in her mouth.

"But after we talked, I thought maybe it was just that you wanted a friend. But then I opened up about my dad, and you talked about your trips. I'm just as confused as ever."

"I see." Lourdes sipped her coffee as she pondered Maddie's confusion. "Let me rephrase the question. What would you like this to be?"

Maddie shook her head, "Nope, I'm not falling for that one."

"It's just a question." Lourdes laughed, and her eyes twinkled. "I can tell you're a thinker. Come on, go for it."

"It's not that easy," Maddie argued. "Not for me."

"Well, perhaps you'll change. It's possible. But the question remains. Do you want this to be a date? It's as simple as that." *Simple?* Nothing was simple about this. However, Maddie knew she wouldn't be the one caught in expressing her thoughts and feelings. That wasn't her. Not now. Not ever. She remained quiet. After a brief moment of hesitation, Lourdes proceeded. "I've done some research at the hospital. It's a mutual love-fest."

Maddie frowned. "What do you mean?"

"I just meant that when I asked around the other day. Everyone said I wouldn't find a better person than you." She snickered, "Especially Eric. He gushes about you. I can see why."

"Eric is a good guy. I've known him awhile."

"That's what I hear. The whole staff loves you."

"Is that so?" Maddie asked quietly.

Lourdes nodded enthusiastically, "I just knew that you were someone I needed to get to know better. I suppose you could say that I was hoping this was a date. I mean, you seemed pretty pumped to grab a coffee with me."

"I did not!" Maddie argued, just as Lourdes winked. Maddie snapped her mouth shut. "You're teasing me."

Lourdes shrugged. "It's so much fun."

Again, a bright red blush crept up her cheeks as Lourdes leaned into her, her eyes fixated. While Maddie knew the temptation was there. The chemistry was on fire, and everything aligned just right. There was still something throwing her off.

"When doing your research, did you happen to find out my age?" Maddie inquired, staring into her coffee.

"Maybe," Lourdes replied. Maddie looked up to catch Lourdes smirking. "Do you know how old I am?"

Maddie snickered and looked away from her. "Not exactly, but I imagine mid-thirties. While I'm—"

"Twenty-five." Lourdes winked. "Age is just a number. So what if there's a ten-year age difference? It doesn't bother me. I hardly notice."

Maddie smiled, sitting back in her seat. Perhaps it wasn't enough to warrant concern. Then why should Maddie make it such a big deal?

The date continued with no break in the conversation, leaving Maddie enthralled about the future. They exited Jolt, walking down a side street to get to Maddie's car. Maddie unlocked her car and awkwardly shifted her weight from one foot to the other.

"So, I had a great time. I must confess I'm happy that we determined date vs. no date," Maddie admitted.

"Me too." Lourdes laughed. "It was nice." Lourdes' laugh and smile were so sexy that Maddie was confident she wanted Lourdes to lean in for a kiss. The feeling was mutual; she could see the desire written all over Lourdes' face.

"Well, Maddie…" Lourdes began.

Maddie snickered. "Well, Lourdes," she replied with a teasing smirk.

Lourdes slowly leaned in. Maddie could smell the scent of Lourdes' perfume and feel her soft breath on her upper lip. But the moment vanished before she could make a move. Instead of closing the distance between them, Lourdes jerked away like a frightened animal.

"I have to get back to work. I'll be seeing you." Lourdes grumbled, affectless.

Maddie's jaw dropped as Lourdes hurried towards her bike. She watched as she got on, rode off, and left Maddie clueless. What just happened, and was the last hour only a dream?

CHAPTER SIX

JOGGING ENCOUNTER

"**A**re you heading out for the night ?" Eric asked as Maddie approached the nurse's station.

"Yep. I'm going for a quick run before heading home. Wanna join me?"

"Thanks for the offer, but James and I have a hot date planned tonight, and I need to shower. Can't be having my man disgusted."

Maddie smirked. "No, you can't. You guys have fun. Don't do anything I wouldn't do." She winked at him and then turned to see Lourdes headed their way. When Lourdes caught her eye, she diverted her direction and walked away from them. Lourdes hadn't said one word to Maddie since their date. Maddie sighed.

"That was awkward," Eric noted.

"Even I felt the chill over here. You guys haven't talked, have you?"

"Nope." Maddie groaned. Lourdes had been avoiding her like the plague for the past week and a half. They had a great time. They both agreed that it was a date. Lourdes paid for it, and all was well until that awkward moment at the car, where their spark fizzled just as quickly as it occurred.

Maddie shrugged, "I don't get it, but I probably never will. And this, my dear friend, is why I'm probably still single."

Eric rolled his eyes. "You just never know what will happen along the way. Maybe you'll meet your Ms. Right. And who knows, maybe that person will still be Lourdes. You guys would be so great together."

"Well, you thinking that and me thinking that does not mean that she's thinking that." Maddie shrugged.

"It is what it is. I best be going. I want to get that run in, and I hear there may be a storm brewing. Catch you later." She waved and hurried out the back way to get to the trail. Once outside, Maddie popped in her earbuds, pulled up her playlist, and started to run. It was already clouding up, so she closed her eyes and ran. The piercing wind invigorated her. She took a deep breath of fresh air. This was exactly what she needed.

A Black Eyed Peas song played in her headphones as she raced around the track adjacent to the hospital's East entrance. With the approaching rain, there weren't many people on the track. It allowed for some clear thinking. Unfortunately, her mind was mush when it came to having an idea of her thoughts.

The song switched to a slow ballad, and Maddie stopped running to change the song. As she skimmed through her playlist, she didn't notice anyone watching her until she heard Lourdes' voice,

"You come here often?"

She jumped and looked up, then laughed. "Oh, you startled me."

She dropped her phone into her pocket and looked around to see if anyone else was around.

"I go for a run here when I want to clear my head. You? I've never seen you running out here before." She regarded Lourdes coolly, tamping down her bubbling irritation. How dare she show up as if nothing happened in Maddie's secret spot of all places?

Lourdes shrugged. "Same situation. I needed to clear my head."

Lourdes looked up at the sky. "And the sky's about to break, so I don't think we have much longer. Care if I join you?"

After almost two weeks of radio silence from Lourdes, Maddie didn't anticipate this moment. Just to get back at her, she left her hanging for a few minutes as Lourdes matched her stride.

"Sure, go ahead," Maddie acquiesced.

They turned and continued to jog together in silence. Maddie could feel the shift in the weather. The sky would let loose at any moment, and they would be running in the rain. Yet, neither one seemed to care, especially Maddie. The thought of getting drenched in the rain brought a hidden desire from within her that she never knew existed. How many romantic movies caught the main couple together in the rain, dancing and kissing? Too many to count. It had been three years since she'd kissed anyone, and she couldn't help but contemplate how good it would feel to kiss Lourdes. "Busy week?" Lourdes asked.

"Yeah, work and life have been hectic. You?" *Seeing that we haven't exchanged a single word in 10 days.* Maddie bit down on her tongue. She would give Lourdes a chance to talk if she had anything to say.

"Same."

That wasn't much of a conversation. A few sprinkles landed on Maddie's nose, and Maddie looked up. "Well, we should head back, or we'll get drenched."

"Yeah, you're right. Let's go."

Once they reached Maddie's car, the rain started to come down even more. "Where are you parked? "Maddie asked.

"My bike is up there." Lourdes pointed to the rack of bikes, where her bike was the last one remaining. Maddie tilted her head and shook it. "I'll be fine."

"Let me take you home and bring you back tomorrow for your bike. You'll never make it before the hurricane hits."

Lourdes snickered. "Aren't you being a bit dramatic?"

Dramatic or not, there wasn't any way she could leave Lourdes there to fend for herself, even if she were irritated with her. She wasn't that petty "Get in the car," she ordered.

With no more convincing than that, Lourdes got into the car, and Maddie headed toward the direction Lourdes mapped for her. She only lived five minutes from the hospital, so it was obvious why she chose to take her bike.

"Best on gas, too," Lourdes reasoned.

"If I lived so close, I'd do the same. Makes sense." Maddie turned into the driveway and stopped her car. The rain started to pelt the windows harder. "See, you would have never made it."

"My hero," Lourdes smiled as she looked over at Maddie. That same flirtation instantly returned, along with the heated gaze they shared. Maddie quickly shifted from it and reached into the backseat for her umbrella.

"I'll walk you up to the door so you don't get drenched ."

"You don't have to do that," Lourdes argued, but Maddie was already out the door and around to help her out of the passenger side. The wind started to pick up, moving her umbrella, but she held it steady as Lourdes exited the car.

"Thank you!" Lourdes turned to her once they reached her porch. "Maddie," Lourdes started. Hearing her name come out of Lourdes' mouth made her melt. It was getting harder to stay mad at her. *Remember what she did.* Maddie coached herself. Lourdes led her on. Now she had the gall to stand here with her gorgeous brown eyes, the color of melting chocolate, and soft, luscious lips.

The rain fell harder, crashing to the pavement. "What's that?" Maddie leaned in closer, their faces inches from one another's. Her eyes locked on Lourdes, and Lourdes smiled.

"I was just going to say I'm sorry I have been avoiding you this week."

At least the truth was out there, and it wasn't all in Maddie's mind. She felt vindicated at that moment. She wasn't crazy.

"The truth is," Lourdes went on. "The other day, I wanted to kiss you."

As Lourdes spoke the words, Maddie listened. She nervously bit down on her lip. In one moment, she has this overly-hyped anticipation of what it'd feel like to be kissed by this beautiful woman.

"Why didn't you?" Maddie asked. "I wouldn't have objected."

"I know you wouldn't have. I saw it in your eyes, but I was scared. I was scared that it would have been too forward and would have pushed you away. I didn't want it to look like I was taking advantage of you. I guess because you mentioned the age difference, it worried me that it would appear like I felt I could overpower you or something." She snickered as Maddie opened her mouth, appalled by the statement.

"I freaked. I'm not too old to admit that. I swear, I wanted to kiss you. Then, the moment I told myself to buck up and do it, I swear, I saw my ex. She just moved back to Chicago from Denver about a month ago, and I didn't think we'd run into each other so soon. It freaked me out, so I bolted." Maddie shook her head, feeling a pang of sympathy settle in her stomach. Lourdes was so confident. It was hard to imagine her being nervous enough to flee a date like it was a crime scene.

"That bad, huh?" Maddie asked.

"It was terrible. I nearly mowed her over on my bike. I biffed it," She showed Maddie her elbow, sporting a nasty multi-colored bruise.

"And then, I was too embarrassed to say anything," Lourdes explained.

"I thought you were pushing me away because as we had gotten close, you realized it wasn't what you wanted. Then when you avoided me, I convinced myself that the date meant nothing."

"The date meant everything." Lourdes brushed her hand against Maddie's cheek as she moved closer.

"I want to see where things can go, Maddie. As long as you feel the same way," Lourdes whispered.

Maddie nodded. Finally, Lourdes leaned in, caressing her lips so softly against Maddie's. The kiss deepened, and Maddie went all in. She drew her arm around Lourdes. Her whole body sparked with the warring forces of pleasure and excitement. This was the romance she longed for, where the two lovers stood in the rain as it showered down over them.

"I'd invite you in," Lourdes teased.

"But then we both know where that would lead."

Maddie pulled back from the kiss. Her eyes lingered passionately on Lourdes'. Lourdes smiled and grabbed Maddie's hand, pulling her back towards her, and their lips reconnected. Lourdes pushed Maddie up against her front door, not breaking from the hold. The rain enveloped them. Nothing was more right than being locked in Lourdes' arms as the rain poured around them.

CHAPTER SEVEN

HIDDEN AFFAIRS

A couple of weeks after their fateful meeting in the rain, a notification sounded on Maddie's phone. Maddie smiled as she read the message.

Lourdes: Hey, Gorgeous. I hope your day is fantastic. Can't wait to see you tonight.

Maddie: Lovely, you are a breath of fresh air. Until tonight …

"I guess I don't have to ask what you're grinning about," Eric said, approaching the nurse's station. Maddie blushed and quickly put her phone in her pocket.

"I don't know what you're referring to." She looked over to where Shannon was leaning against the wall, resting her eyes until her next patient.

"She can't hear a thing. She's in Zen mode." Eric rolled his eyes. "You know exactly what I'm talking about. You've been grinning like a schoolgirl with a crush since Lourdes, and you decided to make this thing work."

Maddie playfully pushed him backward, and he pretended to stumble. She snickered. "Things aren't bad between us."

"Aren't bad." He scoffed.

"That's like someone saying it's not bad that they won the lottery. Please don't kid yourself or me. You are one happy lady, and you love every minute of it. You have been a busy little beaver since things started to heat up between you two. Have you done the deed? Gone downtown? Spent an evening of Sapphic seduction on the 'ol Isle of Lesbos?"

Maddie arched an eyebrow, "Eric, seriously! Get your mind out of the gutter. We are taking things at our own pace, and it's good."

Her grin deepened. "Really good. But I'm beginning to think you know way too much about my love life."

"Come on. You wouldn't want it any other way." Eric teased, bumping his hip against her.

"You like that someone is privy to your secret desires," Eric pretended to swoon.

Maddie sighed and continued. "We went running this morning. I never thought I'd meet someone that could outrace me, but to my surprise, she holds her own." Maddie smiled. She loved the challenge when it came to running with Lourdes. Lourdes could keep her on her toes, and she admired that.

"And you went to dinner the night before last."

"We gotta eat, right?" Maddie looked down at the file in her hand. "And she's making me dinner tonight."

"Oohhh...how cozy. But can she cook?" He arched an eyebrow.

"That would be the question. Guess I'll find out tonight." She laughed.

"Although, I haven't found something she hasn't been amazing at."

"Keep searching. Keep searching." He winked at her, and Maddie shook her head, unable to stifle her giggle.

"Didn't you go wine tasting over the weekend?"

Maddie nodded, "Right after a picnic in the park. Then a cycling event the weekend before."

"What haven't you done?" Eric replied.

"Oh yes...the deed. Don't you think it's about time? It's been just about a month! That's like ten years in lesbian! You have far exceeded the three-date limit."

Maddie rolled her eyes. "When you're playing by your own rules, there are no rules."

She looked behind him as Shannon, a fellow nurse, inched closer to them, most likely interested in their conversation. "Anyway, as I was saying, this pediatric fundraiser will be a huge event. I'm excited to be part of the raffle. How many tickets can I put down for you and James?"

"Depends. What's the winner getting?"

Maddie opened her mouth, shocked that he would inquire about that. "The joy and satisfaction of knowing you are helping make a difference. Isn't that enough?"

He chuckled. "Of course. Put me down for ten."

"That's better," Maddie giggled.

"I'll take five," Shannon piped up. "Sounds like a terrific cause. Good for you."

"Thanks, Shannon."

Shannon spun on her heel and walked away, and Maddie

snickered. "That was a close one. The last thing Lourdes and I need or want is to be ground through the hospital rumor mill.'

"As if people don't already know," Eric teased. "But in all seriousness, Shannon is right. Good for you, but you get involved in so much. I don't know how you do it."

"And I don't know how you do so little," Maddie teased, playfully punching him in the shoulder.

"So little? I'm buying ten raffle tickets, and James and I will come to eat the food. It's all about giving." He winked, and Maddie could hear his laughter ringing as he walked away from her. Still, she couldn't tear the smile from her face. She was a woman intrigued with her new relationship, which was something to celebrate. Her past relationships tended to die down after the initial honeymoon phase of week-long dates, but with Lourdes, it seemed like they would never run out of things to talk about. With Lourdes by her side, Maddie felt she could conquer the world. Still, part of her worried that the other shoe would drop, that Lourdes, just like her previous partners, would find her combination of ambition and anxiety too much to bear.

CHAPTER EIGHT

INTIMATE DINNER

Maddie smelled the earthy scent of Spring rain as she stood on Lourdes' front porch. She smiled, images of their first make-out session coming back to her. That was one night she wouldn't forget, even if it were over three weeks ago. Standing there, drenched, the scent of Lourdes mingling with the smell of heavy rain, it was the closest she had ever been to a perfect moment.

Lourdes opened the door and greeted her with a huge smile. "I thought this night would never get here," she teased, pulling Maddie into the foyer and embracing her. They kissed, and the busy day faded away. Maddie's heart quickened, and she slid her hand up Lourdes' back, feeling her toned back muscles, desperate for the moment to last just a few seconds longer. Her breath escaped loosely through her lips as Lourdes slowly broke away. "You look nice," Lourdes added.

Maddie blushed, ashamed to admit that she had dug through her entire closet in preparation for tonight. She settled on a black turtleneck and jeans, hoping to convey her stylishness. She even started wearing a new flavor of tinted chapstick: cinnamon flush.

The taste of Lourdes' lips lingered on her own. Maddie looked Lourdes over longingly. "You look extra lovely," Maddie said, giving an equal-sized grin. Lourdes stood wearing a black pair of pants and a red blouse that dipped down, revealing her cleavage. It was an outfit that matched her curves splendidly, leaving very little to the imagination.

"Thank you, Gorgeous!" Lourdes winked. "Make yourself at home. Dinner's almost ready."

Maddie dropped her gaze to Lourdes' ass as she walked away. The outfit hugged her curves in all the right places. When Lourdes disappeared around a corner, Maddie glanced around the foyer. There were running shoes by the door and a yoga mat propped in the corner. It was as if she was ready to escape to the realm of physical fitness whenever possible. From the conversations they had, it didn't surprise Maddie one bit. She peeked in a room right off the foyer and saw more exercise equipment, with dumbbells and a treadmill. Perhaps this would be another activity they could do together.

"There you are," Lourdes said.

Maddie jumped and whirled around. "I'm sorry if I was being nosy. You said to be at home and…."

"Calm down … I just missed you! I was wondering where you ran off." She kissed Maddie, calming her racing heart.

Lourdes grabbed Maddie's hand, and they left the room and went back through the foyer and to the kitchen.

Maddie took in a big whiff and nodded with approval. "It smells amazing."

Lourdes looked over her shoulder from where she resumed her place at the stove. "Thanks! I just got a new perfume," she winked before returning to her preparations.

Maddie couldn't believe they had gotten to this point. In just three short weeks, she was already feeling like maybe Lourdes was the one she had been waiting to connect with emotionally and physically. Yet, the mere thought of taking their physical relationship to the next level caused her heart palpitations to increase. Why was she so nervous? When they kissed, it was like the world melted away. Any worries and stress just dissolved. But the minute she contemplated moving forward, she always wanted to take a step back. It had nothing to do with their chemistry and everything to do with her fears and failures. She couldn't shake the feeling that she would be the one to mess this up.

"Uh oh."

Maddie turned back to Lourdes as Lourdes' voice echoed in the kitchen. "Huh? You look worried. Want to share?" Lourdes moved in closer to Maddie.

"I was just thinking about a plethora of stuff. It's nothing you need to worry about." *Plethora of stuff? Why the sudden need to break out a thesaurus in front of Lourdes?*

Lourdes frowned but never pried.

"I'm good. Is dinner ready?" She brushed past Lourdes but felt Lourdes' eyes following her.

"Uh, yeah. It is. Let me grab your seat for you." Maddie

waited as Lourdes pulled out a seat and waited for Maddie to sit down.

"Thank you!" Maddie sank back in her seat and waited for Lourdes to sit across from her.

"How was work today, Gorgeous?" Lourdes asked as she moved in and took the first bite. Maddie sighed, grateful to have any awkwardness behind them.

Maddie was centered and anxious to enjoy the meal and the company. "Busy, but the thought of meeting up with you made the day go smoothly." Maddie took a bite of her spinach salad and sighed. She could now tell Eric that Lourdes was a fantastic chef.

"This salad is amazing. So delicious," Maddie exclaimed.

Along with the salad were tofu and noodles. The tofu was spicy and perfectly crisp. Whenever Maddie tried to make tofu, it tasted like wet cardboard. She made a mental note to get the recipe from Lourdes. She always wanted different healthy ideas.

Lourdes laughed. "I appreciate the satisfied look on your face. I don't recall anyone looking so pleased with a salad," Lourdes took a bite, and Maddie laughed.

"It's not just the salad. This tofu is divine — compliments to the chef. Please remind me to get the recipe to share with my dad. He'll love it." Maddie winked and went back to savoring the meal. She was less nervous than when she arrived, but earlier thoughts and fears circled her mind.

"Thank you! It's a secret family recipe. But I suppose my ancestors wouldn't mind." Lourdes gave a teasing wink.

Maddie took a sip of her water, but her gaze never dropped. "Tell me about your family." Maddie had spent time discussing her dad. It was only fitting that Lourdes discussed hers. "I want to learn about your parents. Do you have any siblings? Tell me everything." While Maddie and Lourdes had been on several dates, they were mostly activity-based. This dinner was the first time since the coffee shop they had the chance to talk.

"There's not much to tell. My mom died when I was young. She immigrated to the United States from Italy in her twenties. Then, she met my dad. I was only a couple of years old when she died. My dad took great care of me. I'm an only child, but I was close with my cousins. A couple of them live in Italy, where my mom grew up. My dad owns an oil company in Texas."

"Wow, he must be rich." Maddie bit down her tongue. "Sorry, I didn't mean to butt in."

Lourdes shook her head. "No worries. He's well-off, indeed. He provided well. He remarried a few years ago, and she's a nice enough woman. I'm glad he's happy, but I don't see any of my family as often as I should. I guess we just drifted apart."

"You travel, so maybe you should make a point to visit Texas and visit them. You could even go to Italy!" Maddie took a bite of her salad.

"Yeah, maybe you're right," Lourdes quietly replied. "But tell me about your mom."

Maddie moved her salad around with her fork. "I don't like to talk about her. She abandoned my father and me when I was six. So, in one aspect, we have that in common, too. I don't have too many vivid memories of her. Until two years ago, I didn't even know my dad knew her whereabouts. It turns out she died of breast cancer. My dad saw the obituary. She lived just about twenty-five miles from here. It's a shame she never wanted to reach out or anything."

"I'm so sorry. Do you know why she left?"

Maddie shrugged. "Possibly depression. Who knows? My dad just said that they grew apart. In one way, I get that. You'd think she'd want to stay in touch with her child. But, it was her loss. She didn't want to be around us, so it is what it is. And no siblings. No cousins." Maddie snickered, "Just me and my dad."

"Depression can put people in a world of hurt that not everyone understands. I'm sorry she chose to leave you and didn't want to get help."

"It's alright. My dad never left me wanting for anything, so I didn't feel deprived."

Lourdes was very easy to talk to; she was a thoughtful and attentive listener. Maddie hadn't shared that information with anyone: even her first love, Raven. After Raven, she dated a couple of other people casually. But Maddie was starting to suspect that this thing with Lourdes was anything but casual. They continued to eat, making idle chit-chat. Maddie never once checked the time. She didn't want the night to end.

"How about I get us some wine and take this conversation to the living room?" Lourdes grinned, standing up and grabbing both of their plates from the kitchen table.

Maddie nodded. She would need the wine if the evening went as far as she thought it could go. After all, three weeks and several dates later, she was ravenous for Lourdes.

"Here you go, Gorgeous."

Maddie jumped when she heard Lourdes' voice. "Oh. Thank you! That was fast."

Lourdes grinned. I didn't want to be away from you longer than necessary." She winked, and Maddie felt the heat building between them, but her nerves didn't lessen. Lourdes moved in closer to her. "Everything is going to be fine," Lourdes whispered. "Trust me." She grabbed Maddie's hand and led her to the couch. They sat just inches from one another and sipped on the wine. A fire softly glowed in the background.

"Everything was great," Maddie choked out through her sip of wine. "The food was wonderful."

"Glad you enjoyed it." Lourdes brushed a strand of hair away from Maddie's eyes and slowly moved in, kissing Maddie with a hunger that Maddie felt tenfold. Maddie released a moan as Lourdes' tongue slipped between her open lips. She tasted the wine on Lourdes' tongue, sending shivers down her spine.

As they kissed, Lourdes slipped her hand up Maddie's shirt, gently caressing her breast. Maddie groaned. She wanted to take things further, but she couldn't relax. It had been over a year since Maddie had slept with someone. What if Lourdes thought she was terrible in bed? Lourdes was experienced. If she knew what good sex was, then surely she'd been able to tell if someone was inexperienced. Maddie quickly pulled back. "We can't."

Lourdes' mouth hung open, and she distanced herself from Maddie as if Maddie had slapped her across the face. "I'm sorry if I moved too fast. I just thought it was going in that direction. I guess I was wrong."

"It's not that. We were going in that direction. But at the same time, I don't want to rush things. Can you understand that?"

Lourdes gave a weak smile. "Honestly, I can respect that. Before we went down this path, I thought maybe we should talk. I had no intention of taking it to that level right here. Right now. But then, as we were kissing…." She smirked.

"I guess I read too much into it and didn't want to do what I've accused you of doing."

"Overthinking?" Maddie asked.

Lourdes sighed. "Exactly. The moment just felt right."

Maddie grimaced. Lourdes wasn't wrong. The moment felt perfect, right up until she pushed her away. Lourdes' suspicions were spot on. Maddie was a thinker, and that was her demise at times.

"Lovely, I would love to go there. But it's been a while…." She quickly stopped herself, dropping her gaze.

"How long?" Lourdes asked, arched eyebrow.

Maddie looked up, then shook her head. "Around a year, but it doesn't matter. I'm not as experienced as you are. I can leave if you want me to."

"What?" Lourdes caressed Maddie's cheek. "I would never do that," Lourdes moved her hand down to cup Maddie's chin in her palm.

"I would never kick you out for that reason. I would never kick you out for any reason. You're not like any other woman I've met, Gorgeous. You are truly someone special."

"You mean that?" Maddie softly asked. Maddie was preparing for a walk of shame to her car. But she could see the sincerity in Lourdes' eyes. Lourdes was being honest.

"Maddie, what kind of woman would I be if I didn't respect you? You think we should wait; then we'll wait." Lourdes stood up from the couch and went over to the overstuffed chair. Maddie watched her, where she now sat halfway across the room. Maddie looked at the fireplace, the soft romantic glow encapsulating the space. She swallowed. She wanted Lourdes to return to her, but she couldn't get the words out. It'd been a long, lonely year. Maddie could feel herself longing for Lourdes. Her heart fluttered in her chest. No one had ever encapsulated her thoughts and desires like Lourdes Russo. She took a deep breath to psych herself up and told herself to be brave.

"Maybe we shouldn't wait," Maddie suggested.

"What?" Lourdes asked.

Maddie got up from the sofa and walked over to the chair. Lourdes stood up. Her eyes narrowed in on Maddie's. "Maybe we are right," Maddie said.

Lourdes paused for a moment, arching her eyebrows. "Maddie, are you sure? Again, I don't want to pressure you."

Maddie took a deep breath, pushing past her anxiety once and for all.

"Yes, I'm sure. Lourdes, I want this. I want you," Maddie said.

Lourdes smiled. Finally, Maddie closed the distance between them, kissing her fiercely. Maddie groaned. She reached up and threaded her fingers through Lourdes' thick hair attempting to demolish any molecule of space between them. At that moment, Maddie had never wanted anything more in her life.

Lourdes wrapped her arms around Maddie, enveloping her in her warmth. Her hands tugged at Maddie's shirt until it was over her breasts. Lourdes kissed her chest, licking the underside of her breasts.

"Yes," Maddie groaned. Lourdes pushed Maddie down to the couch and slid her mouth around her left nipple, hungrily tugging at it before swirling her tongue around it and releasing it with a loud groan. "Lourdes!" Maddie growled just as Lourdes engulfed her other nipple between her teeth. Maddie released a breath, digging her nails into Lourdes' shirt.

"Let's get this off of you," Maddie said. For the first time, she felt confident, sexy even.

She unbuttoned Lourdes' blouse as fast as her fingers let her, revealing Lourdes' ample breasts, pouring out of the top of a black lace bra. Maddie was practically drooling. She kissed Lourdes again, reaching behind her to unhook her bra. She tossed Lourdes' bra behind her and began to lick, trailing her tongue along Lourdes' large, dark nipples, which soon pebbled with desire. Maddie took one of her nipples in her mouth and sucked. She left a trail of kisses along her chest until she finally made her way to Lourdes' lips, slipping her tongue into Lourdes' mouth. Maddie rolled her hips toward her instinctually. She felt her underwear grow slick with desire as she ground her crotch into Lourdes.'

Lourdes pulled away, grinning as she unbuttoned Maddie's jeans.

"Lie back for me, baby," she instructed. Maddie did as she was told and laid back on the couch. Lourdes slid off the couch and knelt in front of Maddie, a devilish grin spread across her face as she yanked Maddie's jeans off her legs, peeling her slick underwear off. She got up onto her knees and started to kiss the muscular plane of Maddie's stomach. Desire formed a molten pool behind her belly button as Lourdes' lips got closer and closer to her center. Maddie's hips bucked, and the back of her thighs ached with anticipation. Her heart hammered inside her chest, but she wasn't nervous … she was enthralled, that same mixture of fear and awe that occurs when you reach the crest of a roller coaster.

Even though it seemed Maddie was about to burst, Lourdes paused, "Is this okay?"

"Yes," Maddie said breathily.

With that, Lourdes slung Maddie's legs over her shoulders,

adjusting her position. She parted the lips of Maddie's sex. She began to lick, slowly exploring the contours of her molten, wet center. Lourdes traced her tongue along the arch of Maddie's clitoral hood. Lourdes took Maddie's clitoris in her mouth and sucked, savoring it as if it was a world-class delicacy. Maddie's hips bucked, pleasure fissured along the backs of her thighs. Encouraged, Lourdes began to increase the speed of her licks, adding more pressure with her tongue. A guttural groan escaped from the back of Maddie's throat. Lourdes licked even faster, swishing her tongue upward around Maddie's clitoris. Maddie could feel her orgasm starting to build. Her legs were beginning to shake, and Lourdes licked even faster. Maddie gasped, her hips rocked upward, and Lourdes grabbed onto her hipbones, meeting the rhythm of her body. Lourdes' sucked at her clit, and Maddie came hard. It was as if every nerve ending in her body had transformed into a firework. There was no such thing as pain, only wave after wave of pleasure. Maddie soared along the crest of her orgasm, crying out, "Lourdes!" in a ragged yell. This was bliss. This was heaven. This was everything. How was she supposed to go to work tomorrow when she knew this existed? Lourdes lapped along her sex, slower now, savoring the taste of Maddie as the last fissures of her orgasm fizzled out. Lourdes looked up at her, grinning, a ring of Maddie's juices shining slick around her mouth.

Maddie was breathless, "What … how did you … when?"

Lourdes shrugged, "What can I say? I've got a couple of years on you," she teased. She got up and sat beside Maddie, who rested her head in her lap. Lourdes stroked her hair, "You're an angel," she whispered.

"No, you," Maddie insisted. She leaned up on her elbows and captured Lourdes' lips in hers.

"Is it your turn now?" She teased.

She got up and straddled Lourdes, leaning forward to kiss her again. But then, Lourdes' phone rang, vibrating against the coffee table.

Lourdes grabbed it, "Shit, it's work. I have to take this," she said.

"Of course," Maddie replied.

She tried not to listen as Lourdes pressed her phone between her cheek and the crook of her shoulder, "Yes, this is Russo. How often? Ugh, that's not good. Okay, I'll be right there." She hung up quickly and turned to Maddie.

"Marilyn is complaining of chest pains and is ordering them to get me. But you know her; it's probably nothing."

"Right…124." Maddie shrugged. "If you need to go, then you need to go."

"But I want to stay here with you," Lourdes whined, pressing her face against Maddie's bare chest. It was cute how indignant she was.

"You have to work. It's okay, I understand," Maddie reassured her.

Lourdes groaned again and bent down, retrieving her bra and top from the floor. Maddie grabbed her clothes that were flung about the living room. Once she was decent, Maddie gave her a quick peck. "Call me later," she instructed Lourdes. They grabbed their coats, and Maddie drove Lourdes to the hospital, silently furious at Marilyn Evans for interrupting her chance to go down on the inimitable Lourdes Russo.

CHAPTER NINE

CRASHING DOWN

Maddie anxiously tapped her fingers alongside her keyboard.

"Don't fail me now." Technology was great, most of the time. However, on this particular day, Maddie could scream at the computer. While it was bad enough that the day was busy, with a full schedule of patients coming in, Shannon called in sick. The hospital had a strict policy on tardiness and sick days, and Shannon had used up her quantity and then some. But what could you do if you weren't feeling well? She said she had a fever, so it was all they could do but believe her. The last thing the patients needed was a nurse to give them their germs. And with Covid still going around, nobody needed to take that chance.

"Hey, Gorgeous. Wanna stop and get some lunch?"

Maddie smiled back at Lourdes' eager grin. They hadn't talked since the previous night's rudely interrupted love-fest. Maddie would have loved to have a few minutes to catch up and find out how Marilyn was doing. "I'd love to, but I'm swamped. I'm not sure I'll get lunch today." Maddie got up from her computer. "The computer's lagging. Plus, Shannon's out sick. I have three new patients in a matter of 2 hours. I'm over-whelmed." Maddie turned, but Lourdes grabbed her arm.

"Calm down, Gorgeous," she whispered. "If you work your-self in a frenzy, it won't be good for anyone." Lourdes rested her head against Maddie's. "You're going to pass out from all this stress. Just take a deep breath and breathe."

Maddie closed her eyes. Feeling Lourdes' hands on her did ground her at that moment, but she quickly came to her senses. If someone saw them, they would think Lourdes was picking favorites, and she couldn't have the staff believing she had the edge over everyone.

"You're right. I'll try my best. How's Marilyn doing? Was everything alright?"

She nodded. "A bit hypertensive, and her EKG was abnor-mal, but I think it was just a case of anxiety. Two hours later, she improved, and I went back home. I'm sorry that it interfered with our night."

"That's alright. The patient has to come first. Speaking of, I really should get to my next one."

"Understood." She felt Lourdes' eyes on her as she darted away from her. While she was getting more comfortable being around Lourdes, she still struggled with how the other employees would handle seeing them together. It's not that she wasn't proud to be a lesbian. Most of her friends at the hospital knew that she was gay. But it was another thing for strangers to know so much about her personal life. She didn't want her sexuality to be the first thing that popped into people's minds when they thought of her. The only thing that worked quicker than triage at CAPMED was the hospital's rumor mill, and she didn't want her and Lourdes to be subject to the relentless scrutiny of the entire hospital, at least not yet.

Maddie focused back on the task and stepped into the packed waiting room, "Jennifer," she called. There weren't any open seats left in the waiting room. When she escorted Jennifer to the room, she saw Lourdes still watching her. She released a breath and looked away. She led Jennifer to the scale and noted her height and weight in her chart. "Please take a seat. My name is Maddie, and I'll be your nurse for the day." She grabbed the blood pressure cart and wrapped the vinyl cuff around Jennifer's arm.

"Now, are you on any medications we should know about?" Maddie prompted.

Jennifer paused, thinking hard, before she responded, "I'm on 15 milligrams of Corgard, and I take 20 milligrams of Lexapro. Plus, I have an albuterol inhaler for seasonal allergies that I use as needed."

Maddie noted the medications on her chart.

"And what brings you here to see us today?" Maddie asked.

"My primary doctor said that my last echo showed an arrhythmia. He wanted a specialist to take a look. However, I heard great things about CAPMED's Cardio therapy department and decided to come to check it out. I'm sure I need some help with breathing exercises, or maybe some meds would help.

I'm exploring this first, and if a specialist is necessary, I will pursue that as a last resort."

"Alright, today you'll get to see one of our finest physical therapists." Maddie escorted her to the physical therapy room, "Tami will be right with you."

"Thank you!" Jennifer replied as Maddie left the room and returned to the nurse's station. To her relief, Lourdes wasn't there anymore. However, Eric was at the computer as she approached.

"Trouble in Sapphic paradise?"

"You saw that?" Maddie mumbled. If anyone saw it, she was glad it was him, though. At least he knew about their relationship. It was the nurse practitioners and doctors that Maddie wanted to steer clear of.

"I tried to look away," he replied. Maddie chuckled. She knew he was lying.

"What's going on?" Eric prompted.

"I'm way too busy to talk. Lourdes wanted to grab lunch, and I didn't have the time. Did you see the waiting room out there?"

"Believe me, I saw it. But you have to eat. You can't run yourself ragged. It sucks that Shannon isn't here, but you and I can only do so much." He touched her arm. "Don't stress yourself out."

"You're sounding like her," Maddie snapped, pulling her hand away.

"I literally write about managing stress and healthy living. You and Lourdes don't have to tell me how to handle my stress levels. Got that?"

Eric frowned. "Got it." He stood up from his chair. "We're

just trying to help because we both care. Don't push us away just because you don't like what we have to say." He headed to the waiting room as Maddie sank into a chair. Maddie clutched her stomach as a pain tugged at her insides. She was hungry, starving. Maddie appreciated their concern, but she had it all under control. She hurriedly put in Jennifer's vitals and the information she gathered at the appointment, then reached for another chart.

Her phone vibrated in her pocket. She grabbed it and looked to find a text from her dad.

Dad: So, I don't want you to worry, but if I didn't tell you, I know you would be upset. I was in a minor car accident today. I'm fine, but the car didn't have it so lucky. Don't worry about me, though. I'm fine.

Maddie swallowed a scream just when it felt like the day couldn't get any more stressful. She called her dad, and he picked up on the first ring.

"Maddie, I already told you I'm fine! It was just a little fender bender," he insisted.

Adding after a beat, "Wait, aren't you at work?"

"Yeah, I'm at work, but leave it to you to downplay a car accident," Maddie snapped. She felt terrible as soon as she said it, but the stress of the day was getting to her.

"Maddie, it's okay. I'm already back home! My car will be in the shop for a few weeks, but I got a rental."

"Dad, this isn't about the rental!"

"Maddie, listen to me. It is okay. I am okay. I feel fine now, but the moment I notice any issues, I'll go ahead and get them checked out. I promise."

"You promise?"

"Yes, now get back to work. Don't you have lives to save?" Her dad teased.

"More like charts to update. It's been a crazy day."

"Well, you better get back to it then. I'll call you later. I love you."

"I love you too, Dad," she hung up the phone and tried to steady her breathing.

Maddie's heart started to pound, and her breathing turned ragged. She slipped her phone back into her pocket. Her stomach clenched, and her chest tightened. A slow breath escaped her lips. "You've got this." She made her way to the waiting room, her legs trying desperately not to shake. She paused at the wall and grabbed onto it to steady herself.

"Robert?" A man that looked about the same age as her dad and a younger woman came walking toward her. "Hello, my name is Maddie, and I'll be the nurse assisting you. Follow me."

They walked to the triage room, and the younger woman put her arm around the older man's waist. "I have you, Dad," she said.

Flashbacks came rushing back to her. Suddenly, it seemed like she was back in high school again, terrified and clutching onto her dad as they sat in an unknown hospital waiting room, frightened about what the future would hold. When the woman looked up, Maddie smiled, then motioned to the chairs against the wall. An image of her dad continued to play in her mind, playing tricks on her. When Maddie turned to the girl, she saw her own face staring back at her. Maddie wondered if it would always be like this if part of her were still stuck in that waiting room today. She thought again about her dad's accident. He was always one to downplay his health. What if he had internal injuries that no one would catch until it was too late? What if the accident made him forgetful? What if he forgot to take his medication? What if he had a concussion and fell asleep, only to not wake up the following day? The myriad ailments and injuries that could occur to the person she loved most flooded her mind. Her brain was a continuous loop of gore and flat-lining vitals. There was no escape. She would never escape. No matter how fast she ran.

Maddie felt a tear stinging the corner of her eyes. "Alright, so what are we seeing you today for?"

"I recently had a heart attack, and now my daughter is forcing me to have therapy." The guy's voice was rough, but his daughter clutched his hand. He gave her a loving look, then offered Maddie a smile. "I think it scared her a bit, and I would do anything for my daughter. So, that's why I'm here."

A tear seeped from Maddie's eye, and she quickly flicked it away. "Um, can you please excuse me?" She hurriedly escaped the room before they would see her tears. Eric sat behind the desk; by this time, she was bawling.

"Eric, please … I have Robert in the triage room. Will you please do his vitals? I just can't. I just can't."

"Maddie? What's wrong?"

Maddie swallowed, but she couldn't speak. She couldn't breathe. Maddie felt her airway beginning to close. She thrust the folder into Eric's hands and rushed away from the desk before someone else could spot her and ask questions.

Maddie collapsed into a chair. The weight on her shoulders had pushed her down entirely. Her sobs echoed in the break room. She heard the door swing open and sighed. So much for alone time.

"Maddie? There you are." Maddie looked up, tears streaming down her cheeks. "What happened?" Lourdes rushed to her side, taking the seat beside her and throwing her arm around her shoulders.

"How'd you find me?" Maddie sobbed. "Or even knew I needed someone to find me?"

"Eric, but that's not important. What's going on?" Lourdes pulled Maddie closer, and Maddie rested her cheek against hers. "Everything is going to be alright. I promise you." The loving words she whispered to Maddie were well-received. Lourdes had no idea how much Maddie needed to hear them at that moment.

"It's my dad," Maddie whispered.

"Your dad? Another health scare?" Lourdes' eyes widened, and Maddie quickly shook her head.

"Well, not exactly." She sniffed and then sat back up, grabbing her phone from her pocket to show the texts to Lourdes. Lourdes read them to herself, then handed the phone back to Maddie.

"At least he's okay."

"Well, that's what he says. He's not planning on getting checked out unless something happens. You know as well as I do that sometimes something happens when it's too late to do anything about it. You work at a hospital; you should get that." Lourdes' eyes darkened, and Maddie winced. "I'm sorry. I shouldn't have snapped."

"No, it's fine. And you're right. Sometimes it can be too late, but you also have to have faith that everything will turn out all right. You can't go around believing that something will automatically go wrong. That's no way to live."

"But…"

Lourdes brushed her finger to Maddie's lips. "I know you're concerned. He's your father."

"He's all I have," Maddie added.

Lourdes looked away from her. Her eyes dimmed. When she turned back, she had a tear in the corner of her eye. She was the strong one, so where did those tears come from?

"There are times when you have to let people in, Maddie. Even if it's difficult."

"I rushed out on a patient earlier. That's not like me." Maddie looked down at her knotted hands.

"Wanna talk about it?" Lourdes asked. Her hand ran along Maddie's fingers as Maddie considered whether she did. But there was one thing for sure. Maddie needed to open up more if she wanted to explore this relationship.

"A man, my father's age. The same situation my father was in several years ago. A loving daughter who looks like her world would come crashing down if something happened to him."

"That piled on top of everything was sure to break you. I get it, but you can lean on me." Maddie moved in closer and put her head on Lourdes' shoulder. Those words were the signal she needed. "What do you say tonight we go for part two? You come to the house, and I'll cook you dinner again. We'll have wine, and we can talk. I think we deserve that much."

"I don't know," Maddie scrunched up her face. Before this nightmare of a day had started, she woke up dreaming of Lourdes. Now the thought of being away from her father, unavailable with her phone shoved in a bag, racked her with guilt. "I should be with my dad. At least check up on the fact of how he's doing. He tends to play things off when they're more serious."

"I get that. So, here's my offer. If tonight doesn't work, you choose the night. I want you to feel comfortable that he's doing alright. Once you know that's the case, I'll wine and dine you. But it's your choice when it happens."

"I love that you're around," Maddie whispered.

Lourdes pulled Maddie to her. "That's always good to hear." Lourdes kissed Maddie and held her for a few moments until Maddie felt ready to return to the floor. After work, she would call her dad to ensure he wasn't just blowing her off. And then, she would gladly take that do-over.

CHAPTER TEN

BURNING HEAT

"You're sure you're doing alright?" Maddie asked for the twentieth time.

"For the eightieth time, I'm doing great. Enjoy yourself tonight, and don't think about your dear old Dad," Dave insisted.

Maddie smiled, the knot in her stomach finally going down in size. "Twentieth," she mumbled.

"What was that?"

"Nothing, Dad. You call me if you need anything. You know how to reach me."

"Honey, if anything changes in my health, you'll be the first to know. Have a good time tonight with your friend." He enunciated friend as Maddie turned to look at Lourdes' house.

She hadn't told her father anything other than Lourdes was

a co-worker she was getting to know. She didn't even mention her name. It was more of a need-to-know basis, and she would surely tell him if there was anything he needed to know in the future.

"Love you, Dad."

"Love you, Kiddo. Talk soon."

She finally relaxed her shoulders. He was good. There wasn't anything to worry about. Now, all she had to do was focus on Lourdes.

The door swung open before Maddie could even finish knocking. Lourdes had a bright grin that lit up the whole night. She wore a classy suit, jet black to match her long eyelashes. She looked elegant. Yet, Maddie wasn't kidding anyone. She also looked ravishing. Maddie stood there, gobsmacked, as her breath caught in her throat. Lourdes had this dimple on her cheek that only appeared when she was excited. Tonight, it was one of the first things Maddie saw.

"Are you going just to stand there looking gorgeous, or are you going to come in?"

Maddie blushed but didn't tear her eyes away from Lourdes' breathtaking gaze. "I'm not nearly as gorgeous as you," she retorted. Lourdes pulled Maddie into her house, barely touching her arm as she tenderly greeted her with a kiss.

"You're wrong about that," Lourdes whispered. "And tonight, you're absolutely radiant." She returned to the kiss, Maddie's lips opening slightly to welcome Lourdes' tongue. Maddie trailed her fingers around Lourdes' neck and held her in place. If she didn't ever have to stop, it would be too soon.

"If we don't stop now, dinner will burn," Lourdes whispered, slowly parting from the kiss.

Maddie inwardly groaned. And? She'd let dinner scorch for a couple more seconds in Lourdes' arms.

Already, Lourdes made Maddie's life infinitely better. Maddie intertwined her fingers with Lourdes'. Lourdes escorted Maddie back to the kitchen. "Have a seat, Gorgeous, and I'll grab the food off the stove. I hope you like salmon?"

"Yum…love it. But I thought you were a vegetarian?"

"Mostly vegetarian," Lourdes corrected. "Sometimes, on special occasions, I make exceptions."

And just like that, they were back to sitting in that kitchen, talking, laughing, and enjoying conversation as if they had known each other for years. Maddie's worries evaporated. Her dad was fine. He wanted her there, and more importantly, she wanted to be there.

As the dinner ended and they lingered in the kitchen sipping on wine, Lourdes turned the conversation to Dave. "Have you spoken with your dad? How's he doing?"

"We've talked, and he's doing alright. He told me to go out and have a good time tonight." Maddie took a sip of her wine as Lourdes arched an eyebrow.

"What?" Maddie asked, giggling.

"Does he know about me? Come on, spill the juicy details."

Maddie laughed. Her face was on fire, and she could only imagine how red she had gotten. She looked down at her hands nestled in her lap. "Let's say he knows you're someone I want to get to know better. And speaking of, tell me more about your travels. It's all so fascinating." She leaned forward. Lourdes laughed and nodded, then started speaking.

Maddie enjoyed that Lourdes could easily carry on a conversation, and this night didn't disappoint. "I would have to say my most recent excursion was one of the most exciting. I went to Iceland."

"Iceland? Wasn't it cold?" Maddie squealed.

Lourdes snickered. "Precisely why I enjoyed the hot springs most of all." She gave Maddie a wink. "Soothing and relaxing. Simply perfect. Iceland, though, was more of a personal trip. Maybe we can go sometime and slip into those hot springs. You wouldn't want to be anywhere else." Lourdes winked, and Maddie imagined them enjoying the hot springs together. Lourdes' foot brushed against Maddie's, and Maddie kept her lower lip clenched between her teeth. If Lourdes continued to flirt like that, she wouldn't be able to pass up any trip with her. She took a sip of her wine, and Lourdes' gaze dropped to Maddie's lips. Maddie opened her mouth slightly, feeling Lourdes' gaze shift up to her eyes.

Lourdes cleared her throat. "Anyway...that wine?" she began, her gaze still locked on Maddie's. Maddie nodded. "It's from France. I volunteered over there and kept it for a special occasion. I can't think of anything more special than this."

"Special?" Maddie softly inquired.

Lourdes nodded. "Special. You've had a rough day. You deserve it." Lourdes took a sip.

Maddie moved in her seat, eager to finish what they had started the other night.

"So, you've talked to your dad and know he's doing alright. And yet, you still seem so stressed."

Maddie looked up into Lourdes' dark eyes. "I'm not," Maddie argued. "I've never felt so relaxed in my life."

Lourdes scrunched up her nose, as in thought, then stood up from the table and reached for Maddie's hand, a soft smirk on her lips. Maddie didn't budge. Lourdes tilted her head. "Even if you're not stressed, I have some great techniques that can help a person ease some tension." She grabbed Lourdes' hand and pushed herself up on her feet. "You and I are similar in so many ways. And yet, there are moments when we're just so different."

"Shhh..." Lourdes cooed. "Relax. You won't even know what tension is once I'm through with you." She winked and pulled Maddie behind her. Those words left a tingling sensation in Maddie's core. As they reached the living room, Lourdes pointed. "Sit on the floor."

"Is that an order?" Maddie asked, curving her lips into a smile. Lourdes snickered but kept pointing. Maddie took a seat on the floor, with Lourdes quickly joining her. Lourdes pulled Maddie back, placing her in between her legs. She promptly found the knot in Maddie's shoulder and began to work at it with her nimble hands.

"Just relax," Lourdes whispered.

"I'm telling you, I'm, oh God."

Lourdes snickered just outside her ear. "You were saying?" Lourdes kneaded Maddie's shoulders, her hands moving deep into her surface. Maddie's head fell to her chest, and she groaned with Lourdes' strong hands kneading her shoulders. She wasn't expecting this once they reached the living room, but she wasn't arguing. Lourdes had magic hands. The knot in Maddie's shoulder melted.

"On some of my adventures, one of the best things I could give myself were these massages. You get out there and do work to help people but catch yourself not taking care of yourself. These massages would always keep me moving. I felt centered and in control."

"I can see why," Maddie moaned, feeling the warmth and strength of Lourdes' hands. Lourdes reached down and touched Maddie's inner thighs. "Oh God," Maddie moaned again.

Lourdes snickered. "Yes, it can be very sensual. But we'll get to that later. Right now, I want you to relax." Lourdes gently massaged her thighs as Maddie felt the pressure building inside her. "Unfortunately, I never had the benefit of being attracted to whoever was massaging me. So, I imagine you're getting a better experience." Maddie looked over her shoulder as Lourdes grinned. "At least, I would hope so."

Maddie twisted around and kissed Lourdes, "It's not so bad," she said. She leaned forward to kiss her again, but Lourdes raised her hand. "Face me." Another order Maddie jumped to follow. Maddie turned around and sat before Lourdes as Lourdes raised one arm and started doing stretches. "As you do this, breathe in and out so your diaphragm slowly rises and falls."

"Like this?" Maddie asked.

Lourdes smiled. "Almost. Just move your arm forward a little." She moved in, touched Maddie's arm, and slowly pulled it forward. "Like this." Their eyes locked, and Lourdes trailed her hand down Maddie's arms, tenderly caressing her, with Maddie closing her eyes, enjoying the sweet and simplest of touches. As Lourdes' hand grazed over the side of Maddie's left breast, Maddie's eyes flung open.

Finally, they kissed. Their tongues darted around one another like a dueling battle until Maddie could barely breathe. She broke away and grabbed her shirt, quickly pulling it up and over her head. She grabbed Lourdes' shirt and pulled it over her head, shooting it in a different direction.

Lourdes continued to grin while Maddie kept possession of the heat in the living room. She pushed herself up and wrapped her legs around Lourdes' waist, then grabbed onto the hook of her bra and released it, sliding it off to press her bare breasts against Lourdes' chest. There was no need for words or questions. She kissed Lourdes again, sucking on her bottom lip.

Slowly, Lourdes massaged Maddie's breasts. Lourdes took Maddie's breasts in her palm and rolled them upward, releasing the tension in her chest. Maddie's nipples pebbled with desire at Lourdes' touch. She leaned in and undid the clasp of Lourdes' bra, allowing it to fall away. She pulled away from the kiss and shifted her attention to Lourdes' breast, grabbing her right nipple into her mouth as Lourdes hungrily kneaded Maddie's breasts through her fingers. Maddie captured Lourdes' lips in a kiss once more. She shifted her hips upward. Lourdes reached down and unzipped her jeans. Deftly, she slipped her middle and ring fingers into the entrance of Maddie's sex, arching her fingers upward in a motion that unleashed a torrent of pleasure within Maddie. Her hips bucked. Maddie felt the back of her neck grow hot as her orgasm fizzled up her spine; emboldened, Lourdes increased her pace. Maddie whimpered, leaning into Lourdes' touch. Finally, she cried out, enveloped in ecstasy and Lourdes' strong arms. When she emerged from the haze of her orgasm, she saw Lourdes smiling.

Lourdes pressed her lips to Maddie's sweaty forehead.

"Feeling Better?" Lourdes asked.

Maddie grinned sheepishly, "Much better."

"See, I told you so. Stress is no match for me," Lourdes quipped.

CHAPTER ELEVEN

MORNING AFTER TEMPTATION

Lourdes' snores echoed in the living room as Maddie quietly pulled her pants on. She turned to look for her shirt and caught it resting against the lamp. Images of Lourdes and her in the wild heat of passion flashed back through her mind. Lourdes' olive skin shone beneath the slither of the crescent moon, barely coming through the front window. She shuddered; that image brought her rushing back into that moment. Maddie looked over as Lourdes continued to sleep on the sofa. Falling asleep in her arms was heavenly.

She reached for her shirt and tugged against the lamp, bringing it crashing to the floor. "No, no, no…." Maddie moaned, rushing around the table and picking it up, sighing when she saw the lamp was still in one piece.

"Gorgeous? What are you doing?"

Maddie groaned. The lamp wasn't broken, but the noise still caused Lourdes to wake up. She situated the lamp and turned to where Lourdes leaned on her elbows, the blanket shielding her naked body.

"I didn't mean to wake you."

"I'm glad you did. What's going on? It's two o'clock in the morning." Lourdes pulled the blanket up, and her nakedness vanished. Maddie made an inward growl, then shook her head, trying to clear away that sexy image.

"It's three thirty. Much later than I should have slept." Maddie pulled on her shirt. "I tried to get out of here before you woke up."

"Early shift?" Lourdes asked. She sat up, the blanket slipping down to reveal her upper half. She leaned over and grabbed her shirt, pulling it over her head and not even making eye contact.

Maddie nodded, "I have to be at work at six this morning. Or rather, I should be at work at six. I left a mess with documentation. Yesterday was a nightmare, and I don't want to start the day off already behind. So, that means getting a shower and dressed, and I think it's best if I get out of here. The earlier, the better. That's all."

Lourdes was now fully dressed and standing in front of her. "Shit, that's too bad! I was hoping we could spend the morning together, possibly take a shower together." She quirked up a smile. "Then have some breakfast before we both go into the hospital. I wanted to spend our first morning together, actually, together. If you know what I mean." She reached for Maddie's hand, and her fingers traced slowly over Maddie's digits. "But that's just how work goes, isn't it? When you think you're caught up, they throw something else at you. I wish you could stay," Lourdes said.

" I know." Maddie sighed

She sighed, not daring to close her eyes for more images to come racing back into her mind. Last night was perfect. Spending the night together strengthened their bond, and Maddie undoubtedly knew she wanted all her nights spent with Lourdes.

"But it's more than just a work thing. I can see it in your eyes."

Maddie sighed. "I don't know, Lovely." She plopped down on the couch, where moments ago she had been cuddled up against this vibrant woman, and she looked over to where the blanket was a chaotic mess. "I guess I worried that you'd think we rushed into things."

"How could I possibly?" Lourdes reached for Maddie's hand and held it as they sat on the couch, staring longingly into one another's eyes.

"Last night, in the heat of the moment, I thought there was silent agreement. We both wanted this week to happen. Maddie, when I'm with you, everything is perfect. There's no doubt in my mind about it." Lourdes dropped her gaze. "If anything, I feared that you would regret it. If we're going to be together, I don't want either of us to be on the fence about it. I'll admit, I've questioned our age difference, but mostly I questioned how someone like you would want to be with me."

"Get that thought out of your mind right now. I'm here with you because it's the only place I want to be. Got that?"

Maddie nodded, and Lourdes brushed her thumb along Maddie's lower lip. Maddie shifted in the seat next to her and moved in, bringing her lips to Lourdes' as they gently kissed one another. All of Maddie's fears melted away.

"When we're together, our connection feels so real." Maddie leaned her head against Lourdes'.

"I don't want this to come across as some fling." Her heart raced as Lourdes' gaze met hers.

"I could never see this as a fling, Maddie. The connection you feel, I feel it, as well. You may see differences, but I focus on just the similarities. We go about things differently, but our similarities are our spark." She winked, and they were making out on the couch before Maddie could stop it; Maddie's hands roamed the soft cotton material of Lourdes' PJs. Just five more minutes, she'd rush out of there and get home and get ready for work. Lourdes slipped her hand up Maddie's shirt and touched the back of her bra, tugging it to try to unclasp it. Lourdes groaned when Maddie's bra wouldn't budge.

Maddie laughed, pushing herself away. "Keep doing that, and I'll never leave."

"Promise?" Lourdes asked, giving a flirtatious smirk.

Maddie stood up from the couch. "I better go. We'll see each other at work."

Lourdes jumped up, snaked her hand through Maddie's, and walked her to the door."So, does this mean that I get to call you my girlfriend at work?" Lourdes asked.

Maddie blushed, "Let's see how things go. I don't want to make everyone jealous right away. See you soon, Lovely."

Lourdes stood at the door, and Maddie felt her eyes on her as she drove away. Maddie was a bit more private than Lourdes. But she would accept whatever happened. She'd never smiled so big.

CHAPTER TWELVE

CALM BEFORE THE STORM

Maddie whistled as she exited the break room, bumping into the person headed the other way. "Oh, sorry, Eric." She laughed and continued to whistle.

Eric tilted his head. "You're in a chipper mood. After your day yesterday, I expected a permanent scowl."

He took a look at his watch and then arched his brow. "And you're here at least two hours early. What gives?"

"Well, I have a boatload of work and thought I would get an early start. As for the scowl, it's supposed to be a beautiful day outside. What's there to scowl about?" She reached up and pinched his cheek, and his jaw dropped.

"Oh, my goodness. Oh, my goodness."

"Oh, my goodness? What are you, an eighty-year-old

woman?" Maddie laughed. She started to push past him, but he reached out and grabbed her arm, knocking her back to him. "You and Lourdes had sex, didn't you? Didn't you?" His eyes narrowed, and there was a devious grin on his face. His smirk deepened. "I'm right, aren't I? You and Lourdes finally banged, and now everything is rainbows and puppy dogs."

Maddie's cheeks were on fire. "Will you be quiet? Rainbows and puppy dogs? Really?" She laughed, unable to hide her grin. "What happened between Lourdes and me is for me to know and you to contemplate."

She whirled on her heel and smirked as Eric's eyes widened. "Have a good day, Maddie. Just remember, your silence speaks volumes."

Maddie rolled her eyes and continued to the elevator. He could inquire all he wanted, but she wouldn't budge. Let him imagine what happened. Once she reached the nurse's station, she saw a pile of charts. Her smile couldn't last much longer.

"Ugh!" she groaned. "And why did I leave these charts until today?" It was a question she didn't need anyone answering. She didn't want to get to Lourdes' house any later than she had to. She reviewed the charts individually to clarify the documentation and get everything into the computer. Over thirty charts were waiting there; this was going to take forever. When eight o'clock rolled around, she still had five charts to do.

"Maddie?"

Maddie looked up and smiled. "Hey, Louisa. Is the first patient here?"

"Actually," Louisa grimaced. "Mike Bishop is here for an add-on."

"Did you see the schedule? There's no way. You can try working with him next week, but we're swamped."

"I told him all that. But the thing is, he had a mild heart attack at the end of last week, and the doc said he needed to work him in right away. But if you insist, I'll let him know. I just thought I should tell you."

Maddie's heart lurched as she stared at the computer, looking at the schedule, hoping that she had miraculously over-looked a cancellation. It was going to be a nightmare, and she immediately put them back behind schedule, but she couldn't be the one to tell him that he'd have to wait.

"Sign him in."

"Thank you." Louisa hurriedly left the nurse's station and returned to the lobby. Maddie glanced at the lobby as Gretchen, one of the nurse practitioners, headed towards her. "First patient here yet?"

"Not quite checked in, but there's been a minor delay in scheduling. We're working with Mike Bishop. He had a heart attack last week, and his PCP told him to get an appointment asap."

Gretchen rolled her eyes. "Everyone's a priority. There's only so much we can do, Maddie. We can't work all the patients in just because they have a story. Everyone has a story." She stared at Maddie, but Maddie couldn't back down. This was Mike; if she wanted to work anyone in, it was him. She didn't like to pull the favoritism card, but she had to take her stand in this case. "Get him roomed, but this will have to be it. We can hardly keep up with the patients we have. I don't mean to be harsh, but it's the truth. Got it?"

Maddie nodded, her cheeks flushing. "Got it." She turned

from Gretchen. Only a few minutes into her actual shift, she was already getting reprimanded over her attempt to help the most patients. "I'll get him checked in." She quickly walked to the waiting room without even bothering to grab his chart. "Mike?" she called.

He walked even slower than usual as he made his way to her. He gave a weak smile. "Hey, Maddie. I appreciate you getting me in."

"That's all right, Mike." On the way to the room, she made conversation to gather some information. "When did you have the heart attack?"

"Last Thursday. Before you freak out, I know I need to be more careful. But I was exerting myself, and it was mild. Nothing much to worry about. I was only in the hospital for a couple of days."

Maddie frowned; why no one was informed of his stay was beyond her. It was just another classic inter-hospital miscommunication.

"Have you been doing the exercises and monitoring your BP? And most importantly, have you remembered to take it easy when you play ball with Myles?"

"Of course," he argued. "But…" His face fell, and Maddie waited for him to continue. "My brother was moving, and I offered to help. I might have overdone that because I wasn't feeling well that night. I thought it was indigestion. It didn't feel anything like the last one…." He gave a short shrug. "Sometimes it's hard to say no."

Maddie knew that phrase all too well. It was hard to say no, especially when the people you loved most asked for help. She saw some of her stubbornness reflected in Mike, making her feel even more sympathy for him. Mike refused to make eye contact with her as she took his blood pressure and pulse, then made a mental note of the numbers. "Gretchen will see you, so follow me."

"Gretchen? I usually see Noelle."

Maddie nodded. "This is a little more serious, as you just had a heart attack, even if only mild. You need to see one of the nurse practitioners, and Gretchen is waiting for you." When she reached the exam room, she turned to him. "I don't want you being here again unless it's for regular therapy. Got that?"

"I'll do my best." He winked, then chuckled as he leaned back in his chair. Her duty for the moment was through, but walking back to the nurse's station, she didn't feel any better about that. If Mike wouldn't listen, what good was it to keep talking? Feeling helpless, she dug through her pocket and retrieved her phone from the pocket of her scrubs. Maddie opened Instagram and scrolled until she found the draft of her latest post about the benefits of stretching. She added a couple more tips about using yoga as a stress management technique and pressed "post." Sometimes posting online felt as useless as chastising repeat patients, like she was talking to a brick wall, but she didn't know what else to do. So much of her life felt uncontrollable. From her workload to her father's health, Instagram was something she could control. She could decide what she wanted to talk about and when. She could encourage strangers to make healthy choices, which had to count for something.

The fax beeped to life as she approached the desk, and she pulled the paper off the machine. Maddie shook her head. "Just a week too late," she murmured. She tossed down the pages to the desk and grabbed a seat.

Shannon came hurrying by as she did, rushing off to the waiting room. Her eyes appeared red, she was frowning, and she looked as pale as the hospital bed sheets. Maddie frowned. It was crazy how staff needed to be there even when they weren't feeling well, and from the look of Shannon, she looked like she wanted to hurl. Sure, Shannon called off way more than hospital rules allowed, but if you're sick, you're sick. Maddie hated that everyone felt obligated to be there because of rules and regulations.

Maddie turned back to the computer and quickly put in Mike's stats, then reached for the first chart of the scheduled patient. She took a glance at her watch and then over to the hallway. Maddie hadn't seen Lourdes yet and hated to admit it, but she missed her. This morning was already turning into a stress fest, and she would have loved to have been able to wake up next to Lourdes and spend the morning together. Instead, she was stuck drowning in paperwork. *Get it together, Maddie. Quit complaining. You'll see her tonight — no need to U-haul.* Maddie grinned as she dug for her phone and pulled up Lourdes' name.

Maddie: Just checking on your morning. Another busy one. Maybe we can grab lunch together?

Maddie stared at her phone, hoping that Lourdes would send her a quick reply, but the response never came. She groaned and tucked her phone back in her pocket. Hopefully, after her next patient, she would return to a text.

Maddie went out to the lobby and grabbed her next patient. As the morning went on, she tried to give each patient the same courtesy she always offered, but she slowly began to get further behind. This only left her more stressed and scrambling through the assessment process. She always smiled but felt depleted with each patient she rushed through. When lunch arrived, she grabbed her phone, disappointed that Lourdes never replied. Besides that, she had yet to see her in the department. This wasn't unusual, especially since the morning had been one big blur of activity. She didn't have much time to take note of anyone. Most of the staff appeared too stressed to focus on anything but work.

Shannon sighed as she sunk into the chair next to Maddie. "Is this day over yet?" she groaned.

"I wish. It's been busy for us all." Maddie side glanced over to Shannon. Shannon's cheeks were peaked, and Maddie felt a pang of regret for her co-worker. "You know, Shannon. Maybe you should go on home. You don't look so great."

"Gee, thanks a lot," Shannon mumbled. "If I went home, then you would be all alone. I'm feeling better. Besides, I don't have any more sick days." She looked up and shrugged. "It's all good. No fever. No contagion. Do you want to go to lunch? Or I can go first, whichever."

Maddie opened her mouth when she spotted Lourdes for the first time. Lourdes grinned and gave a slight wave, then walked over to the desk. "Ready for lunch?" she asked.

"You read my mind …." Maddie's words fell off as she turned to Shannon. "Are you going to be alright here?"

"I'll be just dandy. Enjoy." Shannon turned back to her computer as Maddie and Lourdes left the desk. Once they were alone in a hallway, Lourdes reached for Maddie's hand.

"I missed you," Lourdes whispered. She lifted Maddie's hand to her lips, then frowned.

"Are you okay? You're frowning."

"I'm fine. I haven't seen you at all this morning. And I texted you...."

"And you missed me...." Lourdes replied, grinning, squeezing Maddie's hand.

"Are you being smug?" Maddie teased, quirking up her lips.

They entered the elevator and waited for the doors to close before Lourdes pushed Maddie against the wall. "Never." She hungrily kissed Maddie, and there was a thirty-second gap in time, where Maddie forgot how stressed she was throughout the morning. She slipped her tongue into Lourdes' welcoming mouth, and they kissed until the bell dinged in the elevator. Lourdes pulled away and gave Maddie a wink, and the doors opened. "Sorry, babe. It's been a crazy morning. But I saw you running around like a gorgeous blur."

Maddie blushed. "I know what it's like to be busy, that's for sure. I'm glad we can grab lunch, though." They entered the cafeteria and went in separate directions as Lourdes went to get a salad, and Maddie grabbed a chicken wrap from the deli. Maddie paid and then looked around the cafeteria, locating Lourdes in a secluded corner.

She sunk in the chair, and Lourdes gave a teasing grin. "I wish I could kiss your stress away every day."

"That elevator wasn't a bad start," Maddie replied, smirking. They started eating their lunch, and Maddie picked at her wrap, unsure she had the energy to eat.

"Wanna talk about your day?" Lourdes asked, nibbling on her salad.

"Well, it starts with the last-minute patient. He was seen in the ER last week and then admitted to the hospital for two nights of observation. We never received this information until today. That's a week after they admitted him! The doctor wanted an immediate follow-up. The truth is, he should have been here at minimum four days ago. But how would we know this without getting the information? It's the lack of staff, and it sucks. Patients aren't getting the care they deserve."

"And I feel it's only going to get worse," Lourdes mumbled.

Maddie shook her head. "Why would you say that? Why would you think that?"

Lourdes circled her fork in her salad before glancing up to meet Maddie's gaze. "This morning, I forgot I had a board meeting. The truth is, they're talking about budget cuts. They're asking older nurses to retire early. Other staff members might be laid off. The nursing staff is in danger. That's all across the hospital. I worry about—" Her face fell, and Maddie leaned back in her chair. "Even if you keep your job, there will be many more days like what you're experiencing today. Things are liable to get worse, not better."

"As it stands, we're talking about one nurse to every fifteen patients. How exactly can it get worse than that?"

"It can always get worse."

Lourdes was looking at a worst-case scenario, right? The struggle was already so real, and Maddie feared they hadn't seen anything yet.

CHAPTER THIRTEEN

HEATED CONFRONTATION

An hour after her shift ended, Maddie walked out of the front door of CAPMED and headed to her car. She hadn't stopped thinking once about Lourdes' mention of budget cuts. She knew that it impacted her interactions with the rest of her patients.

"Maddie? Maddie, wait up?" She turned around and saw Lourdes running to her. "Geesh," Lourdes said, stopping short of Maddie's car. "I didn't think you were ever going to stop. I've been hollering for you ever since you clocked out."

Maddie smiled. "Sorry. I've got a lot on my mind. I didn't hear you." She stared at Lourdes' perfect complexion. Her hair was pulled back into a neat ponytail, whereas Maddie felt like a dingy mess. Half her ponytail was undone, and her face smudged with dirt. She could feel a volcanic zit forming under the skin on her chin. Deep purple bags were forming under her eyes from stress and lack of sleep. It was most likely all in her mind, but Maddie felt gross. "You look worried. I didn't mean to freak you out earlier. Let me take you out for dinner. It's the least I could do."

"That's nice of you, but I'm a mess. I should get home. I need to shower, put on some sweatpants and have a frozen dinner. It wouldn't hurt to get to bed earlier tonight, either."

Lourdes frowned. "First off, you look beautiful. You're not a mess. Secondly, don't go home and sulk. It puts on some unnecessary worry lines on your gorgeous face." Lourdes reached up and drew her finger along Maddie's cheekbone. Go out to dinner with me. Nothing fancy. Please. My treat."

"Lourdes, you've done so much for me. I should repay you by picking up the tab."

"If I agree, will you go?" It didn't take much convincing for Maddie to say yes.

Lourdes led the way to a corner diner that was a favorite amongst hospital staff. It would be good to spend another evening just talking with Lourdes. At least she had that to look forward to.

Lourdes held the door open for Maddie as she stepped into the diner. Inside the restaurant, it was downright cozy. A Sam Cooke song warbled through the tinny speakers. The lighting was warm, a perfect contrast to the unforgiving fluorescents of CAPMED. Customers sat in worn vinyl booths. Teens nibbled on French fries as they puzzled over their homework. Couples shared milkshakes, and old men sat at the counter eating pie and drinking steaming mugs of coffee. It was a warm and friendly atmosphere, a welcome change from the dismal mood that hung over the halls of CAPMED like a storm cloud, ready to burst.

They found an open booth near the window and took their seats. A waitress was there to grab their drink orders and food. Once she was gone, Lourdes reached out and held Maddie's hand. "I have a confession," Lourdes began. "I can't stop thinking about these past couple of nights.."

Maddie giggled, "Honestly, same. Work's been hell lately, but the past few nights have been actual dreams come true," Maddie confessed.

"Agreed." Lourdes pulled Maddie's hand to her lips and placed a kiss between her knuckles. "I saw your latest Instagram post. Now that I follow you. Ah, the benefits of stretching. I believe I inspired you there, at least partly."

"Well, my dear, you were the biggest inspiration." Maddie skimmed her fingers over Lourdes'.

"I feel you might inspire me more and more as time goes on."

"I'll certainly do my best," Lourdes wiggled her eyebrows flirtatiously. The food came, a veggie burger for Lourdes and a harvest salad for Maddie. It was a spinach-based salad with gorgonzola cheese, dried cranberries, and walnuts. Maddie poured a small cup of balsamic dressing onto her salad and mixed it up. They ate silently, with Maddie and Lourdes staring at one another between bites and drinking water. "How are the raffle baskets going?" Lourdes asked, causing Maddie to raise an eyebrow.

"What?" Lourdes inquired. "I remember you mentioning them when we were out jogging once."

Maddie grinned. Lourdes wasn't only a great conversationalist. She was also a great listener. Maddie practically glowed from the attention.

"They're coming along great. We've met periodically to go over plans. There's going to be a dance, too. You're more than welcome if you want to come to a meeting."

Lourdes grinned. "Perhaps, but I might leave the talent to you and show up with some money."

"That's always needed, too," Maddie joked.

"The charity is going to be a huge success, though. I can feel it in my bones." Her smile slowly faded. That was if she would still be there once the fundraiser got underway. Maddie knew that she wasn't the best nurse from a technical standpoint. Maddie had to double-check the equations for converting med dosages that her coworkers could do in their heads. Her desire to connect with patients meant that her patient turnaround time was slower than others on staff.

To top it all off, Maddie was significantly behind in planning this fundraiser. She hadn't even started making a list of previous donors to reach out to. Her promotional Instagram post was currently a one-line note on her phone about putting the 'fun' in 'fundraiser.' She was supposed to draft an E-vite to send to the hospital staff, and she hadn't even picked a template.

Maddie felt her chest twinge. Her throat tightened. Was her airway closing up? Did she have a walnut allergy that no one told her about as a child?

"You're eyes instantly darkened," Lourdes commented. "I feel like you're thinking way too much." Lourdes reached across the table to grab her hand, but Maddie shied away from her touch.

Maddie huffed. "Lourdes, did it ever occur to you that I'm

not thinking enough? The fundraiser is a month away, and I haven't even started reaching out to donors! I need to cut down on my patient turnaround time. I still have a huge pile of charts left to update. And now, you come through talking about budget cuts! I'm scared that people are going to start losing their jobs. Maybe I'll lose my job, and then what? So, I'm freaking out a bit? Can you blame me?"

". Maddie, I understand where you're coming from and that you're feeling overwhelmed."

"Don't tell me how I'm feeling," Maddie snapped.

Lourdes continued, "But I don't think worrying about it will help change the situation's outcome. If anything, all it's going to do is stress you out more, and you've already got a lot on your plate," Lourdes' tone was dripping with sympathy, pity even. Suddenly, Maddie was irritated. Did Lourdes think that she was in over her head? Who was she to judge? Maddie didn't see Lourdes taking on extra tasks at the hospital. Her solution during a crisis was to grab a slice of pie and not worry about it!

"Are you trying to suggest that I can't do my job, that I'm incompetent?" Maddie asked.

Lourdes straightened up her spine, adopting a stern demeanor. She took a deep breath, trying to calm herself before continuing, "Maddie, that's not what I'm saying at all. You're a wonderful nurse. But I've been through staffing cuts aplenty. It's all a part of the business world. Nothing much anyone can do about it. Senior nurses never really like to retire early because they don't want to lose their retirement benefits. So, that means they have to find other people to cut. Sometimes they lower a person's hours or give them less desirable shifts. They move them to other departments or fire them on the spot."

"And that's just okay?"

"It is what it is. Such is life." Lourdes shrugged, and Maddie stared at her. Lourdes' nonchalant attitude was appalling. Maddie was genuinely angry now. How dare Lourdes be so blasé, not only about their livelihoods, but the quality of patient care that was sure to plummet as staffing cuts swept the hospital?

"Such is life? No biggie? That's how you feel? So, if I lost my job, it would suck to be me? Politics have no place in healthcare, Lourdes. Money shouldn't take priority over patient care. And I can't believe that you think that's alright. You don't even care about the patients that get lost in the shuffle." Maddie couldn't take it anymore. She couldn't breathe. Maddie had to get out of there. She could feel sweat pooling under her armpits. Maddie slapped her hands on the table, and Lourdes dropped her gaze to Maddie's hands. Maddie's eyes kept locked on Lourdes.

Slowly Lourdes raised her gaze, and her eyes were dim. "It's hard to care about patients when you don't have a job. You have to cut your losses somewhere, Maddie."

"Cut your losses? It's not that simple.

Maddie reached into her pocket for money and tossed it on the table. She stood up, but Lourdes reached out and grabbed her arm.

"Maddie, I know that came across as harsh, and I'm sorry. Do not rush out like this. I don't like this any more than you do, but it's the harsh reality. Now, I'm not saying this will happen to you, but when you lose a job, it's hard to think about the patients suffering. You're out a paycheck and having to put food on the table. You're scrambling to get by. It will be awful if you, or anyone else, loses their job. Yes, I will care about that. It will be a mess for the patients having to deal with even fewer bodies on the floor. But, dammit, my heart can't go out to them when I have to see coworkers getting cut. Or if I lose my job. No one is safe, and that's the harsh reality."

Maddie sighed, shaking her head. "There has to be a balance," Maddie argued.

"Care about yourself, but empathize with the patients. It's not always black and white."

Lourdes slowly pulled her hand away, and Maddie looked towards the door; Lourdes' eyes softened. "Stay. If you leave, it won't solve anything. I don't mean to be callous, but sometimes you can't do everything. It's not always in our hands."

MADDIE SUNK BACK DOWN IN HER CHAIR AND STARED STRAIGHT ahead. Yet, there had to be some way to make a change. There had to be some way to help everyone.

CHAPTER FOURTEEN

TOUGH TIMES WON'T BREAK YOU

addie skimmed through the schedule for the day. It wasn't as intense as the last couple of days, and she'd be lying if she said she wasn't looking for a little reprieve. Even ten minutes she could get back in her day would be well worth her time. She leaned back in her chair and pulled out her phone. It was still on the last text she received.

Lourdes: We're good, right? I didn't mean to freak you out last night or insinuate that you might lose your job. I know it's scary. I'm scared, too. I'm off today, so perhaps we could meet up later for a jog?

Maddie slipped the phone back into her pocket, still contemplating a response. While they ended dinner with a friendly wave, the romance had evaporated. How could Lourdes be so cynical about a profession dedicated to helping others? How could their beliefs be so different, and how could they overcome that?

Eric popped around the corner, and his brown eyes diverted from Maddie's. Plus, there wasn't even a hint of a smile. "Hey there?" Maddie began. He barely acknowledged her with a nod. Did Lourdes get to him first? Was he seriously on her side after having known Maddie for years? Maddie opened her mouth, then snapped it shut. She really didn't want to know if that was the case.

"Let's hope the day flies by," Eric mumbled.

Maddie tilted her head. That wasn't like her jovial friend. "Are you doing alright? You seem, um, a bit out of sorts. We haven't worked the same shift recently, but is everything okay?"

"Not even a little bit," he gruffly replied. He looked up, eventually meeting Maddie's gaze. "Did you hear about Shannon?"

"Ugh. Is Shannon still sick? Poor thing. She didn't look so great the last time I saw her."

"Apparently, you didn't hear." Maddie looked up as Eric turned away from his computer. "She was let go of the department. They said they had to get rid of someone. Frankly, I suspect it has to do because of her absences. They're trying to save face."

"Wow. I hadn't heard that." Maddie sunk back in her chair, recalling Lourdes' concerns about budget cuts. It had already started before she could figure out how to fix things.

"How'd she take it? Was she fired, fired? Or sent to another unit?"

"They offered her geriatrics, but she gave an excuse that she lost her grandma last year and didn't think she could see the patients suffering. Apparently, that was a lie. So, she's gone. How would any of us take it, though? I imagine she was blindsided and didn't know how to deal."

He shook his head. "I'm sorry, Maddie. I'm not taking it out on you. It's just I'm frustrated. With the workload the way it is, we will look at longer hours, and before you know it, we'll be drowning." He stood up from the computer and grabbed a chart. "Speaking of, I have to get to the first patient."

Maddie considered those words all morning as she called her patients and did everything she could to keep that look attentive. With fewer patients, the morning dragged on. She crossed paths with Eric a few times, but they were mostly in separate areas, like two ships passing at sea.

"Mind if I take a break?" Maddie asked when she finally caught up with him just after eleven o'clock.

"Nah! I'll go when you're back." Maddie made sure she had her cell phone tucked in her pocket, then left the nurse's station and headed to the elevator. Her phone vibrated once she had gotten through the elevator doors.

Lourdes: Thinking of you, Maddie. Please give me a call.

Maddie fell back against the elevator and stared straight ahead. On the ride to the break room, the elevator stopped off at another floor, and another pediatric nurse, who Maddie only knew in passing, stepped onto the elevator. She gave Maddie a curt nod, then turned to face the front. Maddie appreciated the silence, and as the doors opened, she waited for her to get off and followed her.

She sighed in relief when the nurse darted to the exit, and

Maddie entered the break room. She was the only one there and could use the moment of solitude. Maddie retrieved her phone again and pulled up her dad's number. Lourdes' messages stared her in the face.

"Hello?" A woman's voice answered.

"Oh. I'm sorry. I think I have the wrong number." She glanced at her phone. Dad flashed across the screen. She frowned and turned her attention back to the phone. "Is this Dave Anderson's phone?"

"Yes, honey. Give me just a minute. David?"

David? Maddie hung onto the phone, trying desperately to hear anything else, but there was silence.

"Maddie? What a nice surprise."

"Hey, Dad. Who was that?"

"Oh, that? Just a friend. I was away from my phone, and she grabbed it." Maddie arched an eyebrow. *Friend?* She couldn't remember the last time he had a woman over to the house. It was probably something like eighteen years ago. Let alone someone comfortable enough to pick up a phone call on his cell.

"How are you doing?"

"Um, I'm fine. I just wanted to check up on you. How are you feeling?" She'd visited him briefly after the accident, stopping by to drop off some salmon filets she'd made with Lourdes' recipe. While he seemed perfectly fine, save for a cut on his forehead, Maddie still wanted to check up on him.

"Oh honey, I'm still fine. Nothing's changed in the past three days! No worries." He hesitated. "But are you sure you're fine? Remember, I'm your father. I can tell if something isn't right."

Maddie huffed. "Well, if you want the truth." Maddie

collapsed into the nearest chair. "I'm not doing so great. I just found out that one of my co-workers, a fellow nurse, was let go from the department. She's had some health problems and had to miss some work, but that's not everything. There's talk about more budget cuts; if I'm being honest, I'm nervous. I'm nervous I'll be the next to go."

"Honey," Maddie's dad's soothing voice came through the receiver. "You are a hard worker, and they know that about you. They would be foolish to let you leave. However, even if they did, you could find another job. There are plenty out there. I have faith in you. Just remember, the world is a better place when you're in it, and you are meant to do great things."

Maddie exhaled. "Thanks, Dad, but I can't imagine having to start all over again. What if I'm not prepared for that? What if I take losing my job as my biggest downfall, and then I spiral, and I can never get another job?"

There was a long hesitation on the other end of the line. Maddie checked her phone twice to ensure the call hadn't been dropped. "I know it's difficult when your mind and heart are struggling. But you have to remember that you and I faced many hard times when you were growing up. Do you remember when I got laid off? You were only eight, and it was Christmas. You feared we would lose the house, but I assured you that as long as we were together, nothing bad could ever happen."

"You got a new job on New Year's Eve, and it was like none of that had ever happened." Maddie tried to smile, though it couldn't even reach her eyes. "I remember"

"And how about college? You swore that you were failing all your classes and would never be able to pass and get your degree. But look at you now. Bad times are inevitable, but you'll get through them. We always do."

Maddie always felt good after talking to her dad. However, in this instance, she was still depleted and too anxious to hold onto hope that all would be well. Her stomach tightened, and she winced.

"Are you there?"

"Yeah, Dad. I'm here. I know you're right. It's just...." Her words trailed off. "I better get back to work. Glad you're still feeling alright. Love you, Dad."

"Love you, too. And please try not to worry. Nothing good will come of that." As soon as he said that, her mind returned to her heated conversation with Lourdes.

"I'll do my best." She hung up the call and looked at Lourdes' two messages. *Just breathe, Maddie.* As Maddie sat there, she did a few breathing exercises, hoping they would lessen the stress that had quickly built inside her. Alongside the breathing, she worked on her stretches, keeping her eyes closed and practically feeling Lourdes right beside her. After ten minutes, she felt a tad better, but still a slight twinge of pain in her gut. "Everything is going to be alright."

Maddie grabbed her phone and pulled up her Instagram. She took a selfie, forcing through a smile, then added her message. *Reminder, don't get caught up in daily stress. You'll only burn yourself out. Do those stretches, and you'll be feeling better in no time. Keep stretching. Keep smiling.*

"And post." She stood up, and her phone vibrated as she headed to the door. Lourdes had left her a like, and Maddie frowned. It would look suspicious if she didn't respond to her texts. She pulled up Lourdes' messages.

Maddie: Hey, babe. We're absolutely swamped over here, so I haven't had time to check my messages. Talk soon?

That should suffice at the moment. Things would be alright with them. She just needed to get out of this funk. Eventually, she'd get there.

CHAPTER FIFTEEN

UNEXPECTED VISITOR

The rain started to fall the minute Maddie exited the hospital. She looked up into the sky, and a splash hit her face. "Go figure!" She ran towards her car but was soaked when she slipped into the front seat. Maddie backed out of her parking spot and drove to her apartment building. Her phone started ringing, and Lourdes' number came over Bluetooth.

"Answer," she mumbled. "Hello?"

"Oh, good. Glad I caught you! Are you going home right after work?"

"Um yeah, but it's been a long day, and I want to rest. So, I'll be home, but I'm not really into...." Her words trailed off as her building came into view. Lourdes parked her car in the first parking spot behind Maddie's building. Maddie lived on the second floor of a two-flat on the outskirts of Little Village. Lourdes stood outside near the back door, umbrella in one hand, roses in another. "And you're here."

"I hope you don't mind. I was just in the neighborhood. I thought I'd surprise you. Surprise."

Maddie smiled. All of the tension that she had been holding in her body evaporated. Maddie worried that her last conversation with Lourdes had left them on bad terms. Even with the rain pouring down and Lourdes struggling to keep her umbrella up, she looked elegant and beautiful. "Glad to see you." Maddie hung up the call and got out of her car. Lourdes held the flowers up, a wide-toothed grin on her lips.

"Okay, hear me out. I know it's cliche, but I had no idea what your favorite flower was. I hope you like roses!"

"They're beautiful. Thank you. But let's get out of the rain." She grabbed the flowers from Lourdes and fished her keys out of her pocket.

"Just one moment." Maddie hurried past Lourdes and to the front door, unaware of what Lourdes was doing, until she reached the stairs to her apartment with a pizza box in her hands. "I brought dinner. I hope you're hungry."

"Famished." They went up the stairs, and Maddie motioned to her door. Maddie opened the door for her, and they were both dripping wet, standing in the narrow front hallway. Once the door was closed, she turned to Lourdes. "Hi," she said again. Lourdes beamed.

"I hope you don't mind an unexpected visitor," Lourdes smirked, and Maddie was in awe of how beautiful someone could appear with wet hair matted around her face. Still, Lourdes took her breath away.

Maddie opened her mouth and looked around her small foyer. This was the first time Lourdes stepped foot in her home, and that realization quickly hit her. She wondered what Lourdes would think of her apartment. While Lourdes lived in an elegantly furnished apartment with framed reproductions of famous paintings and a cloud-soft velvet loveseat, Maddie still used her futon from her college apartment as her couch. She found her kitchen table on Craigslist and the accompanying plastic chairs in the alley behind her apartment. After work, she barely had time to think, let alone decorate. The walls were bare except for a *Love and Basketball* poster that Eric got her for her birthday last year. That movie had been her gay awakening in high school. Lourdes was staring at it now.

She looked back and met Lourdes' inquisitive gaze, then shrugged. "I'm happy to see you. The living room is in there. I'll grab some plates and wine and be there in just a moment."

"Do you have any beer?" Lourdes inquired.

Maddie looked over at her. Once again, she was awe-struck. "You're so elegant. You drink beer?"

Lourdes laughed. "There's still so much you need to learn about me, Maddie." She winked and then disappeared into the living room

Maddie went towards the kitchen and took in a whiff of the roses. And there was so much Maddie wanted to know. The roses smelled just as lovely as Lourdes. Maddie smiled, and suddenly her worries about their relationship vanished. She could compromise. Maddie grabbed a vase, filled it with water, and dropped the roses in it. She grabbed a stack of napkins and two beers and was ready to get the evening going.

Once back in the living room, she stopped short of the couch. Lourdes had lit all three of the candles that Maddie owned, allowing the living room and Lourdes herself to take on a soft, atmospheric glow. Maddie stared at Lourdes from a short distance, where Lourdes was oblivious. She attempted to lean closer and heard Lourdes humming a gentle melody. Maddie couldn't make out the tune, but Lourdes was engrossed.

After several minutes of gawking and listening to the song, Maddie cleared her throat. Lourdes twirled around; her cheeks flushed. "How long were you standing there?"

"Long enough." Maddie quirked up her lips. "Beautiful song."

"Thank you. My mother wrote it."

"Are you ready to eat? Again, I had to guess your pizza preferences. Do you like veggies with black olives?"

" Perfect," she replied, turning back to her guest.

They sat down and began eating and drinking their beers, neither rushing to make any small talk. Maddie wiped her mouth halfway through her slice and smiled. The silence didn't bother her. Even if there was any leftover awkwardness from the previous night, Maddie was already over it. Her mind returned to the song Lourdes had hummed as they sat there. Her mother wrote it. Those words played in a loop in Maddie's mind. Her reverie was interrupted by a soft meow. She turned to her cat, Cheddar, as he entered the living room.

"You have a cat?" Lourdes asked, eyes wide.

"Um yeah, I do. You're not allergic or anything, are you?"

Lourdes laughed. "No, I love cats." She reached out and immediately scratched behind Cheddar's ear. Cheddar started to purr.

"Better watch out," Maddie warned. "He'll think you're here only to see him, and he'll hang all over you."

Lourdes grinned. "What's his name?"

"Cheddar."

"Like the cheese?" Lourdes asked.

"It is my favorite," Maddie confessed.

Lourdes smiled, leaned in, and began baby-talking to Cheddar as he purred and crawled up into her lap. She laughed, snuggling her nose into his fur. Maddie shook her head in disbelief. He was a friendly cat, but sometimes it took days for him to warm up to a stranger. In this instance, it seemed like he knew Lourdes even better than she did. Maddie ate her pizza, with Lourdes seemingly forgetting she was even there. Lourdes continued to talk to Cheddar, leaving Maddie shocked.

After a moment, Maddie caught herself a bit jealous. She would laugh at it later, jealous of a cat, somehow watching Lourdes interact with Cheddar only endeared her to her more. Maddie cleared her throat, patting her mouth with the napkin.

"So, anyway, that song from earlier," Maddie began. "You mentioned your mother, but I thought she died when you were only two."

Lourdes nodded, finally looking up, but still scratching behind Cheddar's ears, then moving to under his chin. "She did, but a few years ago, I started to have flashbacks, memories I never held onto before then. Those memories included thoughts of that song. Then I started to think vividly about her and how she would hum that song to me to get me to fall asleep. I have journals from her younger years discussing singing and writing music. Those journals made me realize that I didn't just have random memories. I remember the days when my mom was alive. I strongly believe that children latch onto early childhood memories."

"Wow! That must be so exciting for you."

Cheddar moved away from them and hopped into his bed, closing his eyes and settling down to snooze. Maddie turned her attention back to Lourdes.

"Memories are sometimes all you have, so you should hold onto those. And I hum the song, so I never forget." She gave a gracious smile.

Maddie smiled. She loved how Lourdes' brain worked. Lourdes' vulnerability inspired her to be more open.

"What about you, Maddie? Do you have memories of when you were a child?"

Maddie considered the question. Outside of what she and her father had discussed earlier, she couldn't recall many memories before she was eight. Maddie had one picture of her mom, but looking at it made her question why her mom had left her. She couldn't remember her face on command.

"I don't know. I guess not. I blocked out most of my childhood. I had a few memories of experiences with my dad when I was eight, then maybe ten. But most of my memory comes from my teenage years." Maddie sipped on her beer.

"Well, I firmly believe that memories have a strange way of working themselves in, so don't ignore them if they happen to pop into your mind one day."

"I won't." Maddie dropped her gaze to her pizza and grabbed an olive, tossing it into her mouth.

After another few minutes, the silence was thick, and Lourdes looked at Maddie. "So," Lourdes began. "The truth is, I didn't just come here for pizza and flowers. Although, I like to believe it cheered you up a bit ."

"Absolutely! I didn't know how much I needed it until you arrived."

Lourdes glanced over to Cheddar, a pensive look overtaking her expression. "But when we left each other at the diner, I got the feeling that things were so awkward with us. Then, I texted you, and you seemed to be avoiding me. I was hoping it wasn't intentional. But then you posted the Instagram picture, and I thought, okay, she's got her phone, so she must be upset. Perhaps even angry."

"I wasn't angry," Maddie argued. "I guess you could say I was upset." Maddie finished off her beer, then shrugged. "I don't want to discuss it. Everything is fine now. Do you want another beer?" She stood up and reached for Lourdes' napkin and beer bottle.

"Nah, I'm good," Lourdes quietly replied. "Every relationship has conflicts, Maddie. It's how we deal with them that matters." Maddie put the bottles and napkins on her coffee table and sat back down. "If you were upset with me, I would prefer we work it out sooner."

Maddie paused. In past relationships, she tended to stuff conflict down and avoid it at all costs, but she could tell that what she had with Lourdes was different.

Maddie took a deep breath, "There are moments when I worry that maybe we're living in a fantasy world."

Lourdes frowned. "How so?" Lourdes' bright eyes had lost their glow.

"You and I are so different. I question how we could keep a connection going when sometimes I wonder if you are too abrupt about your patients. I feel like you sometimes have a business-like sense regarding patient care. Whereas I like to believe that we can save all patients and do what we need to, for the better of the patients, regardless of money matters."

"You are optimistic, and that's a great quality, Maddie. I envy you for that. But I'm not sarcastic, and I'm not pessimistic by nature. And regardless of what you think, I care about the patients just as much as you do." Lourdes sighed.

"Maybe I've become more cynical than I used to be. The fact is, I used to be a lot more like you when it came to patients. I suppose you can say I was a hopeless optimist."

Her eyes softened. "I use a lot of trips as my getaway, so I can truly relax, center myself, and then work even harder when I get back. A couple of years ago, I booked a trip to the Caribbean. I was excited about it. There would be volunteering, but I would also have time for myself." She shook her head, and Maddie saw a tear on her cheek. Lourdes flicked it away like she didn't want Maddie to see.

Maddie touched Lourdes' hand, causing Lourdes to look up and smile briefly. "What happened on the trip?"

"Actually, it happened before the trip," Lourdes quietly recounted.

"I had a patient that I was super close with. You could say she was my favorite patient, even though you're not supposed to have those." She laughed, and Maddie knew the feeling. She didn't interrupt, just listened, waiting for Lourdes to continue.

"The night before I was supposed to leave, I left the hospital I was working at early. She seemed fine. There wasn't any reason to think that something horrible was about to happen. I got the call at eleven o'clock that night that she had a massive heart attack and died instantly. I nearly didn't go on the trip, but her voice played through my mind. You'll regret this, Lourdes. Don't stay on my account. She was young, just a few years older than me. And I questioned life, my Faith, and whether I even wanted to continue this career. Despite missing her funeral, I opted to go on the trip. But you could say her passing changed my life, made me change. Her passing showed me that you couldn't get too involved because if something happens, it can practically kill you. At least kill your spirit."

A tear peeked out of the corner of Lourdes' eye, and Maddie reached up and brushed it away. "Losing a patient is never easy," Maddie quietly replied.

"Some are just harder than others. I don't want you ever to have to feel this way because it ate me up inside. I started to realize that you can't get overly invested. I know it seems callous. But it's not that I don't care. Sometimes I care too much, and I see that inside of you. There's only so much a body can handle." Lourdes' eyes widened, and she stared directly into Maddie's soul. You and I have a lot in common, eating healthy, exercising, and loving life. That's why I feel it far outweighs our differences."

Maddie snaked her hand around Lourdes' neck and pulled her to her. Her forehead rested against Lourdes,' and they stayed in that position for what seemed like an eternity. Lourdes' breath brushed against Maddie's lips, but she didn't move to end their intimate connection.

Cheddar meowed, breaking that moment and causing them both to laugh. Maddie pulled away, and Cheddar scooted onto

Lourdes' lap. Maddie reached out and petted her cat, then looked up at Lourdes. At that moment, she realized that Lourdes and her dad were right. Moments of conflict were a part of life; it wasn't something you had to avoid. If you were lucky, you got to work through it together.

CHAPTER SIXTEEN

READY TO BREAK

Lourdes grabbed Maddie's hand and pulled her into an empty exam room. She pressed Maddie up against the wall and gave her a passionate kiss, her tongue sweeping across Maddie's, causing a deep moan to release through her mouth.

"We have patients," Maddie protested, letting Lourdes' body hover over hers, keeping her warm and safe. Lourdes ignored her, pressing a trail of kisses along her neck. "We should get back," Maddie argued, letting the kiss deepen as Lourdes didn't utter one word.

"Just five minutes," Maddie whispered, snaking her hand up Lourdes' shirt and clamping onto Lourdes' bra. If only five minutes was enough.

"Maddie? Maddie?" A bell sounded, and Maddie jerked

awake from her daydream. Sierra Hinshaw, the head nurse of her department, stared at her, squinting her blue eyes, radiating scrutiny. She'd fallen asleep at the nurses' station! Maddie could have sworn she was resting her eyes. She hadn't slept in days. Every night she went to bed, she tossed and turned as an endless loop of worries and disasters circled her mind. A hot clod of dread settled in her stomach. Maddie wanted to throw up. "Do you have the time to sit around? Did I see your eyes closed?"

"No, Sierra. I was thinking," Maddie insisted.

"About the waiting room full of patients, I hope." Sierra's eyes widened as she gawked at Maddie.

"Something like that," Maddie mumbled. "I'm going." She turned and hurried to the waiting room. The waiting room was packed, and the encounter with Sierra left her reeling.

"Mike?" she called.

Mike came walking up, a grin on his lips. "Hey, Maddie. I've been feeling pretty good now. That should get me at least a sucker. Or, I could go for a cup of Joe."

"We'll see about that," Maddie muttered. "Take a seat, and I'll grab your vitals." Without looking in his direction, she grabbed the blood pressure cuff and pulse oximeter and worked on getting his vitals. "Looks good," Maddie said, quickly jotting some information down. "How are you feeling?"

He frowned. "Uh, pretty good; no complaints this week. I might miss my son's baseball game, but I am trying to get some hours in at work. Overall, just awesome."

"Good!" It'd been nearly two weeks since his latest mild heart attack, and his improvement was a relief. She looked down at his chart and stood up from the stool. "Follow me."

He reached out for her arm before she could get away. "What about you? How are things?"

Maddie's cheeks flushed. "Um yeah, it's great." She couldn't even lie her way through that one. She forced a smile.

"Really good. You said your son has a game coming up. So, he made the team?"

"Was there any doubt," Mike teased. "He'll be a star just like his father. Let's hope a bum shoulder doesn't take him out like his good ol' Dad."

"Hopefully, he'll be fine, but I'm sure he has plenty of years for you to worry about that." Maddie winked, and Mike's grin returned. "Follow me." On the walk to the exam room, she looked over at him, ensuring she kept her steps in line with his. "Anything else new? Diet? Exercise?"

"I'm feeling great, Maddie. I swear. I feel better than I've felt in years. I'm looking forward to living life to the fullest and loving every minute of it." She was glad that at least someone was feeling good. Maddie, on the other hand, was exhausted. She felt like a shell of a human being. She was still behind on her plans for the charity auction. Only one donor had gotten back to her, and it seemed the entire hospital ignored her e-vite, except for Lourdes.

She was too stressed to eat or sleep. Maddie's normally healthy diet had been reduced to protein bars and Red Bull, which she hated, but needed to stay awake. The Red Bull made her jittery, so even though her limbs felt like they were made of lead, her heart pounded a mile a minute. She couldn't keep down any real food. It was impossible to focus on one patient, and her caseload had increased since Shannon's untimely departure.

She forced a smile, "That makes me super happy to hear. Hang out in here, and Noelle will be with you shortly."

"Thanks, Maddie. Good to see you."

"Good seeing you, too, Mike. Take care."

Maddie smiled, feeling relieved that she could return to her old ways. If Mike knew something was off, it could hinder his continued improvement. She needed him to stay as calm as he possibly could.

As she left the room, Lourdes met her outside. "Hey," Maddie replied. She wanted to pull her into an exam room and reenact the fantasy from this morning, but with Sierra watching, nothing of the sort could happen. Even after five weeks, the sparks continued to fly between Maddie and Lourdes.

"I don't want to make you stressed," Lourdes whispered. "But the waiting room is packed, and people are complaining about waiting longer than necessary for their appointment. I'm not sure if you noticed, but Sierra has her eyes on the department."

"I noticed," Maddie mumbled. "I'll pick up the pace." If she wasn't pleased, then no one was pleased.

Lourdes gave Maddie a weak smile, dismissed herself, and rushed in the opposite direction. Maddie turned to see Sierra staring right at her; just another thing to worry about. She quickly walked to the nurse's station and grabbed another chart.

"Maddie?"

Maddie whirled around. "Yes, Sierra?"

"When your shift is over, can I please see you in my office?" Without another word, she turned and walked away.

Maddie looked down at the chart, tears threatening to fall. *Don't cry, Maddie. It's all going to work out.* But Maddie wasn't really sure about that. She had to pick up her pace and get through the rest of her shift, but it would likely be the longest six hours of her life.

MADDIE'S HEART BEAT FASTER AND FASTER AS SHE NEARED Sierra's office. She hesitated right outside the door. What could she possibly need to see her about? *It's obvious. Isn't it? You will be just another rung on the ladder that will be cut.* Maddie released a breath and knocked on the door. She heard a slight murmur but couldn't make out the words, so she opened the door and peeked her head in.

"Is now okay?"

Sierra looked up and motioned for her to enter, then Maddie closed the door behind her. If she was going to be fired, she wanted it when no one could hear it all happening. Maddie sat in the chair directly before her, and her leg started to tap nervously. She touched her knee, willing it to stop moving.

Sierra looked up, zero expression on her face. "I've been going through the documentation in charts and on the computer, and I must admit that I'm disappointed, Maddie."

A punch to the gut wouldn't have hurt anymore. "Excuse me?"

"There are missing holes. The timelines are hard to follow." Sierra shook her head. "It's lackluster work, to say the least."

"I apologize. I'll do better."

Sierra sighed. "It's not even just the documentation. You continuously run behind. I observed most of your day; you took the longest with all your patients. We have a waiting room full of nervous patients waiting to be seen, but you weren't anywhere to be found."

"Sierra, I was in with the patients. I might take more time, but that's because I want to take extra care and show them compassion." Sierra arched an eyebrow, and Maddie bit on her lower lip. It wasn't the time to argue with Sierra, so why even try?

"I will speed up my turnaround time," Maddie mumbled. And right along with that, cut the empathy in half. What about that? She wanted to scream that out, see if Sierra cared, but she continued to bite her lip, holding back everything she longed to say.

"And there's more," Sierra continued. Maddie sunk back in her seat and nodded. "I have noticed that you have worked lots of overtime lately. Unapproved, I might add." Sierra looked down at some papers in front of her. "If you would have gotten the work done while doing overtime, then that'd be one thing, but the way I see it, you haven't. So, the OT needs to stop. Understood?"

"Yes!"

Sierra grimaced. "If I were allowed to not pay you for the extra time you worked, I'd gladly take back the payment. Maybe that would assist with some of the budget issues." The latter part was mainly built-in grumbles and not meant for Maddie to hear. She continued to stay quiet, not inquiring about it further.

"I don't want to let you go, Maddie. You're one of my more compassionate employees, but rules are rules, and we must keep the ship running, or else we'll sink. Got it?"

"Got it." Maddie stood up. "Am I free to go?"

Sierra nodded, and Maddie dismissed herself by quickly leaving the office, the door shutting behind her a little louder than she anticipated. She felt the tears threatening to fall as she hurried to the elevator to take it down to the lobby and out the front door. Before the elevator could close, Lourdes rushed to it and stopped it with her hand.

"Just the person I wanted to see!" Lourdes panted. Maddie quickly flicked away a couple of tears that escaped. "Are you hungry? I thought we could go to Ginkgo. It's been a long day, and we both deserve it. What do you say?"

"I don't know, Lourdes," Maddie whispered. "I don't think I'm great company tonight."

Lourdes tilted her head. "Are you crying?"

Maddie shook her head but then fell back against the elevator wall. "Sierra called me into the office and reprimanded me for taking too much time with patients and extra overtime. I'm just trying to be compassionate, not drain the hospital budget dry! I don't know how much more of this I can take. If I hurry through the patients, then they're upset. If I don't, then my boss is upset."

"Maddie!" Lourdes pulled her into her arms and gave her a warm embrace. "You need dinner tonight! Let me take you out and do whatever I can for you not to think about Sierra and this hospital."

Maddie nodded. That seemed like an enticing offer that Maddie couldn't refuse.

CHAPTER SEVENTEEN

WHAT DOESN'T KILL YOU

Maddie stared at her reflection in the bathroom mirror of Gingko. She had just about got the red out of her eyes, but the conversation with Sierra wouldn't leave her mind. Maddie splashed water on her cheeks and pulled her hair out of her ponytail holder. She fluffed her hair with her hands, hoping she looked more presentable than when she first entered the restaurant's bathroom.

Ginkgo was an upscale vegan restaurant that served home-made Vegan Asian fusion. She'd only been there a couple of times, but their spring rolls were to die for. The soft, sensual lighting and cozy booths made it date-night-ready. She looked down at her scrubs and snickered. Not many customers probably dressed so down, but Lourdes made her baby-blue scrubs look runway ready. She wore her hair in a loose ponytail, her gold hoop earrings peeking out beneath her curls. Unlike Maddie, Lourdes didn't seem bothered by the fact that they were stuck wearing medical-regulation scrubs. The waitress didn't seem to mind.

She gave herself a once over and turned from her reflection. She had to return to the table so Lourdes didn't think she had ditched her.

The waitress had arrived, poured them wine, and dropped off their food by the time Maddie returned. Lourdes ordered spring rolls for the table and lettuce wraps with gochujang-infused jack fruit.

"Thank you," Lourdes replied as the waitress left. "Feeling better?" she asked.

"Absolutely." Maddie grinned, hoping that smile did what she desired. Lourdes smiled, but it didn't even look all that convincing. "The food looks delicious. Thanks for the recommendation." She picked up her fork, but her stomach churned, and she feared she would throw up if she attempted to take a bite.

"You know, Maddie. A boss is there for one reason: to dictate how things should work. I know you feel that Sierra scolded you." She shrugged. "But that's their job." Maddie looked up as Lourdes continued. "With the budget cuts, sadly, the supervisors will have to monitor everyone's actions more closely. I'm not trying to scare you. I don't think you have anything to worry about. Everyone knows how great you are with the patients." Lourdes took a big bite of a spring roll and smiled.

Maddie smiled hesitantly and looked down at the lettuce wraps on her plate. She picked up her fork and deconstructed a lettuce wrap, scraping the filling. "I get what you're saying. I do."

Maddie took a small bite but had to smile through it. "I was worried that the reason I was getting called into her office was my turn to turn in my name badge, no goodbye, nothing. I can't imagine not getting a chance to say goodbye to your friends."

"Well, Maddie, if you're truly friends, you'll see each other after you get fired. Just because you've been let go at the hospital doesn't mean your real friends will abandon you." Again, with that matter-of-fact attitude. It was truthful but still disheartening at the same time. She was always so cynical, yet spoke with grace. After seeing Lourdes' vulnerability, the remarks didn't come across as harsh.

Maddie fished her phone out of her pocket and pulled up her Instagram. She snapped a picture of her food with a thumbs up, then pocketed her phone. Looking up, she saw Lourdes staring at her.

"Why do you do that?"

"Do what?"

"When we're in the middle of a difficult conversation and talking about something serious, you pop out your phone and take a selfie or take a picture of your food, or write something motivational. It feels like you're focusing on your followers instead of me." Lourdes insisted.

"I don't do that," Maddie argued. Lourdes nodded, and Maddie looked down at her food, sensing another scolding about to take place.

"I guess because it's easy. I interact with them because I know they'll always be in my corner. Even when I might lose my job or get reprimanded because someone doesn't like my work, I'll still have my Instagram and all of the friends I've made through my account," Maddie explained.

Lourdes slowly nodded, then smirked. "Just your followers? You think they will be the only ones that stick by you?"

"That's not what I'm saying."

"Well, that's what it sounded like. Maddie, I'm in your corner. I am doing everything I can to help you, but getting a small reprimand from Sierra isn't anything like losing your job. At least she warned you. Now all you have to do is heed that warning. You know how to fix it. She says that you should take less time with each patient."

"And spend more time on documentation. All while making sure I don't go into overtime. That doesn't even seem feasible."

"It's doable. Anything is doable."

"You're always so confident. I don't know how you do it."

Lourdes snickered, "It hasn't always been that way. I've had my fair share of setbacks. I thought if I pushed and pushed, I could do it all. It turns out I was so focused on getting everything done that I was missing out on what life had to offer. Then I was hospitalized for exhaustion when I was in college. Striving to be the best nearly took me out of the running."

"I understand what you're saying." Maddie dropped her gaze to her food. She needed to eat, gather some energy, and relax. But it was all easier said than done. She grabbed her fork and took a small bite. The lettuce was crisp, and the jackfruit absorbed the spice of the gochujang sauce well. It would have been delicious on an average day. Yet, with her stomach lurching and jumping a thousand hurdles, it wouldn't be long before she would have to excuse herself to the restroom. She pushed her fork around her plate, hoping Lourdes didn't notice that her plate was still full.

"Well, I hope you don't worry too much about Sierra."

Lourdes reached out and placed her palm over Maddie's hand. Maddie looked up, and Lourdes winked at her. "We all know that you are the hardest working nurse there. Just appease her for a few days, and she'll move on to someone else to harass. Trust me." She moved her hand against Maddie's, and that quick motion softened Maddie's heart. Lourdes was trying, and that was more than she could acknowledge about other people in her life. She was right, too. Sierra would move on as long as Maddie took a little less time with each patient and didn't log all the overtime. She would find a way to treat the patients with the courtesy they came to know from her, even if she didn't give them as much time. It was all about balance. Maddie would soon have to figure it out or lose everything she had worked for. She wouldn't go down without a fight, and with any luck, she would come out stronger in the end.

CHAPTER EIGHTEEN

BASKETS FOR CHARITY

Maddie stifled a yawn as she left the break room. Her phone buzzed, and she reached into her pocket and checked her texts.

Noelle: Are we still on for tonight in making the baskets?

Maddie: Just leaving the hospital. I'll meet you, ladies, there.

Even though she was exhausted after a long day, she looked forward to getting the raffle baskets made. She reached the elevator and was about to push the button when she felt an arm around her, dragging her towards another direction. She giggled when she recognized the lavender and thyme scent that washed over her.

"Lourdes? What are you doing?"

Lourdes pushed through an empty exam room, startling Maddie. She finally released her, and Maddie turned to see

Lourdes locking the door. Maddie tapped her foot and stared at her captor. Lourdes whirled around and leaned back against the door.

"Hello," she said, smirking as she closed the gap. "We didn't get two minutes alone today, and that's a crying shame." She looped her arms around Maddie's neck and pulled her to her, the hunger dancing in her eyes. She kissed Maddie, sucking on Maddie's lower lip, sending a shiver up and down Maddie's spine.

"Lourdes," Maddie argued, attempting to pull back but to no avail. Granted, she didn't try all that hard. "I was just about to leave. I have plans."

"Break them," Lourdes replied, kissing her harder. She slipped her tongue into Maddie's mouth and weaved her fingers through her hair.

Maddie laughed and snaked her hands up the back of Lourdes' scrubs. She grabbed Lourdes' shirt and pulled it over her breasts. Briefly, Maddie broke from the kiss to unhook Lourdes' bra. She kissed Lourdes once more, surprising herself with the force of her desire. Maddie moved her lips down, tracing the soft skin of her throat with her tongue, peppering her collarbone with kisses. She paused, admiring Lourdes' supple breasts, before taking her nipple in her mouth and sucking. Maddie felt Lourdes' nipple pebble inside of her mouth. Satisfied, she moved onto the left breast; Lourdes groaned. Maddie knelt in front of Lourdes, running her tongue along the smooth plane of her tanned stomach. She toyed with the waistband of Lourdes' scrubs, grinning as she felt Lourdes begin to squirm. Lourdes stepped out of her shoes, and Maddie carefully peeled off her pants, revealing the lacy, dark red waistband of Lourdes' underwear. She tugged on the waistband of Lourdes' underwear with her teeth as Lourdes' leaned back against the bed. Once her panties were on the floor, Maddie could see that Lourdes was dripping wet. The soft flesh of her thighs glistened with desire. Maddie took Lourdes' wrists and shoved her back onto the bed, ready to take charge.

"What's gotten into you?" Lourdes asked as Maddie trailed kisses down her belly.

"I just missed you," Maddie replied. Quickly, Maddie shrugged off her scrubs.

Maddie dropped to her knees and moved in to greet Lourdes' femininity. She slid her tongue into Lourdes, slowly at first. Maddie licked upward, tracing the delicate skin of her clit, lapping up and down, feeling the warmth of Lourdes in her mouth. She licked upward, sucking on the mound of Lourdes' clitoris. Lourdes' breath hitched. She reached down and grabbed Maddie's hands, slinging her legs around Maddie's neck and settling her feet on Maddie's shoulders. Maddie felt Lourdes' thighs begin to shake as she licked, increasing her speed.

"More," Lourdes panted. Maddie was more than happy to oblige. It felt as if she was drowning in Lourdes. Her cheeks were pillowed between Lourdes' impossibly soft thighs. She felt Lourdes' thighs clench around her face; Lourdes was starting to whimper, emboldened. Maddie lapped even harder, sucking on her clit as Lourdes' hips bucked as she rode the waves of her orgasm. The sound of her name echoed as Lourdes came. Time stood still. What would ten minutes hurt?

Forty-five minutes later, they were getting dressed, with generous smiles playing on their lips. "What's the plan?" Lourdes asked.

Maddie laughed, standing at the door of their hospital room. "You were the one that thought up this plan."

Lourdes winked. "I guess our desires took over. But how about you leave first, and I'll wait about ten minutes and duck out of here. Will I see you later?"

"Are you kidding me? After this, you won't be able to get rid of me." Maddie wrapped her arms around Lourdes and kissed her. She could still taste sex on her lips. "I'll call you later."

"I'll be waiting for it."

Maddie opened the door and peeked out into the hallway. The coast was clear, or so she thought. As she stepped into the hallway, two nurses came around the corner. They nodded, but Maddie barely acknowledged them. She rushed to the elevator, all while putting her ponytail back together. Once in the elevator, Maddie fell back against the wall and stood there with a sappy grin. It wasn't until the elevator doors opened and she rushed towards the front door that she heard her phone buzz.

She fished the phone out of her pocket but didn't hesitate to hurry to her car.

Noelle: Hey, Maddie! Just checking in! You were supposed to be here an hour ago.

Maddie: Sorry. Wound up getting called back to the department. Emergency. Leaving now.

Granted, it was less of an emergency than a fulfillment of her wildest fantasies, but Noelle didn't need to know that.

Maddie jumped in her car and quickly backed out of her parking spot. It'd been three days since Sierra had spoken with her. She had tried to abide by all the rules and succeeded. And based on the last encounter with Lourdes, her relationship was thriving. Overall, Maddie was feeling much better. Truthfully, she didn't mind missing the overtime. She missed a few breaks here and there to ensure she got her documentation done, but she could do without her breaks if Sierra left her alone. To her relief, Sierra hadn't seemed to be paying too much attention to how Maddie coped with the reprimand. Maddie's most challenging task was taking less time with her patients, but as each day progressed, she got quicker at the tasks. So, maybe it was all doable, especially with Lourdes by her side.

Maddie turned into the parking lot of Cayman's Event Hall and saw that the parking lot was packed. She parked in the furthest spot away and headed to the front door. Once inside the banquet hall, she saw the other women sitting at tables, working on their creative basket designs. They had already worked hard to plan the event, but the fun part was this: putting the baskets together for the raffle.

"And there's our fearless leader," Noelle remarked. "An hour late, but who's counting?" She winked, and Maddie shrugged.

" I'm hardly the leader. Sorry for my delay. Duty called."

"What was the emergency?" Noelle asked. "I thought I left things relatively quiet."

Maddie opened her mouth, then snapped it shut. *Think, Maddie. Think.* "You know, Marilyn. Well, there's always an issue. She's getting ready to be discharged. She had a panic attack. We couldn't find Lourdes, but crisis averted."

Noelle rolled her eyes. "Yeah, she's sort of a hypochondriac, but glad she's able to get out of there and go to rehab."

Maddie gave a weak smile, but inside, she was beaming. She had gotten away with the small fib, and no one needed to know the real reason behind the delay. Before taking her seat, Maddie opened up the camera on her phone and took a selfie in front of the sign for the Pediatrics event. She quickly typed up a caption. *Tonight we're prepping for the big event. Show your support by purchasing a raffle ticket! Link in bio.* She put out the link and a smiley face, then slumped in her chair. "Those look great!" she exclaimed, glancing at the in-progress baskets.

"Thank you!" The women responded nearly in unison.

"And we have a whole slew of them over there that we've finished," Noelle motioned.

"Wow, you guys have made great progress." Maddie wasn't the least disappointed. She had her forty-five minutes of excitement before arriving at the hall. She wouldn't trade that for anything.

"Here's a basket, Maddie." Gina, a receptionist from the pediatric ICU wing, slid one in front of her.

"Thank you!"

They fell into a steady rhythm of decorating and gossiping. The conversation turned to the topic of the hospital's most eligible bachelor. Maddie always just listened, minding her business, as the other women remained engrossed in their little world.

"Did you see Micah?" Noelle asked. "He looked mighty fine today when I was in the break room."

Maddie laughed, unable to hold it in. "Um, aren't you married, Noelle? Isn't Micah married?" Maddie looked up, mid-bow tie, as she gawked in Noelle's direction.

Noelle smirked. "My hubby and I have an agreement. We can look, not touch." She winked. "And the fact that Micah is married, all the better. I mean, he's not an easy target to snag, so you might as well have a look. No strings attached."

Maddie snickered, looking down at her basket.

"Noelle has a point, though. He is mighty fine. It's good for me that he is married because I would be on the prowl for that one." Maddie didn't know Theresa as well as the others, but her face said it all. She was equally eager to dish about the radiology hottie.

"Speaking of studs," Gina began. "There's a new doctor in the pediatric wing. He's quite the looker. He's straight out of med school. And every sign points to him being single. I think he'd be great for you, Maddie."

"What?" Maddie squealed, looking up. Her jaw dropped.

Gina nodded. "He's a great guy. And did I mention he's a doctor? If I showed him your Insta, I imagine he'd be down to get to know you. Give me the word, and I'll make it my mission."

"Don't bother," Noelle replied, a smirk on her lips. Maddie frowned as Noelle met her eyes.

"Come on, Maddie, everyone in the department knows you and Lourdes are an item. You're not fooling anyone."

Maddie's cheeks flushed. "I don't know what you're talking about." She looked away, but the red on her cheeks was every indication of the truth.

"There's no reason to deny it." Noelle continued to work on her basket. "It's cute the way you two look at each other. And if I were a lesbian and single, I'd go for her, too." Noelle reached across the table, her eyes finally rising to meet Maddie's. "Nothing to be ashamed of there. You love who you love."

"No one said anything about love," Maddie blurted. "We're just exploring things and getting to know one another. That's all," Maddie blushed.

"Love, infatuation, whatever you want to call it. No need to hide from it." Noelle shrugged. "Infatuation can always lead to more, as well. My hubby and I sure were infatuated with each other back in high school."

She laughed. "You should have seen us." She then frowned. "But, even then, I'm not sure that we looked at each other like that. I don't know what we do after ten years of marriage." She laughed loudly.

Maddie opened her mouth to respond, but a familiar sound stopped her.

"Is there room for one more?" Maddie turned and looked towards the sound of Lourdes' voice. She had changed out of her scrubs and into her street clothes, high-waisted jeans, and a red T-shirt. Lourdes slipped her hands in her pockets, giving a sheepish grin, " I thought I'd check this place out." Maddie stared at her. Lourdes was just as radiant, with no sign of how they had sex moments earlier. Maddie only hoped that she looked as well put together.

"Not at all. Plenty of room," Noelle said, a little too eagerly.

"Um yeah, let me get you a basket." Maddie jumped up and grabbed Lourdes' hand, pulling her behind her towards the table of baskets and more decorations. "How'd you know where I was?"

"Your Instagram," Lourdes nonchalantly replied. "After leaving the hospital, I couldn't stop thinking about you."

"So, you're stalking me?" Maddie teased, arching an eyebrow. She lowered it when Lourdes grinned. "I'm glad you're here. I can't stop thinking about you either."

"Good to hear." Maddie dipped her gaze down to Lourdes' lips, longing to kiss her again. "What were you guys talking about? I got the feeling I interrupted something."

Maddie looked past her to the table of women. Everyone was staring at them, but they quickly looked away when Maddie caught them staring. "If you'd believe it, we were talking about you." Lourdes raised her eyebrows. "And how lucky the department is that you came along."

Lourdes smirked. "And that's all?"

Maddie nodded, not wanting to divulge where their conversation went. But she was glad to see Lourdes and the other women were right. If they made each other happy, then maybe that's all that mattered. Noelle seemed to have her own ideas about their relationship, which made Maddie smile. Now, if she could calm her worries, things might be where she needed them, ready to progress.

CHAPTER NINETEEN

SEXUAL INTIMACY AT ITS HIGHEST

They worked on making baskets for two hours, all while laughing and enjoying one another's company. Every time Maddie looked at Lourdes, her breath caught. How could she be so lucky that someone as beautiful as Lourdes was there with her? And it was sweet that Lourdes had shown up at the event hall. After their time in the exam room, it was a new step in their relationship. She had invited her in the past, but Lourdes was adamant that it wasn't her thing. So, it was a pleasant surprise. Maddie was sure it all had to do with their rendezvous. Maddie was disappointed when the evening ended, sulking as she made the long trek back to her car.

"I had a good time," Lourdes replied as she stopped next to Maddie's car

"Granted, nothing beats exam room sex," She smirked. "But it was cool to see you in your element, Ms. Charitable Cause."

Maddie laughed and nodded, "I never thought I'd see the day when you lent a helping hand. I'd say some of your baskets were the best."

Lourdes laughed, "No way. You are the creative one." She gave Maddie a wink; it was undeniably tender.

Lourdes stood up straighter, "So, I thought maybe I could come back to your place. If you wouldn't mind?"

Mind? Maddie couldn't think of one thing she would want more than that.

"I miss Cheddar. I could use some kitty time."

Maddie's jaw dropped. "Oh, well yeah, if that's what you're wanting. I'm sure Cheddar feels the same." Maddie reached for the door handle. "Follow me." Lourdes touched Maddie's hand, then pulled her to her. Maddie's lips caressed Lourdes' before Lourdes returned with a genuine smile. "I guess I'm feeling a little selfish, and I think I'd prefer to give a quick hello to Cheddar and spend the rest of the night with you. If you know what I mean." She quirked up her lips.

Maddie wrapped her hand around Lourdes' neck and pulled her to her, crashing her lips against Lourdes' and dipping her tongue between Lourdes' lips. Lourdes growled, and Maddie smirked. Maddie went ten miles over the speed limit back to her apartment. She kept checking her rearview mirror to ensure Lourdes was still following her. She whipped into her parking spot, and Lourdes grabbed the spot beside her. They laughed all the way, sprinting up the stairs to her apartment, hand in hand. Already, Maddie could feel the palpable heat between her and

Lourdes. They ran into Maddie's elderly downstairs neighbors, slowly creeping down the stairs. "Good evening, Mr. and Mrs. Jenkins," she said, her face flushed, her eyes shining. Her heart was pounding from excitement. Mrs. Jenkins looked perplexed. Maddie gave a quick smile and worked her key on the lock. Lourdes laughed behind her. "I don't think they're used to the noise."

Maddie grinned, looking over her shoulder, "If they think that's noisy, then it's a good thing they're going out." She winked as Lourdes rested her chin against Maddie's shoulder, nuzzling her lips against her ear.

Maddie pushed open the door and pulled Lourdes in after her, letting the door slam behind them as she pulled Lourdes into her arms. She kissed Lourdes with a voracious hunger, already feeling the desire pool deep in her belly. Maddie pressed Lourdes back against the door and wrapped her leg around Lourdes' waist. Two minutes into the kiss, she felt Cheddar's body brush against her leg, and Lourdes laughed.

"Mood. Killer." Maddie groaned, breaking from the kiss.

"Hey there, pretty kitty," Lourdes squealed, kneeling in front of him.

"Aren't you such a good kitty? Yes, you are."

Maddie shot a look at Cheddar, who seemed oblivious to the fact that Maddie and Lourdes were in the middle of something

" Do you want a drink or anything? "She turned back to Lourdes

Are you trying to get me drunk?" Lourdes asked.

"I'm all good. All I want is you," Lourdes stood up and slinked toward Maddie. Maddie felt the heat slowly moving from the bottoms of her feet up her legs and radiating around her midsection. She swallowed, "I just thought you'd be thirsty."

"Hungry is more like it." Lourdes winked and headed towards the living room, Cheddar following closely behind. She looked over her shoulder. "Are you coming?"

Maddie nodded and moved into the living room. Lourdes pulled Cheddar onto her lap and continued to pet her. "You're hungry. I have plenty of choices. I could throw in a pizza or whip up some nachos. You name it, and it's yours."

Lourdes patted the spot next to her. Maddie smirked and plopped down into the seat, reaching over to pet Cheddar as he purred and nestled his nose against Lourdes. For the second time this week, she was jealous of a cat. Suddenly, Lourdes leaned in for a kiss, taking Maddie by surprise. Maddie savored the feeling of Lourdes' soft lips against hers, eagerly slipping her tongue into Lourdes' mouth. Cheddar purred, head-butting the bottom of Maddie's chin. Maddie reluctantly pulled back. She grabbed Cheddar and took him to the laundry room. "You are fine," Maddie snapped the minute Cheddar meowed. She closed the door and hurried back into the living room. Lourdes glanced toward the laundry room, where Cheddar emitted a muffled meow.

"He was killing the mood. Can you blame me?"

Lourdes laughed, "Never."

"Besides," Maddie whispered.

"You said we could be selfish. I want your attention. All of it." Maddie stood before Lourdes and raised her shirt up and over her head. Lourdes' eyes lit up as she saw Maddie's small, pert breasts resting in their light pink bra and her toned stomach.

"You have it, Maddie. You never lost it."

"Good." Maddie pulled off her pants and kicked them to the side. She moved closer to Lourdes. She wrapped her legs around her, straddling her with ease, before capturing her lips once more. As they kissed, Lourdes reached up and withdrew Maddie's hair tie from her hair. Her hair fell in waves around her shoulders. Lourdes splayed her fingers along Maddie's back, unhooking her bra with the flick of her wrist. Maddie grinned through the kiss, slipping out of her bra and letting it fall away. She pulled back, arching her back as Lourdes moved in to kiss her cleavage, running her tongue along the underside of Maddie's breasts, lapping upward to suck on her nipples. Lourdes took her nipple between her teeth, and Maddie groaned. Oh God, yes, she needed to be selfish more often.

Lourdes slipped her hand inside Maddie's panties and slowly parted Maddie's sex, slipping her middle and ring finger into Maddie's molten center. Maddie moaned. She tilted her head upward, and their lips collided with a cosmic force. It was the sort of collision that could create a brand-new galaxy. Instead, Lourdes and Maddie were in their own separate universe. Maddie's hips matched the rhythm of Lourdes' strong, capable hands. Every touch sent a shiver down her spine as her hips started to shake. Lourdes' other hand cupped her ass. She felt herself growing even wetter as Lourdes continued to coax her to explore the depths of her pleasure.

"Come for me, baby," Lourdes whispered, her voice low and soft as her fingers tenderly pressed against her clitoris. The sweetness in Lourdes' voice and the jasmine cloud of her scent mingling with the scent of raw desire sent Maddie over the edge as her lips crashed into Lourdes'. Her hips bucked as she came, and her whole body lit up from within as the fiery tendrils of her orgasm enveloped her. She cried out. Time stopped as she raked her nails down Lourdes' back, desperate to bring her even closer to her.

MADDIE SHIFTED IN BED AND OPENED HER EYES. SHE SMILED when she saw Lourdes sound asleep next to her. Yesterday was the first time she felt like she and Lourdes made sense. From the sexual tryst they shared at the hospital to choose to end the evening in Maddie's apartment, it all just fit. Maddie always longed for the day she would find someone to satisfy her mind, body, and soul. With Lourdes, there seemed to be a mutual and constant fascination that was only further fueled by the fact that they couldn't keep their hands off each other. She moved in and kissed the top of Lourdes' shoulder, the only part of her skin revealed from under the sheets.

Careful not to cause Lourdes to wake up, she slipped out of the covers and grabbed a robe from her dresser. She looked over her shoulder, and Lourdes hadn't moved a muscle. Maddie blew her a kiss, then left her bedroom.

She walked into the kitchen, and Cheddar immediately wound his way around her legs, eager for his breakfast. Maddie scooped some dry food into his bowl and added a bit of wet food on top as an apology. She felt guilty for ignoring him last night. Usually, Cheddar slept on her bed. She'd locked him out last night, so she and Lourdes could continue where they left off in the living room. Cheddar glowered at her as he ate a mouthful of food.

"I'm sorry! We can hang out tomorrow night," Maddie reassured him. Cheddar ignored her apology. Maddie snickered and went back to the living room. She grabbed her pants, still on the living room floor, and retrieved her phone from where it lay on the coffee table. It only had a little battery left, but it was enough. She hurried back to the room, so Lourdes wouldn't wake up and wonder where she went. Maddie pulled up her Instagram and typed. *Breakfast and an early morning jog are a surefire way to start the day off right! Shout out to antioxidants and endorphins.* She skimmed through a list of recipes until she found one for a spinach breakfast shake. She added it and a selfie from one of her morning jogs. She posted it and then read it back.

Lourdes reached out and touched her hand. "What are ya doing, Gorgeous?" she asked.

Maddie shrugged. "Just posting my early morning routine."

Lourdes tilted her head. "At four-thirty in the morning? Is anyone going to be up to see it?"

Maddie laughed. "Some people like to get an early start!" She leaned in and kissed Lourdes. "Speaking of, wanna wake up and go for a jog?"

Lourdes snickered. "Give me a couple of hours. I'm still wanting to be a little bit selfish." She winked and wrapped her arm around Maddie's back, pulling her to her.

"Don't deprive me of that." Maddie opened her mouth to a sensual kiss, grinning as Lourdes pulled back the covers to invite her in. Maddie slipped out of her robe and moved in on top of Lourdes. Lourdes tenderly held Maddie in her arms as they made out under the covers. It was early morning. The moon still lit up the sky, casting a shadow through the bedroom window, and Maddie broke from the kiss, pressing her hands down along Lourdes' side. She rested her head against Lourdes' chest, hearing the faint sound of her heartbeat as she closed her eyes. An early morning makeout sesh definitely beat an early morning run.

CHAPTER TWENTY

VOICE OF REASON

Maddie poured the shake into a glass and snapped a picture of it. She pulled up her message from earlier, editing it to add the photo she just took. *Now off to my jog.* She already had a hundred likes that went along with her post, including her dad and half of the hospital. She sipped on the shake until it was half gone, then dumped the rest into the trash. A little went a long way. Her espresso machine dinged, and she rushed over and grabbed two mugs, then poured them each a cup. She sighed as the espresso went down her throat. *Perfect.* That was enough to get through her day.

"What happened to the shake?" She twirled around and saw Lourdes leaning back against the wall, a smirk on her face.

Maddie looked over her attire, shorts, and a t-shirt that said

CAPMED, courtesy of Maddie's wardrobe. "I see you found something to wear."

"Well, it beats running in my work clothes from yesterday. Seeing that I haven't been home to change." Maddie moved in and held up a mug. "You ignored my question, though. "Per your latest Instagram post, you prefer something a little greener."

"I already had it. But this," Maddie held up the espresso. "Will help me push myself a little further. If I'm going to keep up with you, I must have something that adds a little edge." She winked and turned from Lourdes. "Hope you slept well last night."

"I didn't get much sleep if I remember correctly."

Maddie laughed and looked over her shoulder, downing the rest of her espresso. "Touché," she replied, smirking. "Finish up your drink, and we'll go out and get our jog on." She turned back to the sink as a pang hit her gut. She grabbed onto the counter and leaned forward to try and catch her breath.

"I don't drink this stuff. Too much caffeine for me." Lourdes reached over Maddie's shoulder and poured the espresso down the drain. Maddie tried to smile, but the pain in her gut went a little deep this time. She turned around and leaned back against the counter.

"I envy you."

Lourdes smirked. "Why? Because I pass up on caffeine? It's not too hard to bypass when you have steered clear of it. I'll have a cup of coffee here and there, but tea is more my thing. I'm surprised you chose to drink that in the morning. You go on these health kicks and all. I pegged you for a matcha girl, at least.."

"Are you judging me?" Maddie teased.

"Not judging, just asking." Lourdes looked around the kitchen until her eyes landed back on Maddie's. "Everyone's got their own taste; if you enjoy it, then no argument here."

Maddie shrugged, taking another sip. "Maybe someday I'll give it up." She grabbed her phone and pulled up the group chat for her fellow basket makers.

Maddie: Today at 6 to finalize plans for tomorrow night?

Lourdes reached into the refrigerator and grabbed some water. "You spend a lot of time on your phone, don't you?"

"Social media is the wave of the future; it has been for years. Doesn't everyone?" Lourdes stood there, and Maddie turned away and started washing the two mugs. "I was checking with everyone to see if six o'clock was still a good time to meet at the event center and finalize details." Her phone dinged repeatedly, and she took a look. "Looks like it'll work. Since you were there last night, you're welcome to join us."

Lourdes sighed, "I have to work at noon and don't get off until eight."

"Bummer, I get off at five."

"We'll be there a little bit together. Also, we can still go for a jog before you head to work. Thanks for the offer."

Lourdes took a sip of her water. "Are you ready?"

Maddie nodded. "I'll drive us to the park and bring you back to your car."

"No need." She held up her keys. "I'll follow you."

"I mean, it just makes sense. That way, you don't have to rush home." Lourdes walked over and kissed Maddie. "By the way," she said, grinning. "Yesterday was amazing. And this morning wasn't so bad either." She winked and pushed past Maddie, heading to the front door.

They left the apartment and drove to the park. Maddie led the way and pulled into her familiar parking spot. She and Lourdes walked to the trail, and Maddie was the first to bust out into a jog. It wasn't a slow and easy jog, one where they could chat next to each other. It was a fast run that left Lourdes in her dust. For ten minutes, she ran as fast as she could. She was exhausted, but the espresso was taking over and allowing her to take off. She thought Lourdes was still at the starting line when she felt a hand on her shoulder.

"Maddie, hold up!" Lourdes yelled.

Maddie slowed and laughed when she saw Lourdes breathing heavily, hunched over with her hands on her knees. "What was that about? I thought this was a jog, not the Olympic trials," Lourdes panted.

Maddie grinned. "If you need me to slow down, say it. Perhaps it was because you didn't take advantage of the espresso." Lourdes frowned, and Maddie tried to smile. "Sorry, I guess I can get a little competitive. And you have outrun me in many other cases, so I was trying to show you I could keep up. I guess now's not the time.".

Lourdes shook her head and stood up, clutching her stomach as she grimaced. "I don't know. It just seems like you were running from something. I get being competitive and all. Healthy competition is great, but I didn't realize you could be so fast."

"Only when I want to be." Maddie slowly started to walk, with Lourdes keeping in step. "I sometimes get a little too competitive for my own good."

"A little? If I didn't know better, I would say you were running away from me. Or trying to prove something to yourself."

Maddie stayed silent. From the corner of her eye, she saw Lourdes glancing at her, looking away, opening her mouth to say something but stopping.

"Sometimes it feels like everything I say around you will lead to a misunderstanding. But Maddie, you can only do so much. And while I appreciate that you're ambitious and want to take advantage of every minute of every day, it is a lot to take in." Lourdes released a heavy sigh. "No one can be expected to do all that. I don't want you overextending yourself. You don't have to prove anything to yourself or me."

Maddie stopped walking and turned to Lourdes. "You say I think too much, but maybe I'm not the only one. I'm fine, and you don't have to worry. I only do what I want to do. Everything is great."

"You don't think you're pushing yourself too hard?" Lourdes raised an eyebrow.

Maddie shrugged. "I'm pushing myself because it makes me feel alive and refreshed. Other than that, everything is perfect. Trust me." She then grinned harder.

"Now, let's race." Before Lourdes could respond, Maddie sprinted back toward the cars. Lourdes ran behind her, but once Maddie reached the parking lot, she turned and saw Lourdes was still several yards away. Maddie withdrew her phone from her pocket, panting, sweat dripping down her face, and snapped a couple of selfies. *Perseverance is critical,* she posted, then looked to find Lourdes jogging toward her. "Did you get your next Instagram post?" Lourdes rolled her eyes as she walked past Maddie to get to her car. Maddie whirled around and stared at the back of Lourdes.

"Don't go away like this," Maddie argued.

"Go away like what?" Lourdes rested against her vehicle, locking eyes with Maddie. "Maddie, I'm not trying to chastise you or anything. All I'm saying is that it wouldn't hurt if you tried to relax just a bit. But it's only because I care."

Maddie moved in closer to her. Lourdes had beads of sweat trickling down her cheeks, yet she still looked radiant and beautiful. Maddie had yet to pull something like that off. "If you think I need to chill, I'll try."

Lourdes stood up straighter. "You mean it?"

Maddie smirked, "No one's ever looked out for me like that before. I mean, except for my dad. If anything, I'm always the person who's telling other people to take it easy. And with work and the auction, I guess I really have been spreading myself a little thin these days.

Lourdes grinned. "So, you promise me you'll try to relax?"

Despite both being sweaty, Maddie went in for a kiss. If it upset Lourdes, then she would try to hold back.

"If you're really concerned, I promise I will do what I can to stress less for the both of us.." Maddie kissed her slowly, once again aching to be as close to Lourdes as humanly possible. She caught Lourdes' smile between her lips, which was enough to motivate Maddie to try her best to keep this promise. However, it wouldn't be an easy task, especially when a million things were on her mind.

CHAPTER TWENTY-ONE

A PROMISE FALTERED

Noelle: *Headed to the event hall, running a few minutes behind.*

Maddie: I'm still at work. Getting ready to leave now, so I'll meet ya there.

Gina: I can't be there until 6:30 now. I don't have a babysitter until then.

Noelle: Gina, we might be able to get through without you. I'm just putting some finishing touches on the hall and making sure everything is ready for tomorrow night.

Gina: I appreciate that. I've been neglecting my mini-me and feel that if I could have a few hours with her tonight, she won't forget what her momma looks like, lol.

Maddie: Absolutely. No worries at all. Noelle and I will be there, and so will Jamie. That should be plenty. You have done enough. Take the night off and enjoy your time with your daughter. Rumor has it they don't stay babies forever. ;)

Gina: lol. You girls are the best. I'll see you tomorrow night at the event. I'm excited.

Maddie pushed out of the break room and tossed her bag over her shoulder. Another busy day in the books, but ever since she had gotten reprimanded, she had tried to steer clear of overtime. Today was unavoidable, and she hoped no one noticed since she worked off the clock.

The elevator doors opened, and she stepped on. Maddie heard someone shuffle onto the elevator behind her. "Hold the door!" she hollered. Maddie reached out just before the door closed, and it whipped back open in time for Lourdes to rush in.

"I thought I was going to miss you."

"Glad you didn't." Maddie wrapped her arm around Lourdes' shoulder and drew her into a kiss. Once they broke apart, she sighed, falling back against the door, "Another busy day."

"Too busy." Lourdes crashed back against the wall. "And I still have a couple of hours to go."

She laughed. "I feel like we hardly saw each other." Lourdes' gaze dropped to the numbered keypad as Maddie pressed the button for the main lobby. "I was hoping we would have been able to grab lunch or something. Hell, I would have settled for a five-minute chat or jog along the track. I was busy, but your day seemed to be ten times worse. I don't even know that you took two minutes to yourself." She smirked, her eyes darting back to Maddie's. Her one eyebrow arched up, and Maddie shrugged. "Besides, I thought you were only working until five."

Maddie groaned. "Pretend you didn't see me. Please."

Lourdes shook her head. "I won't say a word, but please tell me you were gentle with your hands" Her voice was syrupy sweet, and she shot Maddie a meek grin.

"I was the only nurse on the floor. They had Eric working admin, stuck in a file room somewhere. It was the only way to manage the day. But I'm good. I promise," Maddie reassured her.

Lourdes crossed her arms and gave Maddie a wary look. "You also promised me this morning that you would take it easy. I'm pretty sure that we have different definitions of easy."

"I will, at least once this event is behind me. Then I'll have one less thing to focus on. Things are bound to get easier from there. The stress will dissipate, and all will be well. You'll see." The elevator bell dinged, and Maddie smiled. "And that's my cue ."

She stepped off the elevator and turned to Lourdes. Lourdes dropped her gaze, which caused Maddie to step in closer, keeping the door from closing behind her. "I know you probably don't trust me."

"It's not you, Maddie. I trust you. I do. But I also know the situation and how difficult it can be when you're spreading yourself thin. It can be impossible not to overdo it, but I don't want you to forget that a human body can only take so much."

"After tomorrow night, things will improve. You'll see." She pulled Lourdes to her, kissing her, finally feeling Lourdes relax in her arms. I have to run."

"How about you coming by the house tonight when you're done with the committee? We can do Netflix and chill. Unless you think that you'll have to work all night."

"It shouldn't be more than an hour or two. I should finish up right when you get out of work."

"Perfect. I'll chill the wine, and you pick the movie. I probably should get back to work. See you tonight, Maddie." She gave a wave, and Maddie turned on her heel and hurried out of the hospital to get to Cayman's Event Hall. She was excited about what the whole night had in store.

As she drew closer to the event hall, she began humming. Why couldn't she have it all? She could slow down, be happy with Lourdes, and life would be great. When she pulled into the parking lot, her face fell, and her anxiety rushed back into her chest. The parking lot was filled with vehicles, from cars to construction trucks -- at least twenty-five more than usual.

She jumped out of the car and hurried towards the door when she saw Noelle and Gina pacing in front of the main entrance. "What's going on?" She looked at Gina. "I thought you weren't coming tonight."

Noelle threw up her hands. "Don't you reply to texts?" Maddie dug in her pocket and withdrew her phone. She had a dozen text messages waiting for her reply. The last one was from Noelle.

Noelle: A pipe burst, and the venue flooded! The whole place is ruined. We've lost the venue.

Maddie gawked at them. "I was a bit distracted. What do you mean we lost the venue? The event is tomorrow night?"

Gina thrust her phone towards Maddie. "We saved most of the baskets. A few were hopeless."

Maddie skimmed through picture after picture, her eyes growing as she saw each one. That panic feeling pumped through her chest as she shook her head. "What now?"

"Jamie is attempting to get a venue, so we can still have it tomorrow, but we're going to have to make calls, send out emails, text people, do whatever we can to let everyone know."

"I can't believe this. It's not salvageable?"

Gina snickered. "Did you see the pictures?" Her voice was thick with sarcasm.

From a distance, Maddie saw Jamie hurrying towards them. "I have an idea, but it will take some work. I hope no one has plans tonight because we'll need all hands on deck."

"We have to do what we have to do," Maddie replied.

"Let's get started." Her anxiety still felt heavy in her chest, but she knew she had to push through it to ensure that tomorrow night was unforgettable. The hospital and the children were counting on her.

EVERY INCH OF MADDIE ACHED AS SHE MADE HER WAY TO HER car. She glanced at her watch and grimaced. How had it gotten so late? What started to be a quick trip ended five hours later. She yawned, but the tension in her shoulders remained.

Maddie slid into the front seat and started the car. Her eyes dipped down to the clock radio, where the time stared her straight in the face. *Lourdes!* Maddie pulled her phone out of her pocket and cringed at the messages on the screen. The last one ended with, *Maybe you just decided tonight wasn't a good night. After considering it, I don't know that tomorrow is a great night either.*

Maddie closed her eyes. It was clear that Lourdes was upset. Maddie felt terrible. Why was everything just so hard? *Maybe you are self-sabotaging the relationship. It wouldn't be the first time.* One voicemail popped up on her phone. Maddie swiped the notification and pressed the phone to her ear.

"Hey, Maddie. So, it's just after ten. I'm starting to worry. You aren't at the event hall, as I've checked. On the verge of checking the hospital. Please call me."

"Call Lourdes!" Maddie yelled into her Bluetooth. She backed out of her parking spot and hurried towards Lourdes' place. Her phone rang once, then; it went straight to voicemail. She disconnected the call and kept driving. Ten minutes later, she pulled up in front of Lourdes' house, barely wasting time to get out of the car. The rain had started to fall just as she reached the porch. Maddie pounded on the door, waiting for the moment Lourdes would open up, and she would talk to her, explain herself, and make sure that Lourdes realized that she didn't mean to bail. "Lourdes? Please open up!" Maddie hollered. She looked over her shoulder; Lourdes' car was still parked in the driveway. She just needed five minutes. "Lourdes!"

Finally, the door flew up as Lourdes stood before her, wearing her hair in a messy bun. She wore a robe hanging open to reveal her pajamas. "Do you know what time it is?" Lourdes asked. She tapped her foot, impatiently waiting for a response.

"I rushed over here as soon as I realized how much I screwed up. I'm sorry." Maddie stepped into the doorway. Lourdes arched an eyebrow. "Things didn't go as planned. We lost the venue. There was a flood, and I know it could have been much worse, but thankfully we could salvage some things. We found a new venue." Maddie rambled, all while Lourdes kept her eyes lowered. "I should have called. I'm sorry."

Lourdes sighed, holding back tears, "Maddie, I was genuinely worried about you!"

"And I can understand if you don't want to forgive me. I shouldn't have screwed up. The truth is...." Her words trailed off, tears threatened to fall, and Maddie clamped down on her lower lip. "I've never been good at relationships. Most likely never will be."

"I don't buy that," Lourdes whispered. "When you have too much on your plate, it's hard for you to focus on everything. You could have at least shot me a text so I didn't have to worry about whether or not you were dead in a ditch somewhere. I guess I felt sort of blindsided, especially after this morning. It felt like you stood me up, that's all." She shrugged. "But you couldn't help it. You lost the venue. Can we talk about it?"

More than anything, Maddie wanted to express her whole heart. Lourdes would comfort her, and they would hold one another. The exhaustion settled in, and Maddie slowly nodded, with Lourdes reaching for her hand and pulling her into the house. They sat in the living room, and Maddie gushed about what had transpired five hours earlier.

"There wasn't any way to save anything! Literally, all of our hard work was wasted."

"Maddie, I'm so sorry. I know how hard you all worked to guarantee it was a perfect night." She reached up and caressed Maddie's tear that had slipped from her eye. "I'm sorry I immediately jumped to the worst conclusions."

Maddie shook her head. "I should have called you instead of letting you freak out. But we found a venue. We only had four hours to put everything together. It's not perfect, but we don't have to cancel the event."

"Is there anything I can do to help?" Lourdes asked. There

she was, once again, trying to calm Maddie down even though she was upset.

"Just one thing," Maddie added.

Lourdes nodded.

"Still take me tomorrow," Maddie pleaded.

A smile crossed Lourdes' lips, and she moved in. "It would be my pleasure." Maddie sighed as the kiss deepened. Lourdes would always be by her side. If only she never doubted that.

CHAPTER TWENTY-TWO

LOVE IS IN THE AIR

It had taken forever to get to this very moment. Maddie could hardly believe they had gotten there. She glanced around the new venue, a convention hall at Jamie's boyfriend's office. They'd decided to go with a pastel color scheme to celebrate Spring. An archway made of flowers, donated by one of Maddie's followers who worked events at the Garfield Park Conservatory, adorned the entrance transporting guests into a Spring wonderland. Centerpieces of paper flowers held down the egg-shell white tablecloths that decorated each table. Thanks to the dozens of paper lanterns that lit up the space, the room was filled with a soft glow. Maddie and the other volunteers had set up a photo booth in the back of the room where guests could pose with props and have the photos air-dropped to their phones. It was a perfect size, even offering an extra room where guests could chill and chat with their partners for the evening. Maddie looked over at Lourdes, and Lourdes offered her a gracious smile.

"You look radiant tonight," Lourdes said, a slight shimmer coming from her lip gloss. Maddie wore a fitted lavender suit. The suit jacket was low-cut, so she wore a sheer crop top beneath it. She gathered her hair in a sleek ponytail at the nape of her neck. A thin gold chain glimmered around her neck. Though she rarely wore heels, she found a comfortable pair of nude wedges online. Now she and Lourdes could look each other in the eye.

"Me?" Maddie asked, her eyes unable to stay away from Lourdes' slight cleavage. The diamonds sparkled just shy of her breasts. Lourdes looked equally dazzling in a slinky aubergine silk cocktail dress. Her hair flowed effortlessly down her back.

Maddie lifted her gaze to meet a beautiful grin. "You always look gorgeous, but tonight you defied all odds. I still can't believe we match."

Neither Maddie nor Lourdes had consulted the other about their outfit before showing up to the hall.

Lourdes laughed, "A classic case of lesbian telepathy."

Maddie laughed along with her and sipped her champagne just before Lourdes leaned in and pressed her lips against Maddie's. She tasted like champagne.

"I couldn't disappoint when you put so much love and effort into this evening."

Maddie braced herself, anticipating that Lourdes would say something about her stress levels. She let out a soft breath, relieved that for the night, at least, Lourdes would keep worrying to a minimum. Perhaps it was because of the night they had shared just eighteen hours earlier. Maybe Lourdes finally under-stood that what she saw as stress was merely Maddie giving it all and that Maddie could handle more than anyone gave her credit for.

Maddie opened her mouth when she spotted Eric and James closing in on their table. They wore pastel blue suits that looked straight out of the seventies. Eric had gelled his hair back. James stood by his side, gorgeous as ever, the blue in his eyes brought out by the powder blue fabric of the suit. His dark, curly hair brushed his shoulders. He was growing his hair out into a mullet. It would have made most people look like truck drivers, but James looked like a model.

"There's the lovely couple," Maddie said, winking.

"Not lovelier than you," he whispered, leaning in and kissing her cheek. Maddie blushed as he parted from her. "You both look great." He gave an approving nod."

"So do you, Eric." Lourdes nodded to James. "As do you. You both clean up quite nicely."

"Thanks! Can you believe these suits? We found them at a Vintage shop on Halstead," James gushed.

Maddie beamed as Eric and Lourdes held the conversation. It was as if they had all been friends this whole time. Eric laughed as Lourdes said something funny. Maddie was too caught up in her thoughts even to recognize the words. Maddie cleared her throat.

"So, Eric, I hope you spent all your money on the raffle tickets for the baskets. It's all for a good cause, you know."

Eric rolled his eyes. "As you have been telling me at least a hundred times." He tossed a look to James, who snaked his arm around Eric's waist.

"James wanted the season passes to the theater. All my tickets went into that. You better not let me down." He held up his finger, and Maddie laughed.

"I'm simply one of the organizers. Good luck, though!"

"Thanks, Maddie. You, ladies, have a great rest of your evening." Eric waved, and they disappeared, with Maddie turning to Lourdes.

"What about you?" Maddie arched an eyebrow, "Anything interests you?"

Lourdes looked over to the baskets and shrugged.

"I don't know. Everything looks pretty dull over there. I'm more enticed by what's in front of me." She leaned in and kissed Maddie again. This time Maddie let her guard down and wrapped her arm around her, unfazed at the prospect of her coworkers watching her and Lourdes make out. If Noelle was right, the whole hospital most likely knew they were a pair, anyway.

The night went better than Maddie could have dreamed. With the venue working its magic and everyone laughing and having a good time, Maddie reminded herself that sometimes stress isn't bad. Without pushing herself to accomplish things, they might not have had this unexpected miracle happen. And she might not have Lourdes in her arms right at that moment.

They had dinner, all catered. The food was divine; scallops, shrimp, roast, potatoes, and a vegan grain bowl with spicy tofu. There wasn't one person that seemed disappointed by the food options. Everyone was thrilled to be there. Even more interesting, Lourdes seemed to know everyone. Maddie didn't mind taking a step back and allowing Lourdes to do her socializing because, in the end, she knew they would have their alone time.

Eventually, Lourdes and Maddie found a secluded table in a corner where disruptions were minimal, and they could enjoy each other's company.

Maddie lowered her hand over Lourdes' chest, barely grazing her cleavage, and Lourdes snickered between their sweet and tender kisses. "The night is still young. Do that again, and I'm liable to pull you into the restroom and make passionate love to you. Screw the party."

"Promise?" Maddie whispered, her breath lingering over Lourdes' smile.

"You naughty girl." Lourdes laughed and started to move in to kiss her again when she abruptly stopped. "You know, Maddie. I'm proud of all this extra work you've put into making this event successful."

Maddie frowned. What happened to going into the restroom and having a party of their own? Maddie was ready to rip Lourdes' dress off in the gender-neutral bathroom. She opened her mouth.

"I hear you have a lot to do with how this evening turned out."

Maddie turned to see Sierra, who was actually smiling for once.

Maddie quickly nodded. "It was a group effort, but I tried to do my part."

"It turned out great. I just wanted to let you know that." She nodded, then shot a look at Lourdes.

"You both have a good night."

Maddie turned and watched Sierra walking away. Her jaw dropped. "Well, it would've been a little awkward to make out with you in front of Sierra." Lourdes took a sip of her champagne and then laughed, covering her mouth. "I can only imagine the look on her face."

Maddie felt her cheeks burn. "Then I suppose I should thank you for pulling away. Even though I was slightly disappointed."

"Slightly?" Lourdes tilted her head.

"Maybe a smidge more," Maddie teased.

Lourdes looked around the room, and her eyes got a faraway distant look. "What you did to transform this place is quite impressive. You had less than twenty-four hours. Kudos to you."

Maddie's smile grew brighter. "You know, the truth is, I wanted to make tonight special for you" Lourdes frowned.

Maddie continued, "I wanted to share this night with you. Knowing that we'd be here together pushed me to make sure everything turned out magnificently. And I can't wait to do more of these types of events. As long as we're there together, I know they'll be special."

Lourdes' smile faded, and Maddie heard a faint sigh leave Lourdes' lips. "You know, Maddie...." Lourdes began. Her eyes dropped, and she shrugged. "Nevermind. Let's dance." She stood up, still frowning. Maddie didn't budge, despite Lourdes reaching out for her hand. Lourdes eventually took her seat while Maddie stayed seated. "When you do things, I want you to do them solely because it's what you want to do. Because it's what will make you happy; after all, that's the greatest gift you can give me."

"I think you misunderstood me. This event never felt like a burden. It didn't feel like I was doing too much. I loved seeing the smile on everyone's faces. That's what makes me the happiest."

Lourdes shook her head, "But all the hard work and stress isn't good for you."

"That's just it. I might be stressed, but this wasn't one of the reasons." Maddie reached out for Lourdes' hand.

"You're right. We need to dance." Her fingers grazed over Lourdes' hand until she grabbed on and pulled Lourdes to her feet.

"But if you try to do everything, you'll never want to plan another event. I'm only looking out for your best interest, Gorgeous."

Maddie smirked. "One of the many reasons I love you." Lourdes' eyes widened. "I mean, I love that about you." She cringed. "You know what I mean." She nervously laughed. "Now, let's dance." With those words still lingering, she pulled Lourdes onto the dance floor. When she turned to face her, Lourdes had a giddy grin, and she pulled Maddie into her arms just as a slow song played over the stereo. Maddie wanted to be here in Lourdes' arms; if the whole world saw, she wouldn't even care.

MADDIE LOOKED OVER TO LOURDES, WHO HAD GAZED AT HER the whole way back to her house. Maddie gave a smile and looked up to the front door. "I'll walk you home." She winked, and that caused Lourdes to laugh.

"All that way? Such a lady." Lourdes grabbed Maddie's hand and kissed her softly between the knuckles. "I'm a lucky woman."

Maddie giggled, and they exited her car. Before they reached the sidewalk, Lourdes reached for her hand, and they slowly made their way to the porch. Maddie didn't want the evening to end. The way Lourdes held back, she seemed to feel the same way.

Maddie stopped at the porch and turned to face Lourdes. "I had a wonderful evening."

"As did I." Lourdes continued to caress Maddie's fingers between hers, and her warmth lingered. Lourdes' eyes latched on hers; they were always magnificent. Every time she stared into them, it was like she had discovered a new shade of green. Their lovely hue transfixed Maddie.

"Maddie," Lourdes whispered, leaving Maddie no choice but drop her gaze to her lips as she nodded. "What do you want out of life?"

"You!" Maddie blurted. Lourdes smiled sincerely.

"What else?" Lourdes squeezed Maddie's hands.

"I want to help people," Maddie admitted, the seriousness in the question showing its face.

"You are a vibrant woman full of life, wonder, and a beautiful soul. Your kindness knows no bounds, which scares me. But that heart, that's what makes me love you."

Maddie grinned. "You love me?"

"I might have said that." Lourdes laughed.

Maddie relaxed as those words played gleefully in her mind. "I know you heard me earlier tonight, but I played it off. Call me scared or confused or just plain stupid...." Her words trailed off as Lourdes moved in closer to her. She kissed her passionately, taking Maddie's breath away. "I love you!" Maddie gasped, sliding her tongue into Lourdes' open mouth.

"I'd love to have you back in my bed," Lourdes replied between kisses.

Maddie wrapped her arm around Lourdes as Lourdes worked on the door, their lips still entangled on one another's. They stumbled their way into the foyer, and the darkness faded. It was a beautiful thing to be in love.

CHAPTER TWENTY-THREE

CRASH AND BURN

Maddie wiped the beads of sweat off her brow as she quickly typed out her notes. "Maddie!" Noelle hissed, approaching the counter.

"Yes?" Maddie asked, unable to look up, the words running together. How could the week start like a dream only to turn into a nightmare? Between understaffing and the constant rollover of patients coming in and out of the department, Maddie was ready to pull her hair out. Not to mention, it felt like everyone had a bigger problem than the patient before. Her stomach clenched, and she braced herself against an accompanying wave of nausea.

"Do you have Mr. Johnson roomed?"

Maddie looked up. "Johnson?" She returned to her list and

saw that he had arrived an hour earlier, but she still had two patients she needed to room before him. "He got here early."

"But his appointment was forty-five minutes ago." Noelle arched an eyebrow.

"I'll grab him next," Maddie mumbled, standing up from the desk. "Sorry." She pushed past her before rushing back to the desk, realizing she'd forgotten his chart. She was so frazzled it was a miracle that her head was still attached to her shoulders. The recent staffing turnover left a mountain of work for the remaining nurses. For starters, they had to pull all their own charts. The only nurses left in the department were Eric and Maddie. They would fill in with staffing from around the hospital. None of this was a genius plan.

"Johnson!" she called.

A man and woman stood up, one on the left side of the waiting room and one on the right. Maddie mentally groaned. "David," she called.

"I've been waiting over thirty minutes," the woman complained. "If I don't get seen soon, I will reschedule; this is ridiculous." The woman crossed her arms and glared back at Maddie. Maddie looked at Rachel behind the front desk, who shrugged. What did she care? Her only responsibility was to check the patient in. As far as she was concerned, her job was done. Maddie tossed a look back to the woman.

"I apologize. I'll be calling you next. I swear." David rolled his eyes as he approached Maddie, and Maddie wanted to do the same, but she had to keep her composure. The day would be over soon enough, and she could forget this monstrosity even occurred. "Follow me."

Maddie heard the huffing behind her and felt her feet dragging behind her as she made her way to the triage room. As long as Sierra didn't come out of her office and offer her words of advice, she might be able to make it through the rest of the day.

"My name is Maddie," she began.

"Have a seat, and we'll get you through relatively quickly. What are you being seen today for?"

"Isn't that in my chart?" he asked. "I would think you would have some idea of why I am here. I was referred, after all. Isn't that part of your job?" His face was red, but not nearly as red as Maddie's probably was. Trying to be friendly to the patients was one thing, but when they insinuated that you were dumb, it made an already awkward situation even worse.

"I apologize, but we're given the bare minimum. If you could give me a brief synopsis, that would be most helpful."

"Fine," he muttered. "Just a little on edge. I was diagnosed with a heart murmur, and they said I needed to come to see someone. I don't even know what that means." His eyes narrowed in, and Maddie sat back in her seat.

"I understand you're concerned, but rest assured that many people live a long and happy life. I can guarantee that you are in the right place."

A small smile graced his lips, and he fell back into his chair. "I've always been healthy. My parents never had any health issues, and I fear I'll pass this down to my kids. Thought it's best not to take it lightly."

"And you are correct. The earlier we can get you a diagnosis, the better we can do to manage the symptoms. Let's take a look at your BP. Do you have hypertension?"

His eyes widened, and Maddie smiled, "High blood pressure," she explained.

"Oh. No. I never had any concerns. Sometimes it runs low, but it's usually normal. "

"That's a good thing. We'll have all your questions answered before the end of your appointment. I promise you that." He relaxed, and Maddie was able to get his vitals without fail. The assessment lasted ten minutes longer, but when Maddie walked him to meet up with Noelle, she felt a tad better.

"Here's your patient, Noelle." Maddie's voice was chipper, but Noelle shook her head and kept her eyes on the chart. Maddie glanced back at him. "It was nice to meet you, Mr. Johnson. I'm sure I'll be seeing you." She patted his shoulder, and he left her with a kind exit.

Maddie returned to the nurse's station, where Eric sat at the desk. "You're looking too happy for the number of patients in that waiting room." The tension in his voice didn't even upset her.

"I saw the charts and nearly went running." He smirked.

Maddie scowled at the charts as her heart started to pound again. "Ugh." She plopped down into the seat and logged into the computer.

"I'm glad you didn't because, as you mentioned, it's been a nightmare."

Eric laughed, "That's better."

He shook his head. "I don't know how much more we're going to be able to do to keep up running this office this way. We might have to utilize the hospital more. They said we can get someone here when the patients outweigh the employees."

"That's every minute of every day," Maddie grumbled. "Besides, if we show them we can't keep up, that will give them a reason to push us out the door and bring in someone that can do the job of ten nurses."

"I'd like to see them try," Eric scoffed.

When they couldn't find a reason to joke around, that's when Maddie knew things were getting worse.

Maddie continued to type in notes for David's appointment, her stomach churning. It was another day with nothing to eat. She hadn't even been able to stop to have a cup of coffee, and she could feel the exhaustion settling in her bones. "Remember" patient in, patient out, patient in, patient out, like it's a factory of sorts. Who cares if we don't give every patient the same amount of time?"

He shrugged. "It's all in how we manage our time. And if patients complain, we'll look at Sierra and the physicians and say, "You're the ones that wanted this.""

Maddie turned from her documentation and stared at him. "How do you do it, Eric? How do you whip through your patients like it's nothing more than snapping your fingers? We have a stack of charts, and even though you grumble about it, you act like it's no big deal. Who cares if we don't give every patient the same amount of time? Is it like a factory? How do you do that? Just snap your fingers and shrug your shoulders like it's so easy."

"Well, it's like this…." He clenched his fists together. "I think I need to give you a lesson in being a cold-hearted bitch. It's not that hard, and it might do you wonders." He winked, and Maddie rolled her eyes.

"Not helping."

She stood up and reached for the next chart, "Ugh, do you want to do this, patient? Consider it a gift from me to you." Maddie held up Marisa Johnson's chart.

Eric grabbed the chart, looked at it, and then turned his attention to her. "If you're this eager, then I would say no thank you" He handed the chart back, then laughed.

"We had a moment earlier. She had some complaints, and I just stood there like a bumbling fool. Either way, I don't want to deal with the glares this woman will give me."

"Sorry, Maddie. I have to finish up this before I grab my first patient. I'm sure you'll be fine, though. Just remember, you don't have to be nice to everyone." He winked and left the station.

Maddie was a nurse by nature. She wanted to fulfill the patient's needs, all while doing the best job she could. The idea of deliberately rushing with a patient made her skin crawl. Maddie looked at the walkway, where Lourdes ran from room to room. They hadn't even had ten minutes to talk, and now she was forced to be nice to a stranger who wanted to chop her head off. She pushed through with a smile and made her way to the waiting room. "Johnson!" she called out.

"It's about time," the woman mumbled. Her frown stayed on her face as she looked down at the floor and marched over to where Maddie stood.

"My name is Maddie, and I'll be assisting you before you get to the practitioner. Follow me."

Again, with a groan, the woman continued to mumble as they walked back to the room. Maddie tossed a look in her direction as they entered the room, and the woman marched over to the chair and sat down.

"So, let's see. Why are we seeing you today?"

The woman stared, just as she expected. "I have to do your job for you? Is that what you're saying?" She sighed. "I had a heart attack a year ago, and I'm starting to have an arrhythmia. My cardiologist told me to come here, and now I think it would be more pleasant to die at home." The woman dropped her gaze, and Maddie's heart went out to her.

"Ma'am. Surely you have loved ones at home that wouldn't want to hear you say that. I understand this is a stressful situation, but we're here to help you. I promise you that." Marisa looked up and cocked an eyebrow, and at that moment, they reached a silent agreement.

Maddie finished up with Marisa and got her back to where she needed to be, then tried her best to ensure the rest of the day went without a hitch. She could feel that it was a losing battle. Her co-workers kept glaring at her. Her anxiety and stomachache returned. Maybe this was all her fault. She clearly couldn't balance good patient care and rushing them through like they were only a number.

She clocked out late, which only added to her stress. Tears stung the backs of her eyes as she rushed to the elevator, fearful she would crumble in front of her co-workers, desperate to get behind those closed doors where she could fully crash and no one would be the wiser.

When the doors opened, Lourdes stood there, ready to enter the break room. "Maddie?" Maddie fell into Lourdes' waiting arms, and she couldn't hold back the tears that had her riddled with anguish.

"I'll never be able to do enough. I'll never be enough." She sobbed, her cheek resting against Lourdes' shoulder.

"It will be okay," Lourdes whispered. "Trust me." No words would calm Maddie's worries. Maddie's mind was set; she was a complete and total failure.

CHAPTER TWENTY-FOUR

TWO SIDES OF A RELATIONSHIP

Maddie inhaled a whiff of fresh air and slowly exhaled. Lourdes remained extra quiet next to her. As they slowly walked, Maddie reflected on the day: the rush, and the fury, how she fell into Lourdes' arms as Lourdes attempted to console her. Even so, Maddie was still reeling. She couldn't calm her pounding heart or her racing thoughts. "I needed to come here," Maddie began. She glanced over to Lourdes. "The fresh air has done me some good."

"I'm glad, Maddie." Lourdes smiled weakly.

"You had me worried back there," Lourdes admitted.

Maddie sighed and turned straight ahead. She was used to running in this park, but now the one coffee she had for sustenance wasn't giving her the strength to move. Perhaps a shot of espresso would have given her that push. But walking out in the fresh air wasn't so bad. At least it was a place she could clear her head.

"I feel like whatever I do. It's not enough at the hospital. As a nurse, I want, or rather, I should do more. But I don't want to rush patients through the triage process. It's just not right. We should want to do more for these patients. They deserve at least that much."

Lourdes remained quiet, her eyes set straight ahead. Maddie sighed, continuing the slow jaunt along the trail. Why didn't Lourdes understand that? Why was this so foreign to all other employees? Sure, Maddie had a leg up. She had experienced the world of lackluster patient care when her Dad went through it, but that was ten years ago! Maddie would have hoped that there would be growth in patient care. If anything, Maddie had hoped she would be the difference.

"We should probably head back to the cars," Maddie mumbled, turning to walk in the opposite direction. After several more minutes of silence, she stopped walking and turned to Lourdes.

"Am I alone here? Am I foolish in thinking that patient care should be our top priority?"

Lourdes huffed, "No, Maddie."

Lourdes hesitated and tilted her head, "Sweetheart, you're not the only one that cares about the patients. I care, too. But I couldn't spend as much time with the patients because your assessments took too long. Maybe you should consider this a group effort, not just an individual task."

Maddie's jaw dropped, more tears threatening to fall. She began to sprint. Her legs carried her only so far. But she couldn't dare let Lourdes see how the words stung. She considered herself a good nurse, but perhaps that was part of her foolish nature. What if Maddie was the annoying one? What if she was the reason why the senior staff was left hanging, wanting to know where their patients were?

It was one thing for all the other staff to question this, but Lourdes? She believed Lourdes was on her side. She stopped at her car, her head racing as fast as her heart. She turned and jogged back toward Lourdes, who was now in a solid sprint. Maddie looked away. She could get in the car and leave, never looking back. That was one idea. She swallowed the lump that had grown in her throat and looked over her shoulder. Lourdes stopped, her breathing heavy as she stared at Maddie. Maddie didn't want to run. Not away from Lourdes. Not away from anyone.

"I'm sorry if I sounded harsh." Lourdes shook her head. "But I'm trying to be realistic. When you're with the patients, they are in great hands, but since we are short-handed, we must move it along. Does it stink? Yes, of course, it does." Lourdes grabbed Maddie's hand, and Maddie instinctively pulled back.

"I don't know how to do that," Maddie spoke.

"That's where your heart comes into play. Maddie, I love your heart. I hate when you think I don't understand where you're coming from. When I watch you with the patients, my heart swells, and you know what I think?"

Maddie slowly shook her head.

"I think that's my girl! That's the woman that the patients need. That's your girlfriend talking. Heaven knows I wish with all my might that that's the only person in play here. Unfortunately, I also have a job to do. I don't particularly appreciate when Sierra, Noelle, or other doctors look down on and judge you. I want to protect your heart. But, on the other hand, I can see where they're coming from. When one person gets behind, we all get behind. That puts more stress on the department, as a whole."

"And that's all my fault."

Lourdes shook her head. "No, it's not all your fault. We all have to take responsibility. But there's a team effort. If one person falters, the whole team goes down. If we're not all doing our part, then a part of the team will crumble. That's where you come into the equation."

Hearing Lourdes' breakdown, it all made sense. "I just don't know if I'm cut out for nursing if that's how it's going to be," Maddie confessed.

"You have to think about what you're truly passionate about, Maddie. Things have changed. There's no doubt about that." Lourdes reached up and cupped Maddie's chin in her palm. "But everyone should take inventory of their lives and if they're pleased. Just remember that I am on your side, Maddie. Even if you don't always see it."

Maddie dropped her gaze. Suddenly, she had even more things to think about. "I should get going."

Lourdes scrunched up her nose, "Wanna go get a bite to eat or something? My treat!"

She gave a genuine smile, but Maddie just shook her head.

"I'm not hungry," she leaned in and kissed Lourdes, hoping the kiss didn't feel forced on Lourdes' side. "Goodbye!"

"Bye, Maddie." Maddie saw Lourdes staring after her from her rearview mirror, unmoving, but the tears couldn't be delayed. She flicked a tear away and kept on driving. She was so exhausted that she could barely keep her eyes open. When

Maddie returned to her apartment, she tossed a frozen dinner into the microwave. She couldn't even bring herself to cook something healthy, but if she didn't eat, she was liable to pass out.

As she went through the evening, Lourdes' words were heavy on Maddie's heart. In many ways, Lourdes was right. Just as much as they were romantic partners, they were also co-workers. Maddie would have to decipher between the two, or it would never truly work out. A call came through from Lourdes at ten o'clock, and Maddie stared at the phone until she had no other option.

"Hello?"

"Hey, Maddie. I just wanted to check up on you. Do you want to talk?"

"Actually, I was just about to go to bed."

The phone went still, and Maddie leaned back against the couch, rubbing the back of Cheddar's ear. "But you've given me a lot to consider. I guess I never contemplated how we have two relationships. Maybe we just need some more distinct boundaries. That makes much more sense in my eyes."

"In a good way or bad?" Lourdes asked.

"Guess I haven't decided that yet. But I love you, Lourdes. I know that. "

"I love you, too, Maddie. Rest easy."

Lourdes hung up, and Maddie tossed her phone to the side. While rest was necessary, she wasn't sure it was possible. With everything running through her mind, sleep was rough. Maddie tossed and turned before finally settling back on the couch, pulling Cheddar into her lap. If she couldn't sleep, why force it?

CHAPTER TWENTY-FIVE

RECOIL

Maddie closed her eyes, if for just a second. She felt like a walking zombie driving to the hospital the following day. She could make it through the day on less than an hour of sleep, but she had no choice. The patients needed her as the staff shortage was already too overwhelming for those who were left. She pushed away from the wall, her coffee still in hand.

"You've got this, Maddie. Don't let the lack of sleep consume you." Maddie downed the last of her coffee and tossed the cup away. Her stomach tightened as she reached the break room door to go out onto her long shift. Maddie grabbed the wall for her support. She closed her eyes briefly, straightened herself, and exited the room. To her relief, the hallways were empty, and she could ride the elevator up to her floor without interruptions. When the doors opened, she was greeted by the familiar commotion. Maddie felt her chest tighten and took a deep breath, trying to center herself as she approached the nurses' station. Eric was already behind the desk, working and looking frazzled. He looked up and scrunched up his face.

"Sierra wants to see you."

"What now?" Maddie murmured. He shrugged, grabbed a chart, and went out to the lobby.

Maddie made her way to Sierra's office and knocked. Sierra looked up and, with no emotion. She pointed to the chair.

"Sierra, with all due respect, there's a madhouse out there. Eric is alone. Can this wait?"

"Not really." The tense words came out in one breath. Maddie entered the office, closing the door behind her, her stomach clenching again. She sank into the chair. She couldn't bring herself to look Sierra in the eye. "I won't take any longer than I need. Maddie, you are good with the patients, but you have had your warning. I noticed you worked overtime again over the past week, and I have been forced to put you on a seven-day probation."

"Seven days?" Maddie squealed. "Like if I don't shape up in seven days, you ship me out?" Tears stung her eyes as she finally looked up.

"It's not technically like that. But you have seven days to make a change." She pushed a paper in front of Maddie, and Maddie skimmed her eyes over it, her tears blurring her vision.

"And if I don't sign?"

Sierra sighed. "Maddie, don't make this more difficult than it already is. No one likes reprimanding someone, but I have given you ample time, and it doesn't look like it's gotten through to you. The biggest thing is you have to move your patients through more quickly. If you take more time, you are depriving the physician of their time. That's your first step. And you have got to monitor your time better. You can't have any overtime unless we approve it. Your documentation has gotten better, but not by much. If you don't sign this paper stating that we went over this, I'll have no choice but to let you go, effective immediately. I'm hoping you don't put me in that situation."

Maddie picked up the contract and stared at it, making out some more of the words. It was a lot of legal mumbo jumbo that Maddie didn't even quite understand. Essentially, if she didn't change her ways, she was out. If she didn't sign the papers, she was out. Either way, the same result was imminent. She shook her head and tossed the papers down on the desk.

"So, basically, I'm screwed. Unless I can find some way to change in seven days miraculously?"

"Eric isn't having any trouble following the department's rules."

He also doesn't care if he's deemed a cold-hearted bitch. "How long do I have to decide?"

"What's there to decide, Maddie? You need this job, don't you?" Maddie looked down at the contract as Sierra continued, "Sign the papers, Maddie. Go back to work and do your best. The way I see it, that's your only option here."

Maddie rolled her eyes and pulled the contract towards her. Sierra held a pen out to her, and Maddie reluctantly grabbed it. Her hand trembled as she signed the contract. She pushed it back towards Sierra and stood up from her chair. Her arm wrapped around her stomach as it tightened.

"Maddie, don't think about it. Just go out there and do your job."

Maddie looked over to Sierra as she pondered those words. That wasn't her. How could she not think about it? She turned and left the office, leaving the door ajar. Eric wasn't around when she returned to the nurse's station, just a stack of charts. She grabbed the chart off of the top and saw Mike's name. Maddie couldn't even smile as she recognized the patient's name. She would have to force her way through a smile, which was impossible.

She kept a smile as she made her way to the lobby. "Mike?" she called out.

He came up, a grin on his lips. "Hey, Maddie."

"Hi, Mike." She lost the smile and turned away from him. "Follow me." When they reached the triage room, he hitched up an eyebrow.

"Everything okay?" he asked.

Maddie smiled, quickly moving to the stethoscope and blood pressure cuff. "All good." When she started to pump up the cuff, he cocked his head.

"I'll be fine," she replied.

Her regular patients wouldn't believe her even if she was a great actress. She had to put the probation out of her mind until her shift was over and she could fully reflect on it. It wouldn't be easy, but she had to do it.

"Maddie, it's Lourdes. I heard about the probation, and I just wanted to check up on you. Please call me back."

Maddie dropped the phone on the counter and downed the rest of her coffee. She took a bite of her burger and dipped a French Fry in a small container of ranch dressing. Maddie had listened to Lourdes' message at least a dozen times but couldn't force herself to make that call. She took a bite of the fry but dropped it into the paper container, her appetite quickly fading.

She poured herself another coffee and sipped it, hoping it would take off the edge. The more she considered the probation and her job, the more she questioned if she wanted to be there. Why settle for a company that was willing to put its patients second? She grabbed her phone and pulled up Indeed once she got home. She wasn't sure what that would entail if she decided to find something else. She suspected that even if she switched hospitals, she would still run into the same problems. All places would likely have the same rules, and she wasn't thrilled about the prospect of dealing with another Sierra. "Who are you kidding?" She tossed her phone to the side. At that moment, the phone rang. She quickly grabbed it, realizing she hoped it would be Lourdes on the other end of the line. "Hey, Dad? How are you doing?"

"Doing well, Sweetheart. How are you?"

I've been better. I'm not doing great. What have you heard? "I'm doing great!" The words tasted stale, rolling off her tongue. "How are you doing?"

He laughed. "You already asked me that. I'm doing well. No complaints here." The phone went silent for an extra-long time. Maddie slowly nodded, waiting for him to continue. She glanced at her watch. It was only nine o'clock, but she wanted to urge him off the line and give a lame excuse that she needed to get to bed or some nonsense like that.

"I just thought I'd reach out. It's been a few days. You haven't even posted on Instagram," he noted.

She snapped her mouth shut, seconds from inquiring if anything was new.

"Are you sure you're okay?" he prodded.

"Oh yes. Of course. I didn't have anything new to post." She frowned, not even realizing time had passed since her last post.

"I was going to post something right before you called." Another lie. When did it become so easy to spew these fibs out of nowhere? She clenched her teeth together. "I didn't know you were that invested in my posts."

He snickered from the other end of the line. "I guess I am, more than I ever even imagined."

They laughed for a few seconds, the laughter aching as she sat there. "

I love you, Dad."

"Love you too, baby girl."

He paused again. "So, I'd like us to catch up with dinner or something. I have a couple of things I want to run by you."

"Oh? What's up?" Maddie could use the break from worrying about her own life.

"Forget about it. We'll catch up later -- nothing major or anything. I just miss you."

He chuckled, "You take care of yourself until then."

"Alright. Be on the lookout for my new post."

"I'll be looking forward to it. Talk soon."

She disconnected the call before she opened up her Instagram and stared at the post from nearly a week ago. She began typing but then stalled, unable to find the words to motivate her followers. She quickly erased them, then started again.

"Life is…" Her words trailed off, and she closed her eyes and leaned back against the couch. *Think, Maddie, think.* The longer she sat there, the more those words faded from her mind. She had no desire to add to that post, which startled her. A task that once was ingrained in her brain was now a heavy weight she had to carry.

Her phone rang, and she looked at it and saw Lourdes' name.

"I was just thinking about you," Maddie replied, answering the call.

"You were? I wasn't sure if I should try you again or wait until you called me. How are you doing?"

"I'm okay now, but it was definitely a shock at first. I needed some time to take it all in. Ultimately, I know that it will push me and make me stronger. So, I don't want to take it as a negative."

"I'm glad to hear you say that, Maddie."

Maddie took a deep breath. She would make the best of the situation, even if it seemed difficult to fathom right now. Maddie appreciated the call from Lourdes. She promised herself that she would keep her head up and not let the probation get her down.

CHAPTER TWENTY-SIX

SHATTERED HEART

E ric approached the nurse's station, a sheepish grin on his face. "Hey, Girl!"

Maddie glanced up and nodded, "Long time since we've had thirty seconds to talk. How are you? How's James?" She checked the computer and looked up again. They could talk while she was waiting for the next patient, but that was about it. At least today, she could finally relax for a few minutes between being bombarded with more work. It helped that two patients did not show up, and the afternoon was just beginning.

"I'm doing well. James, even better." He winked, and that got a laugh from her. It'd been a while since she'd been able to laugh. If only there were more days like this.

"And how are you?" He leaned forward, checking both ways before smirking, "And Lourdes."

Maddie looked back down at the computer. Truthfully, she had no idea how Lourdes was doing. It'd been three days since their last serious conversation; they hadn't even worked the same shift for two of those days. They worked the same shift today, but the influx of patients and the lack of staff left virtually no downtime. There'd been no calls, no late-night rendezvous' and certainly no clandestine hook-ups in exam rooms. It'd been disappointing, but with work being so crazy, there was only so much they could do.

On cue, Lourdes walked out of her room. They made eye contact. She glanced at Eric, turned the other way, and disappeared into another room. Maddie looked up at Eric, who had instantly taken note. "Does that answer your question?"

"Trouble in paradise?" He scrunched his nose.

"It all depends on your take. As far as I can tell, we're not angry with each other. We're just busy, and since the probation, it's hard to really get a chance to communicate. You know as well as anyone else. If you can't communicate, sustaining a relationship is hard."

"But you're talking, just not talking." He put his fingers up in quotations, and Maddie laughed.

"Let's just say we haven't had any ... sensual conversations lately," Maddie felt a blush creeping up her cheeks.

He groaned. "Sorry to hear." He reached out and touched her arm. "Give it time. Before you know it, you two will be back on better terms. Mark my words. You'll see. This probation will be behind you, and you'll be back on cloud nine with your lady."

The computer lit up, signaling her next patient, and Maddie shrugged. "At this point, I'm not going to worry too much about it." She turned, and her stomach tightened; so much for not worrying about it.

"Baker?" She called out.

The new patient got up and gave her a welcoming smile. Things at work were a bit better. She kept up, moving the patients along and slowly finding that balance. With only a few days left on her probation, the timing couldn't be better. Maddie coasted along the afternoon, feeling a smoother transition between patients. None of the providers seemed upset with her. Sierra didn't have reason to pull her into the office. She even had five more minutes on break than usual, which allowed her to chow down on a sandwich before returning to work.

Two hours before the end of her shift, she spotted Lourdes again. This time Lourdes tossed up a simple wave and started to turn away. However, she slowly turned and made her way to the nurses' station, where Maddie stood alone.

Lourdes' lips curved up slightly. "How are you?"

"I'm doing pretty good." Maddie rocked back and forth in her chair. "You? I meant to call, but time has gotten away from me."

"I'm doing pretty good. But yeah, I've wanted to call, too."

"Lour…"

"Madd…"

They then laughed, and Maddie bit down on her tongue. "You go first."

"Well, I was hoping we could meet up after work. Perhaps grab some coffee or tea or whatever you desire. I think we need to talk."

Maddie nodded. "Agreed. We do."

"Okay. Meet you outside in two hours? Next to door 4?"

"I'll be there." Lourdes nodded, then turned away and seemed to hurry further away from Maddie. Maddie watched her, mixed emotions welling up inside. Maybe the meeting was a good thing, right? They could reconnect, have some good conversations, and possibly rekindle their spark. Yet, there was a heavy feeling in the pit of her stomach, and the longer she stared at Lourdes' disappearing frame, the bigger the pit grew.

MADDIE'S TIMER DINGED, SIGNALING THAT HER SHIFT WAS OVER. She quickly finished off the documentation and practically sprinted to the elevator. She didn't see Lourdes when she got onto the elevator, clocked out in the break room, and returned to the elevator to take it to the lobby. She was probably already outside the door, anxiously awaiting Maddie's arrival. Maddie hoped Lourdes was anxious, indicating that not all hope was lost. When she got outside, though, Lourdes wasn't waiting. Maddie checked her watch, sat on the bench, and did her best to look comfortable. She flipped her legs across, from one side to the other, posing in various ways, wanting the least nonchalant position. After several minutes, Maddie got up and began pacing, checking her watch a few times. "Where are you?" she muttered.

"I hope you weren't waiting too long?"

Maddie whirled around, and Lourdes had two cups in her hand. "Caramel Mocha, extra Caramel. I hope that sounds alright."

"Oh. Delicious. I thought we were going to go to the diner or something."

Lourdes shrugged. "It's a beautiful evening. We have an hour of daylight left. I thought I would grab some drinks from the cart. I hope you're not too disappointed."

Maddie shook her head, taking the coffee from her. "This is great. Thank you." She sipped on it and nodded. "Perfect."

"Let's walk, shall we?" Lourdes motioned in the direction of the trail. Maddie fell into step and casually drank her coffee as they walked silently. The birds chirped overhead, and the sun rested low in the sky. It was beautiful out, and the longer they walked, the more certain it was the best place for them to be, one with nature. "Thanks for agreeing to meet up with me."

"I was glad to meet. We're both so busy we haven't had the chance. I've missed our alone time— this is perfect."

"I'm glad to hear you say that. The truth is, I know you've had things on your mind. I've had things on mine. I sort of felt this coming.."

"Right. I've had things on my mind, but I should have made a better effort for us to communicate. With this probation, I've just been so focused on improving, so the probation ended victoriously. I should have sought you out more. I haven't been the girlfriend that you deserved."

"It goes both ways, Maddie. I could have made more of an effort, as well. It's just…." Her words died down, and Lourdes hesitated, sipping her tea. When she swallowed, she turned to face Maddie, pausing.

"The thing is, Maddie, I've taken the past few days and put a lot of thought into life and relationships. I've thought about everything happening in not only my life but yours. Seeing you get so stressed out all the time gets to me. I want to be there for you and support you in any way possible. And, if I'm being completely honest, you're all I ever think about. I'm consumed by how you are and what you're doing. I hope you feel me there with you in your soul, even when I'm far away. And Maddie, I love you. I love you so much that it kills me to see you in pain."

Lourdes took a long drink of her coffee and sighed. "Remember during the beginning of the pandemic when there were so many cases of nurses getting burned out? All these nurses felt stressed because of the environment around them. They didn't know how to deal with it, and Maddie, it worries me that the stress will get to you in ways that your body isn't going to know how to deal with it."

"I'm fine. Really I am. Today has been a good day, and things have been improving gradually."

Lourdes nodded. "I'm happy to hear that. Today you seemed to be smiling more. Your posture is relaxed. You're carrying less tension. Those are the moments I long for. Unfortunately, I fear those days are so slim that tomorrow you'll be right back to stress. You're an idealist, Maddie. That's one thing I love about you. But sometimes you're too idealistic, which can cause your demise."

Maddie swallowed hard. What could she say to that? She nodded, not wanting to face the criticism that the words seemed to dictate.

"The last thing I want to do is hurt you, Maddie."

Maddie frowned. "I would hope that's true." Lourdes shifted her gaze to the ground. "What are you trying to say?"

Lourdes looked back up at Maddie's wondering eyes. She looked like she was on the verge of tears for the first time. Her eyes were red, almost bloodshot. Maddie had never seen her this vulnerable before; she looked wounded.

"You have to take care of yourself, Maddie. So you can be resilient when times get tough." A rush of air left Lourdes' lungs, and Maddie heard it.

She continued, "I wish things were different. I do. This would never happen in a perfect world. But, Maddie, I'm only thinking of your best interest. A relationship between us won't work. Not now, anyway."

Maddie opened her mouth, then quickly shut it, dropping her gaze to the ground. "Before fully committing to a healthy relationship, you have to learn how to take care of yourself."

"Lourdes, I beg to differ." Maddie looked up, the tears threatening to fall, "Maddie, for three days, I've thought about this. I've considered all options. I went down several avenues in my mind. They all led me back to this one decision. Our relationship isn't going to work when there's so much uncertainty. You must take care of yourself before you can let anyone into your heart. We both know this. If things could work between us right now, you would have reached out to me. And, in turn, I would have reached out to you. I know that this decision is the right decision. I'm sorry, Maddie." She backed away from Maddie. "So very sorry." Lourdes turned and sprinted away from Maddie. Maddie stared after her. Her heart shattered into a hundred pieces, but she couldn't bring herself to beg Lourdes to stay.

CHAPTER TWENTY-SEVEN

LATE-NIGHT EMERGENCY

Cheddar meowed as Maddie fell onto her bed. Her tears hadn't once subsided, and she sniffled as she looked down at her cat. She remembered how lovingly Lourdes interacted with Cheddar, and she was immediately hit with another tidal wave of sadness.

Maddie grabbed Cheddar and pulled him into the bed with her. "Lourdes and I are so different. This is just for the best. I could never be satisfied with a woman with no empathy for her patients and their treatment."

Cheddar snuggled up against her as the tears continued to flow. She knew that wasn't fair. Lourdes had empathy, but she was also practical. Maybe Maddie's heart was in the right place, but she didn't know how the business aspects worked. Cheddar purred and cuddled against her. Her tears dampened his fur.

Lourdes failed her, giving up on her when the going got tough. That, alone, should tell her they weren't suitable for one another. Maddie was too disappointed to console herself.

Cheddar moved away from her and made a bed at her feet, snuggling into a comfortable spot as the tears stung Maddie's eyes. A notification popped up on her phone, and Maddie quickly grabbed it and pulled it up. *Lourdes?* Her face fell -- just an advertisement for shoes. Maddie pulled up her Instagram and sifted through her old posts. Each selfie looked more and more positive. Yet, none of those pictures conveyed how she truly felt nowadays. Her gaze dropped to the photo of her at the finish line, the crowd behind her cheering her on, the smile on her face. Briefly, she remembered how it felt to be happy and fulfilled. She scrolled through hours and hours of pictures, most filled with likes and comments, people thanking her for her help. Maddie felt the love behind each one of them. But that was over a week earlier. Lately, she had steered clear from Instagram and her followers. She had missed a lot, as each new post reminded her of how she had stepped away from social media.

"Just me and my daughter," she read aloud. Her father had posted a picture. It was the only time he had ever posted on Instagram, and it was a picture of them together. Was it from Christmas last year or the year before that? They were grinning, with wide eyes and mischievous smiles, enjoying the holiday as they always did. She hadn't gotten the notification of the picture. But he had made a valiant effort to take part in social media. Maddie never thought she'd see that day. She forced a smile, running her fingers over the outline of their photo. Her face fell. She didn't even look like the picture anymore. The stress had overtaken her body, leaving her a shell of the person she once was. The Maddie on the screen was unrecognizable. She never smiled like that anymore.

Her followers showered her with likes and positive comments, but it still wasn't enough. Maybe Lourdes was right; she had to focus on caring for herself. But how exactly should she do that? Maddie always felt positive; lately, her optimism faded. She pulled up her Instagram again and typed out a message.

Just remember that just because someone always smiles doesn't mean they're not struggling. Take care of each other, online and off. Sending y'all love and positive vibes. XOXO.

She stared at the message for what felt like hours and then ultimately deleted it. Maddie pulled up her dad's texts and sent him a message.

Maddie: Love you, Dad.

Dad: Love you, too, Sweetheart.

Maddie grabbed her pillow and sobbed into it as the tears suddenly took over her body, causing massive convulsions. She hadn't cried this hard for as long as she could remember.

THE PHONE RANG, THE SOUND DEAFENING THE DARK BEDROOM. Or was it just in her dream? The longer the ringing continued, the more convinced Maddie was that it wasn't just in her dream. Her eyes shot open, and the moon crept into the bedroom window.

Maddie grabbed her phone and squinted to see the name on the screen. "Dad?" she quickly answered. According to the alarm clock on her bedside table, it was 2:30 A.M. "What's wrong?" Maddie's heartbeat quickened.

"I don't want you to worry." Maddie sat up in bed. The phrase immediately caused her to panic. "My chest is a little tight. I'm sure it's fine, nothing more than indigestion."

Maddie tossed the covers back, glancing down at her outfit. She was still fully dressed. Suddenly better just in time to help her dad.

"Are you there?" he asked.

"You can't possibly tell me not to worry. I won't have you lessen the severity of the issue on my account. Stay on the phone with me. I'm on my way."

"Honey, you don't have to do that," he argued as Maddie grabbed her keys and purse and quickly left her apartment. She had to be there for him. If anything happened, she shuddered at the thought, another tear threatening to fall on her cheek. "Just be careful," he murmured. "Again, I'm sure it's fine. I had spicy chili for supper, and I'm sure that's all it is. Please be careful."

The words drowned in her ears as she nodded, concentrating on her drive to his house. She arrived at his house ten minutes later, with him still trying to console her. "I'm here." She disconnected the call and hurried to the front door, her heart never stopping its race. The door was unlocked, and she burst through the front door, spotting him at the kitchen table.

He looked up, sheepishly grinning. "See? I'm fine. You really shouldn't have rushed over here like this." He reached out for the table and closed his eyes.

"Dad!" She rushed over and grabbed his arm. "We're getting you to the hospital."

He mumbled some words that Maddie was still curious

about, but she couldn't decipher what he was saying when she carefully walked him out the front door and got him to her car.

"You don't have to do this," he whined.

"Dad, if anything happens to you, I'd be lost. Don't ask me not to." She looked at him, and he slowly nodded and slipped into the passenger side. Maddie helped him with his seatbelt and then closed the door. Her mind was a mess as she rushed him to CAPMED. What would she want to say to him if this was the last time she saw him? She watched him as he closed his eyes and rested the whole way.

She pulled him up in front of the Emergency Room doors, where a man brought a wheelchair out as if he were waiting for that moment.

"Dad, they'll get you checked in, and I'll park and be right there."

He nodded. "Honey, don't worry. I'm sure it's just indigestion."

Maddie would feel better hearing the doctor say that over her father. She loved her dad, but he wasn't a physician. Maddie parked the car in the nearest spot, which was still too far. When she got inside, she looked around and couldn't see her father.

"Good morning. May I help you?" The woman behind the desk asked in greeting.

"My father just came in here. He's having shortness of breath, tightness…."

"Room E-3," the woman replied before Maddie could even continue. Maddie went through a set of double doors and made her way down the hallway until she reached the room. He was alone, sitting on the bed, his phone to his ear.

"I'll let you know once I hear what's going on. Talk soon." He disconnected the call, and Maddie frowned.

"Who was that? It's nearly three in the morning."

He gave a weak smile. "It's just a friend." He reached out and touched Maddie's hand, but his whole face lit up the way he said, friend. "The nurse said she would grab the EKG machine and get me checked out." Maddie's face clouded over. "Honey, I'm fine. My chest isn't nearly as tight as it was. I promise you."

Maddie nodded, but it wasn't doing much to convince her. Once she was given the green light from the doctor, she would feel better. She opened her mouth when there was a knock on the door.

"Come in," she said, snapping her mouth shut. She stepped back and out of the way when the nurse came in with the EKG machine. She nodded and then worked on it with her dad. Maddie sunk into the chair, watching the whole scene play out. It brought about a bit of déjà vu while she waited.

"The nurse practitioner is finishing and will be with you, but I'll get your EKG monitor on. How long has the pain been for?"

"About four hours. It happened after I had supper. I'm telling my daughter that I'm sure it's just indigestion."

"Even so, it's best to have it checked out," the nurse said. She looked over her shoulder and smiled. "My name is Tiffany."

"Maddie," she mumbled.

"My daughter works here," her father boasted. "Cardio area."

She smiled. "Is that right? It's a good place to work."

Maddie kept her mouth shut. Instead of being stuck in this rut, she wanted to feel that way. Maddie wanted to be proud of the place where she worked. Perhaps she needed to change departments if the other staff disagreed with Maddie's approach to patient care.

A knock on the door, and Maddie jerked out of her thoughts.

"Is this a good time?"

Maddie looked towards the door as Lourdes entered, smiling until she turned and spotted the woman staring back at her. Lourdes' face instantly dropped.

"We're ready for you, Lourdes," Tiffany remarked, upbeat and completely oblivious. Lourdes cleared her throat and turned to Maddie's father.

"My name is Lourdes, and I'll be the nurse practitioner on duty this morning. Why don't you start telling me how you're feeling now."

Maddie dropped her gaze to the floor. Instantly tears wanted to spring back to her eyes. What was Lourdes doing there, and how could she stop her heart from yearning for her?

CHAPTER TWENTY-EIGHT

PROPER ASSESSMENT

I*ndigestion.* Maddie finally allowed herself to unclench her jaw once Lourdes confirmed her father's suspicion. Lourdes had deduced a full hour of panic using a single word.

"See, I told you." Her father smiled with pride. "I guess from years of being around my nurse daughter, I was able to pick up a few things. But she was worried."

Lourdes smiled. "The heart is something you shouldn't mess around with, so I can understand her fears. Just rest for a couple of days, and try not to eat anything spicy, and you should be good as new." Lourdes shook his hand, then glanced over at Maddie.

Maddie quickly looked away. She had spent the last hour

ignoring Lourdes' attempts at eye contact. She didn't intend on reading too much into them now. After some awkward silence, Maddie glanced over and saw that Lourdes was still looking in her direction. Maddie gave a weak smile as Lourdes stood to her feet.

"Um, may I speak privately with you for a minute?" Lourdes asked.

Maddie's brows furrowed, and she looked over to her dad, who had his eyes on both of them. He nodded, which pushed Maddie to follow Lourdes into the hallway.

"What are you doing here?" Maddie asked.

Lourdes spun around and shrugged. "They were short-staffed and didn't have anyone to fill the department. They called me in a panic. I had no idea this was your father when I went in."

"I'm sure it was strange to see me."

"Something like that." Lourdes looked down at the floor. "But Maddie, I couldn't stop thinking about you and how things were left yesterday. I'm sorry if I hurt you. I would never want to cause you more pain. I'm only...."

"Putting my best interest at heart." Maddie finished for her. She shoved her hands in her pocket and looked at her father's room.

"The truth is, I have done some thinking since we parted ways, and I guess I am starting to understand where you're coming from. I was terrified when I got the call from my dad. My stress levels are through the roof."

"At least it was only indigestion," Lourdes replied, comforting. Her hand reached out, and she touched Maddie's arm, "In this case, I can understand why you would be worried. I mean, I know you don't want to lose your father. That could stress anyone out, but managing our stress matters."

"Lourdes," Maddie started before catching her eye. "I want you to know that I have never loved another woman the way I loved you."

Lourdes smiled. "The feeling is mutual."

"But you're right that I can't be with someone until I fully care for myself. This morning has made me see that."

"I'm glad you see that." To Maddie's surprise, Lourdes leaned in and hugged Maddie. Maddie rested her head on Lourdes' shoulder, wishing she could stay there forever. Eventually, she pulled back. Lourdes' eyes were dark, but she smiled, "See you around, Maddie." She moved past her, and Maddie tossed a look over her shoulder.

"See you around."

Maddie's breath hitched, and she returned to her dad's room. He was on his phone, texting someone in a frenzy. Maddie reached for the phone, but he pulled it away, causing Maddie to tilt her head.

"You heard her. You should be resting." He looked up and grinned, slipping his phone into his pocket.

"Believe me. Texting won't give me a heart attack. Are you ready? I've got the papers, and I'm raring to go."

Compared to how she found him at his house, he was good as new. They headed towards the front of the hospital, but she reached out for his arm to steady him.

"Should I get you a wheelchair?"

"I'm fine. Much better than when we arrived," he insisted.

She shrugged, and they kept on walking.

"Who was that woman? She said her name was Lourdes, right?"

Maddie smirked. "You heard her right. Just a co-worker in my department."

He snickered, "Looked more chummy than just that."

Maddie stopped at the car and turned to him. "You think?"

He shrugged, "Us fathers know these things. She looked at you like she was interested. I just thought maybe there was a story to tell. That's all."

Maddie grinned. She liked that her father noticed that, but she wasn't quite sure where she could take the story. "Let's not change the subject. Tell me about that phone call and the texts. Who are you talking to? Looks like maybe someone you're quite interested in."

He laughed, "Perhaps I have something I need to tell you. Only if you'll tell me about Lourdes first." He winked, and Maddie was grateful that he was in better spirits.

MADDIE DOWNED HER COFFEE AND GLANCED AT HER REFLECTION in the mirror. Outside of the bags under her eyes, she didn't look half bad. No one could tell that she had been up most of the night.

"Are you sure you should be going to work?" She fumbled with her cup and laughed as she looked over her shoulder, gently placing the cup on the counter.

"You startled me."

Her dad smiled. "Well, I would say you haven't slept a wink

because of me. I would feel much better if you stayed home. Surely the hospital can manage without you for one day."

Maddie shrugged. "I'm good, honestly." She left it at that. Giving the hospital another reason to get rid of her during this probation wouldn't be beneficial.

"But how are you doing?" She raised an eyebrow, and he grinned.

"Can't complain. I'm at least a nine on a scale of one to ten."

Maddie turned away from him. If only she could believe that. Maddie would stay home with him in the perfect world and not worry about rushing off to work. But, as she knew, this wasn't a perfect world. "Can I get you anything?"

"Coffee," her dad replied.

Maddie shook her head, "Not happening. I can't have you back in the hospital."

"Not fair," he whined, like a little kid, then laughed. "I'll just take water."

"As you wish." She poured him a glass from the filtered water jug and handed it over. "Please rest today. I don't want to find out that you overdid it. Understood?"

"Aye, aye, doctor." He teased, offering up a wink. "I promise. I will be a good patient."

"Good." She kissed his cheek. "I'll stop by after work. Love you!"

"Love you, too."

She hurried out of the kitchen and straight out the front door. As she drove to the hospital, she remembered their conversation at home. For the first time all week, Maddie smiled. She couldn't believe her father had a woman in his life after all these years. She also couldn't believe this was the first she had heard about it. She had answered the call the one time Maddie called, and Maddie suspected something was up between all those secret texts and calls. She was grateful to see him so happy.

The hospital employee parking lot was dead once she arrived at her usual spot. She waited a few minutes before getting out of the car, her eyes surveying the hospital momentarily. "Just get me through the day," she muttered.

She headed to the elevator without encountering one person. The hospital used to be so lively. Who would have ever thought they would get to this point? She exited the elevator and spotted Eric at the nurses' station. At least she wasn't alone for her whole shift. Eric looked up, though, instantly tilting his head.

"What are you doing here?"

"What do you mean? I work here." She snickered, attempting her hand at a joke, no matter how small.

"Is it a busy morning?"

"A tad. Nothing record-breaking. But I'm confused. I heard about your father and the early morning ER visit."

"Word travels fast," Maddie replied, skimming through the patient list. I'll grab Roma, and you grab Noah?" She jumped up from the desk, and he reached out and touched her arm.

"You should be home resting, Maddie. I can handle this. If we get backed up, I'll call down for help. You must be exhausted, and now you're rushing through like breaking the triage record is imperative. This isn't like you."

"Well, maybe it needs to be," Maddie argued. "I need this job, and if my probation depends on me rushing through like I don't care, then so be it. It's all about that cash, right?" She turned, but he still had his hand grasped around her arm. She closed her eyes and waited for him to release her.

"How many coffees?" he asked.

"Three, but what does that matter?"

"Maddie!" he argued.

She turned around and glanced at him. "I'm fine. And you should know Lourdes and I broke up. It's all good. Grab Noah, and I'll grab Roma." She spun on her heel and hurried out to the waiting room. Before calling out her name, she leaned against the wall. The walls wobbled in her field of vision. *You can't lose it now, Maddie.* She took a deep breath and counted to ten to steady herself.

"Roma?" she called. She had this, no matter what anyone else believed.

CHAPTER TWENTY-NINE

A NEW CHANGE

Maddie was extremely frazzled the rest of the week, but she had no choice but to continue to work. She would try hard to get the work done; otherwise, she'd lose her job. Was it ideal? Not particularly, but it got easier as the days slowly moved by. When Friday hit, she was confident she had done enough to keep her job and get off probation. She only encountered Lourdes a couple of times. They greeted each other with a friendly nod before continuing with their days. After seeing each other in the emergency department, Maddie knew it was for the best. At least for now, until they got their bearings. Her heart hurt every time she thought about the breakup, but until Maddie proved that she could take care of herself, there was no need to even wish for it. Part of her knew she was in no shape to be someone's partner right now. The stressors were piling up around her. Every time she took care of a problem, five new ones appeared. She had to figure out how to manage her workload without putting herself on the back burner, like that dumb cliche about loving yourself before you could love someone else. Maddie dragged herself into work on Friday morning. Her jaw ached, and she'd started grinding her teeth in her sleep. Maddie could barely keep her eyes open. Still, she had to be on her A-game. There was no saying when Sierra would want to have their meeting about the probation. She continued working throughout the morning, keeping the extra speed in her step, ensuring all documentation was done, and practically bending over backward to transform into Sierra's ideal employee. Sierra approached her right before lunchtime.

"Here it goes," Maddie mumbled.

"Good luck," Eric replied before skirting off to the next patient and leaving them alone.

"Hey, Sierra," Maddie wanted to portray the hopeful employee her voice attempted to portray. Sierra gave a quick nod, then motioned with her finger for Maddie to follow her.

"We can talk out here," Maddie argued.

"After all, I feel like things have greatly improved. The staff doesn't seem rushed, and I apologize for the part I played in bringing us to this point."

Sierra turned as they reached her office, and Maddie dropped her gaze and entered the office. She jumped when Sierra closed the door behind them, and Maddie could feel her frustration mounting. She had worked hard to get to this point. Just another situation for Maddie to see that hard work was never enough.

"I have decided to transfer you to post-op recovery."

Immediately, Maddie's heart sank. Post-op recovery was the sterile, unfeeling part of nursing care she had always disliked. Instead of interacting with patients, she'd monitor patients as they awoke from surgery. If she talked with patients at all, they would most likely be coming out of anesthesia. She'd barely get to interact with patients, which is what Maddie loved the most about her job. She loved caring for people and making them smile. Now she'd only be talking to doctors. Her patients probably wouldn't even know her name. And who would look after Mike, Noelle, or even Eric back in her department? She'd be on the opposite shift schedule of all her friends. . The apathetic nature of the work, combined with the loneliness of a new department, would crush her spirits in a matter of days.

"What? I don't understand. Sierra, I have done everything you have asked of me. Just ask Eric and the other nurses. Ask Lourdes or Noelle. Come on. You can't do this to me."

Sierra looked up with that same grimace that stopped everyone in their footsteps. Maddie looked down, her cheeks burning. It just wasn't enough.

"I have seen improvement, Maddie. I will give you that." Maddie looked up as Sierra's eyes softened. "This isn't about the probation or the fact that you haven't improved, but you still haven't improved enough, Maddie. I think you'll find this isn't a bad thing in time. You'll like post-op recovery. I think it'll be a bit more," Maddie could have sworn she saw her grimace, "Your pace."

Maddie gulped back tears, "What do you mean my pace?"

Sierra sighed, "Maddie, I know you've worked really hard to improve, but I can see that you're struggling to keep up."

"I'm not!" Maddie insisted.

Sierra continued, "Maddie, yes, you are. I know you think you have it all together, but anyone can see you're drowning. I'm not doing this as a punishment for you. I'm doing this as a favor. If you keep going at the pace that you're going, you'll burn yourself out and never want to touch a stethoscope again. I've seen it happen to far too many nurses in my day. And you're a good nurse. I don't want it to happen to you, too."

Maddie couldn't believe it. This was her worst-case scenario playing out before her. Well, second worst-case scenario. She swallowed the lump growing in her throat and nodded numbly.

"We all wish you the best, Maddie." Even Sierra's tone didn't convey that she was speaking the truth. She signed the papers in front of Maddie, then pushed them towards her, waiting for Maddie to do the same. Maddie stared at them.

"When does this go into effect?"

"They expect you in the department on Monday morning. You can leave for the day. We canceled your shift, and you'll have the weekend off. That should give you some much-needed rest. I heard about your father."

Maddie mentally groaned. Everyone said she needed to rest, everyone except her. Maddie signed the papers and stood up from her chair. Without a word, she turned and left Sierra's office. Maybe she should see Eric or call Lourdes? However, neither thought seemed to add much enthusiasm to her step. She clocked out and left the hospital. Her mind was a blur. What would she do in a department she knew nothing about? Tears sprung to her eyes as she drove the long way to her apartment. It wasn't until she got there that she could let the tears dry.

Maddie dialed her father's number, "Hey, Pop. How ya feeling?"

"Are you at work, worrying, again?"

He gave a light-hearted chuckle. "Sweetheart, I'm doing well. I promise you that. How's work?"

Again the tears stung. Maddie released a slow breath. "Actually, great. I just got some exciting news. I've been transferred to Post-op recovery. It's a great department to be a part of. I'm super excited."

"Really? That's great. You never even mentioned that you put in for a transfer. I look forward to hearing all about it."

Maddie sunk back in the seat of her car. She couldn't fool her dad. Now what? He would see right through her lies. She flicked a tear away. "Maybe we can grab some lunch this weekend, and I'll share the details. I have to go. Talk to you soon!"

Her phone dinged with a text message, and she looked to find a message from Eric.

Eric: I just heard the news. How are you doing? Can we talk? I get off in an hour. Text me.

Maddie didn't reply as she got out of the car and hurried to her apartment. What could she say? Her heart now had two reasons to shatter.

ERIC'S FACETIME CALL CAME THROUGH JUST OVER AN HOUR later. Maddie stared at the request, nearly missing out on taking the call, but in her heart, she knew that pushing Eric away wouldn't help. She needed someone in her corner who wasn't her dad.

"Hey!" Maddie answered. Her tone was hopeful and confident, unlike the onslaught of tears she had experienced over the past hour and a half.

"How's it going? How was work?"

"Maddie! Don't even get me started. How are you doing? Are you okay? I see your eyes are red. I'm so sorry. Tell me how things have been. We haven't been able to talk. Spill the tea. Do we hate Sierra now? I think I hate Sierra now. Whatever, screw her. I'm here to listen."

"You're driving. You need to focus."

"Don't even try that. I just reached my destination."

Maddie frowned when she recognized the trees and stairs and heard the knock on her door. "You're here?" She ran downstairs and unlocked the front door. He smiled at her.

" I thought you could use a hug." He disconnected the call, and she threw her arms around him. The tears quickly started to flow once more. He let her cry it out as he held her.

"It's going to be okay," Eric whispered.

Maddie sniffled and pulled back from the hug, pulling Eric into the apartment. "Is James upset that I'm keeping you away from him?" Maddie asked.

Eric smirked. "James knows he'll see me tonight, and I'll make it up to him. Just don't you worry about that."

Maddie pulled him into the living room, and they sat on the couch. "I have so much to tell you. My heart has been a cluttered and shattered mess. I don't even know where to start."

"Let's start with Lourdes," Eric dropped his gaze to Maddie's hands as he laced his fingers between them. Maddie watched Eric as he didn't give her a condescending look like so many people would if they were in the same situation. He was soothing, comforting, and gentle. Maddie could speak with him with no judgment.

"I don't know where to begin," Maddie huffed.

"Well, I'll tell you what I know. I know that Lourdes cares a great deal about you. And I know that anything that happened between you is because she only wants the best for you. So, please remember that."

Maddie arched her eyebrow. "What do you know? What have you heard?"

He shrugged. "I know what you told me. You guys broke up."

She arched an eyebrow. "That's all?"

He shrugged. "Also, maybe I heard that Lourdes is worried that the breakup only stressed you out more. Maddie groaned, "Well, you know more than I expected you to. You have the courtesy of hearing from her and me. Ain't that lovely." Maddie grabbed a pillow and wrapped her arms around it, releasing her fingers from Eric's.

"Don't be upset. Lourdes was worried about you. She came into work a couple of hours ago, heard the news, and knew you would need a friend. I'm pretty sure Lourdes thought you'd already told me everything. She probably thinks we chat every night. It's not a big deal. When she started talking, she immediately changed the subject once she figured out that you hadn't told me everything. I'm the one that forced her to spill the tea. It doesn't matter. She was concerned and wanted you to know that she only has your best interest at heart. She even said that she fears changing departments could negatively impact your mental health, so she does care."

Maddie looked up at the ceiling, her eyes picking out various dots from the markings above her. "I wish I could be sure about that. Getting the news from Sierra today practically crushed me. Then I thought about Lourdes and how this would put the nail in our coffin. At least periodically, I would see her, and we would have reason to interact. But now, what would that reason be?"

"After speaking with her, I believe you two will end up back together. I really do."

Maddie looked over at him. For some reason, Eric was beaming, "You know, it's going to be tough not seeing you every day. But I know that you and I will remain friends."

Maddie groaned, "I can't imagine starting over in a new department. I won't know anyone up there."

"You'll know Jamie. Didn't the two of you work on the charity event together? That's her department."

Maddie hadn't considered that. She didn't know who worked on the floor, but it wouldn't be the same. She had made so many friends in her current department. And it took some time to make that happen.

"I don't know if my heart will be into this change. I mean, maybe now's the chance I have to break out and do something else?"

"Like what?" Eric inquired softly.

Maddie shrugged. That was one of the many questions she had running through her mind. *What?*

"I appreciate you coming here. I did need the company." Maddie reached out and grabbed Eric's hand, then stood to her feet.

"But James needs it more than I do." She leaned in and gave him a bear hug.

"Go on and make out and make up for the lost time. Tell James I said thanks for letting me steal you for a bit."

He smirked, leading the way to the front door. "I will! Let me know if you need anything." He turned and faced her, "And remember that just because you and Lourdes aren't currently together doesn't mean it won't eventually work out. Trust me on that. Take care of yourself."

"I will. Talk soon." Maddie watched until Eric disappeared, then looked down at her phone and pulled up Lourdes' number. If she called her, it could be the first step to rekindling their relationship. *Or it could be a sign of desperation.* Maddie longed to hear Lourdes' voice, though, telling her she wasn't saying goodbye.

CHAPTER THIRTY

DEPARTMENT CHALLENGES

Maddie's first week in Post-op was off to a rocky start. As Maddie decided to go forward, she wanted to make a good impression and make sure that no one thought she didn't deserve the transfer. The department placed her with Jamie for training, which was a relief, but even knowing the one person she worked closely with left some challenging moments.

"Maddie," Jamie began approaching her, her eyes looking down at the chart. "It says here you just put in a request for Hydrocodone after surgery for George Bartlett."

"Yeah? I thought that's what the notations said."

"George is allergic to Hydrocodone. Misty Bartlett is supposed to get the Hydrocodone, while George gets the Fentanyl. It's the little details that you have to be most concerned with. If it would have made it through to the pharmacy and he took it, there could have been dire consequences."

"Sorry," Maddie mumbled.

"Don't apologize. Just be more vigilant. Bed 6 is complaining about being cold. Will you get her a warming blanket and finish the documentation for these four charts?" She handed the charts over to Maddie, and Maddie nodded, barely able to make eye contact with Jamie. That was how the week seemed to be going. The only time anyone talked to her was to tell her about the mistakes she was making, which made her want to cry. And she couldn't stop thinking about her patients in the Cardio-Pulmonary department, especially the regulars, who she couldn't even say goodbye to.

How was Mike? Did he understand that she didn't just suddenly ditch him? She hoped Eric would be sure to let him know it wasn't her choice. She would give anything to be back there and do the job that she had become accustomed to doing.

Nathan Scott, one of the doctors, approached the nurses' station as Maddie's mind wandered to the floor a few floors down. "Is someone getting Bev her blanket? She's freezing."

"I'm on it." Maddie quickly left the station, grabbed the blanket, and rushed to deliver it. The day-to-day routines of each department were remarkably different. Her day was now an endless barrage of IVs that needed placing and medication orders. She felt like she was drowning in a sea of IV bags and charts. It took her longer than she anticipated to get into a rhythm when assessing post-op patients. Maddie longed to have the issues she had faced the previous week rather than being forced to learn a new structure altogether.

Maddie returned to the station and began the documentation Jamie had left for her. Another instance that Maddie didn't quite comprehend. Why was it the new person's job to ensure that everyone else looked good? She didn't even work with half the patients Jamie had left her. Although, she was sure that probably made sense to all of them. Let them deal with the more intense job tasks, especially when Maddie seemed to fall short in understanding various aspects of her training.

Apparently, she couldn't even transcribe one medication correctly. *They had the same last name, and it could happen to anyone.* Maddie wanted to prove it wouldn't happen to her. Not again.

When she took her lunch, she finally used the time to decompress. She grabbed her phone and pulled up the texts she missed from Eric as he flooded her phone with cat memes, bringing a smile to her face. One of the few times she had smiled —not including the fake smiles she tossed her patients. That thought left a scowl on her face. She scrolled through the memes, laughing at each cat she encountered. She then loaded them into her gallery in case she needed a reason to smile again.

She continued to scroll as she spotted several pictures she had practically forgotten. She and Lourdes smiled back at the phone as they snapped selfies. Each time their smiles grew more prominent and filled with more enthusiasm. Maddie closed out the photos and pushed her phone to the side. Being reminded of the relationship only brought another cloud over her. As she sat there, nibbling on her salad, she returned to her conversation with Eric. Apparently, Lourdes still cared about her if he wasn't messing with her. Even with the sudden flood of changes, Maddie had been trying her best to care for herself. She fought the constant need to work overtime to catch up on charts and silenced the anxious voice that told her she was just another burden for her overworked co-workers in Post-op.

She made good on her promise to relax after the charity auction. Now, she concentrated on relaxing every night after her shift. Her next race wasn't until May, and she had plenty of time to reach out to donors. Instead of pushing herself to the limit when she was already exhausted from trying to learn new things all day, she started taking advantage of the extra daylight and going for leisurely jogs around her neighborhood after her shifts. She couldn't remember the last time she ran or did anything for fun. Much to her chagrin, she invested in a puzzle to work on to entice her to relax and stay off her phone after work. Though it made her feel like an elderly woman, she had to admit that she was having fun, even though Cheddar accidentally ate one of the pieces.

When her dad suggested meditation, she laughed in his face at first, but eventually, she discovered that having a dedicated time to relax was actually relaxing. Slowly yet surely, she was learning how to sit with her feelings, realizing that what she told herself about herself might not be accurate.

Maddie grabbed her phone and pulled up Lourdes' number.

Maddie: I just want you to know I'll be alright. I hope you're okay, too. Maddie hit send and exhaled, determined to keep moving forward.

CHAPTER THIRTY-ONE

EMBRACING THE POSITIVITY

Maddie woke up to the sound of the text message. She glanced at her phone, and her face fell.

Lourdes: The post-op patients are lucky to have you. Take care of yourself!

Nothing in those two lines told Maddie that Lourdes cared more for her than a mere colleague. As she rolled out of bed and got ready for her day, she continued contemplating Lourdes' text. Why did Lourdes have to sound so cold? Perhaps she shouldn't have wasted her energy by sending Lourdes a text.

You're just disappointed. That's all. You feel let down that she's not falling all over you. But what can you expect? She broke up with you.

Maddie finished off her double shot of espresso and grabbed her keys. A morning jog was just what the doctor ordered. She only had an hour before she had to go to work, so Maddie settled on the hospital track and was grateful that she was the only one getting her run in. By the time she rounded the track three times, she had to get inside. She was undoubtedly a sweaty, energized mess. She ducked inside the bathroom to redo her hair and get ready for the day. Today was going to be the start of her healing journey. Maddie was determined to feel better, even if it was the last thing she did. She grabbed her phone and pulled up her Instagram. It'd been weeks since her latest post. It was time to get back on it. She typed out a message to her followers: *One of the hardest parts about maintaining a healthy lifestyle is finding balance. Remember to take time to actually enjoy your workout!* She snapped a sweaty selfie of her beaming in her scrubs. *Perfect.* She posted it and pocketed her phone, something new for her followers to read was always a great motivation.

She poured herself a cup of coffee and grabbed the last chocolate donut. She was already off to a great start. As she approached the elevator, her stomach tightened, and she clutched it, closing her eyes as the pain subsided. It was only the stress reminding her she still needed to take it easy. She popped the last bite of her donut in her mouth, hoping that getting some food in her stomach would make her feel better, and swallowed. Gradually, the pang in her stomach started to subside. The elevator doors opened, and Lourdes stood there.

The moment they met each other's gaze, Maddie felt her stomach twinge. "Uh, hey," she mumbled. They still worked in the same hospital. It was bound to happen.

"Hey, Maddie." Lourdes stepped off of the elevator, holding the door open for her.

"Have a great day at work."

"Um yeah, thanks." Maddie stepped on, and the doors

closed, blocking them from one another, and Maddie clutched her stomach. *Don't let the sight of Lourdes stress you out.* She stayed in that position for a while, not remembering that she still hadn't pushed the button to her floor. Her head ached, and she frowned. Where did the headache come from? She gulped down another gulp of her coffee. If that continued, she'd have to reach for some aspirin.

When the doors opened, she spotted Jamie rushing in one direction as Sophie, another nurse, ran by in the other.

"Where's the fire?" Maddie asked, reaching for Sophie's arm.

Sophie glanced over her shoulder. Her face scrunched up. "A lot of emergencies through the night. One patient went into cardiac arrest. Another checked themselves out of the unit way too early." She shook her head, distressed, "I'm glad you're here. You'll be on your own today. Good luck." She rushed off as Maddie took another sip of her coffee and hurried to the nurses' station. Already, her head was spinning as she calculated her next steps, but she could do this. She took a deep, calming breath and reminded herself that as long as she put her mind to it, she would do well.

That theory was short-lived, though, when she rushed to the bed of Jack Porter, 59 years old, who had undergone emergency hernia surgery at three o'clock in the morning. He had chest pain and some heart arrhythmias after surgery and was at high risk for complications. The team was preparing to transfer him to the cardiac ward. This wasn't supposed to happen. He was supposed to be a quick recovery from hernia surgery, and now the goal was to ensure his heart returned to normal function. When she walked behind the curtain, Maddie was awash with a wave of sudden nostalgia. He was lying down, now hooked to an EKG and BiPAP. A woman, who looked to be his same age, was right next to his side. Maddie looked back at him and saw that his features reminded her of her father's. He had dark hair, a touch of gray, and a beard; even with the machines and the mask, she could almost see a smile.

"How are you doing?" Maddie asked, turning to the woman.

She gave a weak smile, "I've been better. I don't know what could have happened. Last night he was laughing, and within a few hours, he had such horrible pain and couldn't stop vomiting. Then I got a call he was having heart problems in recovery.Everything changed overnight."

"I understand how you're feeling," Maddie began. The woman looked up, her eyes glazed. Maddie went over to the machine and documented his vitals, "But I can see his numbers look good here, and he's improving. Heart problems may be a side effect of the anesthesia medications. He will be okay. You'll see. Besides, he's moving to the best department to handle his care. By these notes, we'll be able to move him as soon as a bed opens. We're looking at no more than an hour."

She nodded. "Thank you! Everyone has been so nice to me."

"We do our best around here, that's for sure. But I know it's still scary. My dad had a heart attack when I was in high school, and he's okay now. He's doing great, actually. But that fear stays with you. I want you to know that your husband is in the best possible place. Cardio is great, I worked there in outpatient for a bit, and the nurses there are going to do everything in their power to assure that your husband gets the best possible care," Maddie reassured her.

She sniffled, "I don't know what I'd do if something happened to him."

Maddie touched her shoulder and gave a slight squeeze. "You're not going to have to find out. I'll leave you for a bit, but let me know if you need anything. Got it?" One of the things that surprised her about post-op was that she had yet to be chastised for spending more time with patients and their loved ones. If anything, the other nurses on the floor encouraged it, especially during times like these when they were left trying to kill time before a transfer.

"Thank you…um…"

"My name is Maddie. Just give me a holler." Maddie left. This was the first time work made her smile since she transferred. She felt relief and pride knowing she had helped ease that woman's fears. For a moment, the pain in her stomach lessened. She reminded herself to drink some water, stay hydrated, and not get caught up in the chaos of the day. She was still a nurse. Even if the department differed, she could still help patients and their loved ones. Maybe Post-op wouldn't be so bad after all.

CHAPTER THIRTY-TWO

AGAINST ALL ODDS

Maddie's spirits continued to brighten as the days went on. The patients needed her. Some Covid restrictions still kept patients from having too many visitors except in dire circumstances. Most patients couldn't have any. She spent most of her time with those patients that seemed scared. Whenever they smiled, Maddie felt a swell of joy and hope. Maybe Post-op would actually appreciate her and her people skills. As the second week ended, she came into her element and, for the first time since the breakup, believed that maybe this was the best department for her. It was a rewarding feeling.

Maddie walked to Bed 12, where a little girl, Abby, seven years old, lay, looking sleepily around the room. Maddie approached the bed. "Hello, Abby. My name is Maddie."

The little girl looked up; her eyes were the deepest blue Maddie had ever seen. "Hello."

"Are you here alone?" Maddie asked, pulling up the chair next to the bed and taking a seat on the girl's right side.

"Mommy had to work. And daddy…" Abby's eyes dimmed.

"Mommy will be here when she's done."

Maddie nodded and looked down at the chart. Her left arm had a severe break that had to be repaired before she was left with worse issues as she grew older and her bones developed more. It wasn't typical for anyone to stay overnight for a procedure like that. However, the hospital had a policy that if the patient couldn't get proper care after the surgery, they would open a bed.

"How's your arm feeling?"

"Okay." She looked up, and her brows furrowed. "Will it always hurt?" she asked.

"Not in the slightest." Maddie closed the chart and leaned in to check the book on Abby's stomach. "*The Velveteen Rabbit?* That's one of my favorite stories."

Abby's smile deepened. "Daddy bought it for me right before…." Her words trailed off, and her eyes grew dim once more.

I'm hungry," she said, changing the subject.

"Alright. What would you like? You have to start with liquids. I can get you some juice or water Or perhaps a popsicle. You name it."

Maddie stood up as Abby lay there in thought.

Her eyes widened, "Popsicle!"

Maddie smiled. "I've gotcha. Give me just one minute."

Abby's eyes closed once more as Maddie left the room and

went to the refrigerator at the nurse's station. Jamie looked up and nodded, "Just came out of Abby's room, I see."

"Yeah, the poor thing. She's here alone. I don't know how a family could leave their child right before surgery. It doesn't make any sense."

"Well, in these circumstances, I suspect it makes quite a lot of sense." Jamie looked back at the computer, but Maddie didn't even move a muscle, waiting for Jamie to continue. Jamie looked up and smiled. "Her mother is a single mother, attempting to get by. Abby has five other brothers and sisters. They're all older. Abby's father passed away a year ago. Abby's mom wasn't working at the time. Now, she has two jobs, and she's doing her best. Unfortunately, it's hard for her to manage when trying to maintain a household, put food on the table, etc."

"How do you know so much about the situation?" Maddie grabbed the popsicle from the refrigerator freezer and turned back to Jamie.

"Abby's my niece. My brother died in a motorcycle accident, which shocked everyone. Abby didn't have anyone else to watch her. The others aren't old enough to manage a rambunctious seven-year-old who needs to recover from a major surgery."

Jamie stood up from her computer. "Her mother will be here but not until after ten, and she has to stay in bed until then. Will you ensure they bring her what she can eat before eight?"

Maddie held the items in her hand, "You mean more than this popsicle?"

She smiled, "You betcha. I'll give the cafeteria a call as long as she does ok with liquids."

"Thank you!" Jamie called as Maddie headed back to Abby's room. Abby looked up and grinned.

"You're back?"

"I sure am! And if you do okay with liquids, you get to have real food for dinner! You name it, and I'll make sure it's ready for you." The smile on Abby's face was enough to light up the room. As Abby hungrily sucked on the red popsicles that Maddie provided her, Maddie left and went to the front desk. She dialed the cafeteria and gave them her order. "Chicken tenders, Mac and Cheese, French fries, and chocolate milk. Have it up here by 7:15. Thank you!"

Treva, another fellow nurse, approached the desk as Maddie hung up the call. "You're all smiley," Treva observed.

Maddie shrugged. "I guess it's just a good day. Mind if I take a break?"

"I'll be here - forever. Charting." Treva barely broke a smile before looking down at her computer. Maddie rolled her eyes. Nothing was going to hurt her good mood. A sharp pain returned to her gut when she got on the elevator. She held onto the side of the elevator and closed her eyes. Her stress was working its way out of her system. She had to give it time. Rome wasn't built in a day.

When she got to the break room, she went straight to her locker and grabbed some aspirin from her purse. She opened her bottle of water and downed the two pills. It wasn't coffee, but she would make do. Maddie fell against the locker and slowly massaged her temples until the pain subsided partially.

"Maddie?"

Maddie whirled around to find Eric. He ran over to her and threw his arms around her, knocking her back against the lockers. "Hey there!" Maddie closed her eyes. The pounding in her skull was only a dull knocking at that point.

"I'm so glad to see you. How are things going? Tell me everything." Maddie barely had the door slammed shut on her locker before Eric pulled her over to one of the tables and sat them down. "How's Post-op? How are you? How's your dad? Well, you get the gist. How's life?"

Maddie smiled. "Things are good." *Despite the massive headache I just came down from.* "There's this sweet seven-year-old I'm managing today. She's all alone, and I can tell she needs someone to look out for her. And all the other patients have been amazing. I love my boss up there. Jamie and I are getting along great. And I'm slowly getting to know the other staff. There are a few obnoxious docs, but they're fine. She took a sip of her water. "All in all, though, things are pretty stellar."

"You're smiling, so that's a great sign." Eric reached out and squeezed her arm.

He continued, "Work has been going well, too. It's been busy, busier since you, well, you know."

Maddie sipped on her water, staring at the bottle. She'd be ecstatic if only the bottle would turn into a strong cup of coffee.

"Lourdes asked about you," Eric blurted.

Maddie frowned. "Oh yeah?" She took a long, drawn-out drink while staring at Eric. "What'd she say?"

Eric grinned. "That is proof you haven't forgotten her. You're brimming with hope, desire … dare I say, love?"

Maddie's cheeks burned as she looked down at her bottle. "It was a simple question. When I hear that anyone is asking about me, I give the same response."

"Uh yeah, sure. But, anyway, Lourdes said that she hopes you are flourishing in Post-op and to tell you that she says hi."

Maddie's eyes widened.

"Well, I added that last part, but I'm sure she'd want me to tell you that," Eric admitted.

Maddie shook her head. "The hopeless romantic. But, if you get the chance, tell her I'm flourishing, so no worries there." She stood up from the table and tossed her water bottle into the trash can.

"It can't possibly be time for you to go back yet, can it?"

"I'm only on a break." She hesitated before smiling. "It was good to see you, Eric. Tell everyone I said hey." She winked and then hurried towards the door before she could change her mind on that last remark. If he wanted to share that with Lourdes, he could, and she wouldn't mind.

Maddie thought about it. She felt relieved that Lourdes even bothered to ask about her. Yet, she didn't want to get her hopes up. Maybe Eric was exaggerating. If she overthought the matter, she would send Lourdes another awkward text, which would get them nowhere.

Maddie stepped off the elevator and spotted Treva and Jamie at the nurses' station. The closer she got, she heard Treva's voice, "Maddie seems nice and all, but she really needs to up her game. I feel like I'm caring for triple the number of patients she does. I get she's new, but I'm tired of covering for her. She's slowing down the workflow. You know it as well as I do. If she doesn't change something soon, I will have to say something to Pauline. I'll have no choice."

Maddie's gut tightened as Treva's words rang in her ears. For the first time, she thought she was making a difference in a place where everyone understood her, but now Maddie was right back where she came from.

CHAPTER THIRTY-THREE

DISCOURAGED AND ANGERED

Maddie backed away from the nurses' station when she heard Treva talking about her. She felt hurt that Jamie didn't even stick up for her once. Maddie thought they were friends. It was disappointing to see how wrong she was. If she had been in the same situation as Jamie, she would have at least acknowledged that maybe everyone needed to evaluate their work ethic and patient relationships. Why was it that Maddie was the one that was in the wrong?

After overhearing the conversation, she tried to avoid Jamie and Treva. It would be awkward to run into them, and if Jamie caught her eavesdropping, Maddie would be mortified. To her relief, it was easy. Everyone was also avoiding her.

Two hours after she was supposed to be out of the hospital,

she spotted the cafeteria worker bringing the food to Abby's room. Maddie greeted her at the door, "I'll take this for her."

"As you wish." The woman left the tray with Maddie, and Maddie entered Abby's room.

"Your dinner is here. Everything you asked for." She stopped when she saw Jamie sitting beside Abby.

Jamie frowned, "Your shift was over a couple of hours ago."

"Well, I had a few things I needed to get done."

Maddie pushed the tray closer to the bed. " I didn't know you were still here."

Jamie looked down at her niece, "I thought I would stick it out until my sister-in-law gets here." She then looked up. "But you probably should get out of here. I heard they're not happy now with anyone working OT."

Maddie shrugged, "I'll handle it. Have a good night." She turned and left Abby's room, a sharp pain caught in her stomach. She shook it off and made her way to the nurses' station. She was about to leave when she spotted Bill Bristow headed her way. Maddie groaned and looked around to see where she could dart or go unnoticed. It was too late as he stopped at the desk. Bill was the union rep for the hospital. It was never a good sign whenever he came out in the open, "Hello, Bill."

"Maddie." He stopped at the desk and looked down at the clipboard. "I'm just here to give you a friendly reminder. No OT is allowed, especially when you plan on working without pay. You have to stop this immediately, Maddie. And I know you have been warned about this before."

Maddie nodded, unable to muster up much strength to give her response.

"I need to know you truly understand the consequences that can come of this if you don't stop."

"I understand." Maddie dropped her gaze, and he nodded.

"I hope we don't have to see each other again. If I do, then you'll know…." His words trailed off as Maddie looked up and watched him leave. Just another negative mark on her record, and it broke her heart. She grabbed her water and hurried away from the desk, ready to go home even with her wounded dignity.

After clocking out and grabbing her things, she made her way to the elevator to get out of the hospital and to a safe place where she could cry. To her surprise, though, the tears didn't come. She sat in her car waiting for them, but she might have finally gotten to the point where she couldn't shed any more tears. Also, the anger inside her might have something to do with the tears staying away. She grabbed her phone and pulled up her father's number. She leaned back in her seat and waited for him to answer.

"Hello?"

"Hey, Dad. How are you doing?"

"Hey, Sweetheart. I'm doing well; no complaints here. How are you?"

Maddie sighed. "I wish I could say the same. The fact is, though, I'm just frustrated with work."

"Oh? I thought you said that the department was going well. You seemed positive about it. Something's changed?"

"It's just. I'm beginning to think I'm the only one that cares about patients. My boss reprimanded me for working overtime and not getting paid for it. But they don't allow paid overtime, so I don't know how exactly they expect me to get everything done, manage the care the patients deserve, and do it in a regular work shift. It annoys me."

"Honey, you sound stressed. I know You have been working late again. It hardly seems fair to you if you're not getting paid for it. Whatever happened to your puzzle? Did you listen to that meditation I sent you?" Maddie listened to what he said, but it wasn't fully sinking in. Granted, she was taking better care of herself than she was a month ago, but it was hard to resist the temptation to slip back into old patterns, especially when Maddie already felt like she was playing catch-up with her new department. She didn't mind going the extra mile for her patients.

"Okay, I haven't had time to work on my puzzle lately. I'll admit I've been pulling more than a couple of late nights. But it's fine. I'm fine. Everything's fine. Except it's not. But I'm fine," she insisted.

"Are you sure you're alright?"

"Yes, I'm fine." Maddie's stomach twinged again. It felt like her intestines were trying to eat each other. She made a mental note to run by Walgreens on her way home and buy more Tums. She held her stomach as if trying to tamp down the lies she spewed. "I'm just frustrated, but anyone that has to work for a living has to understand that. It's all good, though."

"I hope so."

"I promise you. I'm doing alright. I'll let you go. I love you."

"Love you, too, Sweetheart. Let me know if you need anything, okay?"

"I will," Maddie promised. She hung up the call, her hands clenching the steering wheel although she hadn't inched out of the parking lot. Maddie couldn't believe how alone she was when she thought she had finally turned a corner. She stared straight ahead, the hospital lights shining back at her. Why doesn't anyone care about her hard work, relieved that someone is finally picking up the slack for everyone? She shook her head. She got into nursing to be a beacon for everyone who needed help, but it wouldn't work if she were the only one who noted those struggling. And someone had to do something to make a change. Maddie didn't want to be the only one doing her part.

CHAPTER THIRTY-FOUR

HER WEAKENING

Maddie grabbed her keys and purse and headed for the car. She had plenty of time to get an extra long run in. After her double shot of espresso, Maddie was rearing to go. She had just reached the park when her phone started ringing. Eric's number came through her Bluetooth. She sighed. She had intended to ignore his calls. After the way her shift ended yesterday, she wanted to do what she could to avoid anyone, at least until she got to work.

"Hello?" She turned into the park and waited in the parking spot.

"Hey there? How's it going?"

"Since yesterday? I guess it's going alright. And you?"

"Great! So, my sister is in town. I thought you might want to come over for dinner or something when you have a free night.

She'll be here a couple of weeks, and I think it'd do you good to hang with some friends. What do you say?"

"I don't know, Eric." Maddie got out of the car and started a slight jog as she slipped her earpiece into place. "I think I'd rather sit around and sulk."

"Come on, Maddie. That's no fun. I think you guys would get along splendidly. Wouldn't you want to meet my sister? After all, we've been friends for a while. I'd love for you to meet my family. You know, branch out a little bit.

"I've been out with you and James a few times." She continued to jog, this time picking up the pace. "It's just not a great time. Maybe sometime in the future."

He huffed. "I guess if I can't change your mind...."

"You really can't." Her breathing turned a little more ragged as she ran harder. "But it's not a no, just a not now sort of thing. Your sister's here for business all the time, right? I'm sure we'll catch up sometime soon. But I gotta go. I'm in the middle of a run. Talk soon, Eric." She disconnected the call and continued to run, the intensity burning in her legs and then her lungs. She wouldn't mind meeting his sister, but it wasn't the right time. As she ran, she squinted, drawing nearer to a man no more than a thousand feet from her. *I don't believe it.* The closer she got, the more she knew her eyes weren't deceiving her. She looked around, diverting her gaze from one side of the park to the other. Yet, she couldn't escape the awkward encounter, especially when his eyes closed on her.

"Maddie?"

Maddie came to a halt, and she smiled at him. "Mike! How are you doing?"

He pulled her into a hug, surprising her. "I was sad when I

got the news," he said, slowly releasing from the grasp, "They said you wanted to transfer departments."

So that was the story they were going with. Maddie nodded, wanting to make it a little more bearable. "But I've missed seeing you! How are you? What's been going on? How have you been feeling?"

He stretched and grinned. "I've been staying healthy and fit, doing the exercises." His eyes dipped. "It hasn't been the same, though."

Those words tore at her, and she took in a breath. She couldn't cry, not when Mike was staring at her, expecting to see a woman who asked for this. "Honestly, I've missed you and all my other regular patients. I'm sorry I'm not there to greet you at your appointments."

He grinned. "As long as I know you're doing well."

"I'm doing alright." She glanced around, her eyes catching the distance. When she turned back to him, he had his arm around a boy who looked like his spitting image.

"This is my son, Myles."

"Myles, it is a pleasure. I've heard a lot of things about you." She shook his hand. ". Are you still playing baseball together?"

"We are." Mike beamed. "It was great to see you, Maddie."

"Likewise, Mike. You take care. Nice to meet you, Myles!" She waved to them both, then took back off on her jog.

As she left them, she felt the tears stinging the back of her eyes and forced herself to speed up into a sprint. She missed her patients. And she missed Lourdes. But neither would return to her if she didn't give it some time. When she returned to her car an hour later, Maddie was exhausted. She collapsed against the car and stood there, her legs wobbly and aching, her chest burning. Maddie clutched her stomach as the pain seeped through her body. She should have eaten the yogurt, along with the coffee. Maddie was hungry, no doubt. She'd have to grab a sandwich sometime soon. Her phone buzzed., It was a text from Eric with a photo that read, *My sister.* Maddie rolled her eyes and stuffed her phone back into her pocket. She couldn't handle the prospect of meeting someone new right now. *See? You do know your* limits, she consoled herself. Maddie opened the car door and reached into the console, retrieving some Ibuprofen and popping them into her mouth. She downed them with a large gulp of water and touched her forehead. She was soaked with sweat and needed to get to the hospital for her eight-hour shift. Maybe it wasn't wise to take such a long run on an empty stomach right before work. She'd also been inhaling aspirin. She collapsed into the driver's seat and lowered her head to the steering wheel, unable to stifle the sobs. She tried a breathing technique, but that just made her pay even more attention to the feeling that her throat was closing up into the size of a pinhole. Still, she had to be there for her patients if that was her only reason to persevere.

CHAPTER THIRTY-FIVE

OVERWORKED AND DROWNING

Maddie stifled a yawn as her alarm clock continued to ring. She groaned. *Why?* She finally had a day off, and she'd made sure to shut off her alarm the night before. Still, the alarm sounded. However, as the sound droned on, she realized it wasn't her alarm clock. She kept her eyes closed and reached for her phone. After a few seconds, her hand finally latched onto the phone and opened her eyes to answer the call.

"Hello?"

"Hello, Maddie? This is Pauline."

Maddie sat up in her bed, her supervisor's voice ringing in her ear.

"Hello, Pauline?" She glanced at her watch. Had she misread the schedule? Was she supposed to be at the hospital right now? It was just after nine o'clock, an hour after she'd usually be there. But she was confident that she had the day off. She'd been relieved that she had the day off. She'd planned her whole day the night before a healthy breakfast of avocado toast, followed by some quick morning yoga and a jog around her neighborhood, before finally dusting off her puzzle. Granted, she'd only had the edges finished, but at least her dad could finally stop badgering her to get a hobby.

"I'm sorry to bother you at home. I know you've worked seven days straight, but would it be possible for you to come in today? I'll ensure you have tomorrow off if you can come in this morning and work until seven. I know it's short notice, but Jamie has food poisoning, and Sophie has a fever. It's all a mess. I'm really in a bind. I understand if you have plans, but I was hoping you could do me a favor, just this once," She rambled on so long, leaving little opportunity for Maddie to respond. As exhausted as she was, she couldn't turn down the invitation to work. Maddie was still trying to prove herself as an asset to the department. If she worked today, it would make her look dependable and seem invaluable.

After a beat, Maddie responded, "I'll do it. It's not a problem at all. And if you need me tomorrow, I'll be there, too,"

Pauline breathed a heavy sigh from the other end of the line. "That hopefully won't be necessary. I'm sorry I had to call you in on your day off. So, what time do you think you can get here?"

Maddie tossed back her covers and caught a glimpse of her clock. "I'll shoot for ten-fifteen. See you in a bit." She disconnected the call and didn't hesitate to hurry to the kitchen and put on her espresso machine. She hopped in the shower while it brewed. Maddie was showered and dressed in five minutes flat. Maddie poured herself two cups of coffee and raced out the door. She had plenty of time to get to the hospital when she quoted her boss. Once inside the hospital, Maddie hurried to the break room to clock in, then stepped into the bathroom to finally get a few minutes of deep breaths.

Maddie stared at her reflection in the restroom mirror. Her eyes were still red from crying all night. She was exhausted, and she couldn't fathom going on another minute. She raised her hand and filled it with two pills, placing them in her mouth, then downing it with her second cup of coffee. After all, it was the only thing that would help her to survive the day. She tossed the cup and leaned forward into the mirror.

"This is your eighth and final day, Maddie. You've got this. You are not going to fail now." It was an easy fix. She didn't have to be at the hospital this morning, but something in Pauline's voice tore at her, and she knew that if she helped her out, it would be a saving grace.

It took every ounce of her being to drive to the hospital just now. Maddie's hands shook as she covered her face, pulling her cheeks down to stare at her red eyes. No matter what, she would have to stand her ground if Pauline returned and said she needed to work again tomorrow. What Maddie needed was a good twenty-four hours in bed.

Maddie shook her head furiously. "Oh, brother." She reached for the knob on the sink, barely able to control it because her hands were shaking so badly. Once the water was falling, she loaded her palms and splashed some water onto her face. All she had to do was make it through the next nine hours. Then she'd get a twenty-four-hour break. She could do this.

As she left the bathroom, she spotted two nurses in scrubs walking past. They both glanced at her and nodded but kept on walking. Maddie's legs shook as she walked down the hall and to the elevator. As she waited for the elevator to come down to meet her, she leaned against the wall, her eyes zoned in on the numbers counting down. She started to feel lightheaded and looked at the floor. The elevator dinged, and the doors opened. Luckily, she had the elevator to herself.

As the doors closed, she fell back against the wall. The dizziness continued, and she felt like the walls were slowly closing on her. Maddie's chest started to feel heavy, and her body went numb. *Is this how it feels to have a heart attack?* Maddie lowered herself to the elevator's corner, her knees to her chest, her heart racing. She rocked back and forth, desperate for her heart to stop racing.

"You've got this… you've got this…" she kept reciting, but the tears told her otherwise. The bell on the elevator dinged, and the doors opened. Maddie couldn't even look up as the pain in her body took over, and her eyes blurred. She looked down, her head nestled nicely against her lap. "You've got this…you've got this…"

"Maddie?" As she continued to rock, her head comfortably pressed between her legs, she felt arms around her. "Go get a wheelchair. Stat!"

"You've got this… you've got this…they need me. I have to get to work. You've got this."

"I have you, Maddie. You're going to be just fine."

Maddie swallowed, her eyes closing ever tighter. She had to get through this day. She was in a fog, and her body was full of tremors.

"You're safe. Just hang in there." The voice was soothing and controlling, but Maddie's tears were freely running down her cheeks. Her heart continued racing, and she felt the world caving around her.

"You've got this... you've got this... you've got this...I have to get to work. Pauline's expecting me. You've got this."

It felt like an eternity before the wheelchair appeared, and two people were lifting her into a seated position. Maddie dropped her head as someone took charge and helped her to another floor. It was all a blur, but before she could look up, she was being taken from the elevator and pushed through a set of double doors.

"We need help!" They called out, and then a crew of people came running toward them. Someone hauled Maddie onto a bed, her eyes finally attempting to open to stare at the ceiling.

"You've got this!" Maddie mumbled. "They need me. Pauline called me. I have to get to work. Where's Pauline? Someone needs to tell Pauline. You've got this."

Two nurses stood opposite her. One hooked her up to the EKG, and another worked on her blood pressure cuff and pulse machine. The beeping sound lingered in her mind as she felt her head swaying back and forth.

"Her BP has skyrocketed." The nurse helped her to open her mouth, and Maddie barely registered the dissolvable pill she slipped inside.

"We should call her family," a man spoke up.

"Someone needs to be here."

Tears stuck in the corner of Maddie's eyes as she held onto those words. What was happening? Was it a heart attack? She forced herself to push that thought to the side. Her dad would be devastated if that was what took her out of this world. As the staff ran around her, checking her vitals, the pain in Maddie's gut nearly jolted her out of bed. She grunted, but she wasn't able to move. The pain seared through her body, and darkness overcame her.

Maddie wasn't sure how long she had been out. But when she opened her eyes, a pain shot through her arm, and she looked down to see an IV stuck into her vein. When did that happen? She looked around. A nurse was documenting something in her chart. She looked up and gave a bright smile.

"There you are." The soothing woman's voice came to her, and Maddie blinked. Maddie looked around the room. She had wires coming out of her. A faint beep filled the room, deafening her ears. Maddie had no recollection of getting hooked up to the machines. She turned to the nurse. She vaguely remembered her. Susan, was it? Perhaps, Susie.

She opened her mouth, but words failed her.

"Don't try to talk. Have a drink of water." The woman thrust the cup in front of her and gently helped her to take a sip. Maddie swallowed and nodded, spotting her name tag as she did. Sue, close enough. She licked her dry lips and turned back to the machine. The numbers went up, then down, then back up again. Her blood pressure was a bit elevated.

"What?" she squeaked out.

The woman raised an eyebrow and once again tried to give Maddie water. Maddie pushed it away, swallowing hard, and took a deep breath.

"Why am I here?" Maddie whispered. "What happened? I have to get to work."

The woman tilted her head, "You don't remember?"

Maddie shook her head, frowning as she tried to focus on what brought her to that bed. The monitor beeped faster, and Maddie shot a look to her right.

"Just calm down," Sue replied.

"Everything is going to be alright."

"What?" Maddie pulled back as Sue moved in and hovered over her.

"You're restless, and your B/P is still high. I'll see if I can start you on pain medicine."

Maddie shifted in bed. She was in horrible pain. Her stomach clenched, and her heart started pounding. Maddie leaned back, and her eyes narrowed at the ceiling. Why wouldn't the pain go away? As her jaw tightened, she closed her eyes. Her head started spinning, and she couldn't hang on any longer. The darkness returned.

CHAPTER THIRTY-SIX

BREAKING POINT

Maddie woke with a start. She looked down at the IV and groaned. For a moment, Maddie thought it was all a dream. She frowned as she realized one crucial detail. She wasn't feeling any pain. They must've drugged her, and she wasn't sorry about that. She closed her eyes. She was so tired, though. The medication was doing its job, but why was she here? What brought her to need to be in the hospital bed, and how did she get there?

"You're awake!" She drew her eyes to the door as Sue came in, a smile on her face. "How are you feeling?" Maddie opened her mouth. Her throat was so dry. She swallowed and leaned back against her pillow as Sue rushed to her side. "Take this." She helped her suck on a straw, and Maddie sighed in relief as she sipped the cool water. It was like she hadn't had a drink in years.

"Thank you," Maddie whispered. "I'm feeling a tad better."

"That's what I like to hear." How was it that Sue was so cheery and happy? She wasn't in a rush to get out of there. She was handling Maddie's case with care. It was how Maddie recalled nursing should be without hospital politics.

"I'm going to step out and grab the doctor. He wanted to see you when you woke up."

Maddie nodded, closing her eyes. It wouldn't be long enough if she could sleep for a thousand years. "Maddie?"

She opened her eyes and saw a young man at her door. He couldn't be more than twenty-five. She gave him a once-over and glared. He smirked when she met his gaze.

"I'm Dr. Mallone. And I know what you're thinking, but I assure you I received my MD and everything." He winked, and Maddie dropped her gaze, feeling two feet tall. Why was she being sarcastic? She didn't have a thing to base her prejudice on other than he looked to be twelve. Okay, twenty-five, but still. He didn't seem like a seasoned professional. Yet, she wasn't there to judge. She was there to find out what had happened. And more importantly, who brought her to the ER to get help?

"So, that was quite a scary experience you faced earlier. I imagine you have questions, and I have questions."

He pulled up a rolling stool right up to her bedside. "Shall we get started?"

"I don't know," she barely squeaked out. "I'm not even sure how I got here, let alone why I'm here." She swallowed again and shot a look at the cup of water.

"Here. Allow me." He grabbed the cup and helped it up to her lips. She nodded as she took a quick sip.

"Thank you," she mumbled.

"So, I'm not sure if I'll be able to provide you with much insight." He'd have more luck talking to a wall. Or possibly the person that brought her to the ER, but for that to happen, they would both have to do some investigating.

"I see. Well, let's start with what you do remember. I mean, before waking up in the ER. Surely you've had some symptoms. When did they occur? What symptoms were you having? Maddie frowned. "What kind of symptoms? I mean, people have headaches and stomachaches all the time. It doesn't necessarily mean something's wrong with them." Maddie's heart picked up in speed, and she dropped her gaze. She knew what he was referring to, but if she confessed all, she was admitting that she had a problem. Still, it was nothing she couldn't work out herself. If she got home, she would be just fine.

"Dr. Mallone, I appreciate people's concern. I do. But if someone can get this IV out of me and let me go home, I will surely recuperate much better. I'm fine. I feel perfectly normal." Her head started spinning, and Maddie leaned back on her pillow and closed her eyes.

"Shall we continue?" he asked. Maddie groaned but nodded. "What you were most likely experiencing in the elevator was a standard panic attack. But I will run a couple of tests to rule out any other issues. This is a serious matter, Maddie. And my gut is telling me that you waited too long to be seen."

"Panic attacks? Elevator?"

His brows furrowed. "You really don't remember, do you? You must have lost time."

Maddie sighed. The only thing she remembered was waking up in the hospital room. She closed her eyes, dizziness creeping back into her brain.

"Dr. Mallone," she began. "Have things been stressful over the last month or so? Sure. Have I been handling it poorly? Undoubtedly."

She opened her eyes and shrugged. "But if I promise to take a couple of days off, don't you think I can get out of here?"

"Maddie, you do not quite understand the complexity of the issue. You're going to need off more than a couple of days. We have drawn your blood and are running more tests. The panic attack is merely the one conclusion I'm drawing here. I have diagnosed you with GERD. Gastro…"

She waved him away. "I'm a nurse. I know what it is."

She dropped her gaze to the blankets that covered her, "But I also know that doesn't usually require a hospital stay."

He raised his hand. "And a possible ulcer. Later today, they will come in and prepare you for an EGD." Maddie dropped her mouth, and he arched an eyebrow.

"We have to confirm or deny if it's bleeding. Again, this is a serious matter. And if you can't remember anything…." He stood up from his stool.

Maddie tossed her head back, "I've been under some stress." He slowly sat down on the stool. "That's been going on for almost two months. I've been supplementing the stress with coffee, soda, and a less than complimentary diet. But I've been trying to manage my stress better! I downloaded a meditation app!" He didn't need to know that Maddie never had time to open the app. She wasn't proud of how she'd been handling herself. She didn't even want to admit it, but if she was going to have any hope of getting out of the hospital anytime soon, she needed to start talking. Dr. Mallone continued to take notes, and Maddie felt this burden slowly lifting off of her.

"Maybe I needed to seek out help, but frankly, there haven't been enough hours in the day to have time to get that help."

He nodded and looked up, "So, you continued to do what was putting the stress on you. Day by day, week by week. And it led you to this hospital bed."

"You're the doctor," she muttered.

He smirked. "Well, it was only a matter of time before it would all catch up to you." He stood back up. "We'll get the EGD scheduled and possibly run some more blood work later. If you feel the pain return, call for the nurse, and she'll get you another round."

"As for this bed...." Her words trailed off.

"After the EGD, you'll be admitted and put in another room. You'll need to stay for at least another night of observation, no matter what the EGD points out. Staying overnight will give you time to really rest. Take it as your vacation."

"Some vacation." Maddie rolled her eyes.

He continued to smile. "You have a couple of guests that have been waiting until you were able to have visitors. I'll send one of them in now."

Maddie looked up. Guests? Who? She yawned as he left her room. She had to put on a smile and smile at whoever walked through the door. She could sleep once she had a few minutes alone. As she waited, she looked over at the monitor. Her BP was regulated now, perhaps because they gave her some medicine to lower it. Maddie released a shallow breath and nervously twisted her hands together. The last thing she remembered was stepping out of the restroom to rush off to her eighth day of work. *Work!* Surely the department knew what had transpired earlier and why she didn't show up to her shift.

Her thoughts were interrupted when her father rushed around the corner and into her room. "Maddie! I was so worried." He ran over to the bed, and Maddie couldn't control the tears as her father held her in her arms and consoled her. It was good to see her dad, but all she wanted to do was go home.

HER DAD CONTINUED TO STARE AT HER LIKE SHE WAS GOING TO break at any minute. She cringed. "Don't look at me like I'm some porcelain doll."

He laughed. "So, in other words, don't look at you the way you looked at me when I was in the hospital."

Maddie scoffed. "That was different." He shook his head, and Maddie continued to wring her hands. He had been there only half an hour, but they hadn't said much to one another. Mostly he just watched her, observed her, and didn't bother making too many remarks. She was alright with that because she mostly feared that at any given moment, he would scold her, tell her she needed to take better care of herself and admonish her for letting it get to this point.

"Well, honey, as much as I wish I could stay here all day...." He got up from his chair, and Maddie followed him with her eyes. "There's someone else outside that is itching to see you." Maddie's eyes widened. Who could that be? *Lourdes?*

"He's been waiting just as long as I have."

"He?" Maddie asked, sudden disappointment hitting her straight to the gut.

"Eric. I'll send him right in."

Maddie smiled. Of course, Eric would want to come to see her. That was sweet of him to make an appearance. Her father gave her a quick hug and then was out the door to retrieve Eric from the waiting room. It would have been nice if Lourdes had decided to visit her, but she couldn't expect that to happen overnight. She and Lourdes were still in such a strange place. Lourdes probably thought she deserved this.

Eric rounded the corner, his face crumpling with worry. He sighed as he reached her. "Don't you ever freak me out like that again? You hear?" He wrapped his arms around her, and Maddie sighed with happiness that he was there.

"I have been pacing in the waiting room. I've nearly worn a hole in the carpeting. I get it. We still have COVID restrictions. You can only have one guest at a time, but I was about to break some knees if they didn't allow me in here."

Maddie laughed, then clutched her stomach as she shook her head. "Don't make me laugh."

"Do you want me to leave?" he teased.

"No!" She reached for his hand and pulled him closer to the bed, and he fell into the bedside chair. "I'm glad you're here. And I'm not surprised that the rumor mill went rampant, and you found out what happened."

Maddie shook her head. "What was it? Ten seconds flat?"

He quirked up his eyebrow. "Found out what happened? I was there when it happened, you goof. Of course, I knew you were here." He shook his head. "You had the whole department in a fury. Do you know that even Sierra blames herself? Don't get me started on Lourdes. She was screaming off orders like a drill sergeant.."

Maddie frowned. "Huh?"

They stared at one another, neither one's eyes diverting from the other until Eric frowned. "Don't you remember?"

"Frankly, I can't remember much of anything. I remember coming out of the restroom after taking three ibuprofen with my coffee. Then everything goes black."

He smacked his forehead. "Well, right there, explains it. Three ibuprofen with your coffee? Maddie, Maddie, Maddie." He shook his head. His nose scrunched up. "The elevator doors opened on our floor. I may never know why, seeing you no longer work in that department. You were huddled up in the corner of the elevator, just bawling. Lourdes was the first one to see you. She came running to your aid, barking orders, and wouldn't leave your side until she knew you were in good hands and she had a stream of waiting patients." He shook his head. "If that isn't love, I don't know what is."

For a moment, Maddie felt reassured. She knew that Lourdes loved her. Only Lourdes could make a breakup seem like kindness. But it felt nice to know that Lourdes was by her side. Still, she didn't want to get her hopes up. "She's compassionate and caring," Maddie argued. "I was probably just a patient in her eyes."

Eric huffed. "If that's the case, then why did she specifically grab me and ask me to relay the message on how you're doing? Maddie, you may think what you want. I'm telling you, seeing you struggle broke Lourdes' heart. She cares about you still. I think she's always going to care about you."

Maddie had a lump that wouldn't dissipate from her throat. She swallowed hard, but it remained. "Water."

He grabbed the cup and helped her to drink, but Maddie used it as her moment to think about his words. She wanted to believe them, but as her heart raced a little more, she wasn't sure if it was her illness or thoughts of Lourdes. Either way, Maddie wished she could talk to Lourdes right then. But Maddie's wishes weren't realistic. Lourdes was right to break things off. Maddie needed to learn how to take better care of herself, or her job and health would be at risk. Her shoddy attempts at self-care weren't enough. She had to make serious changes unless she wanted to wind up in another hospital bed. Lourdes saw the signs of Maddie's deterioration, even if Maddie was oblivious. It was funny, almost. Maddie had built up a following instructing others how to live their best lives, but she was the one who needed to make some lifestyle changes.

CHAPTER THIRTY-SEVEN

MUCH NEEDED VACATION

The past twenty-four hours were a flurry of activity, from the EGD to more blood tests, a nurse rushing in periodically to check on her vitals, and Dr. Mallone peeking in a couple of times to check on her. As it stood, there wasn't any news. While Maddie did have an ulcer, it wasn't bleeding. The only meds she needed were acid-relieving medications and a light regimen of antibiotics. Doctors were also adamant that Maddie had to fix her diet. Nutrition used to be so high on Maddie's list, so Maddie was confident that she could return to where she once was.

The next day after lunch, Dr. Mallone paid her another visit. Maddie was comforted by his confident smile. At least she was comfortable in her temporary surroundings.

"Hello, Dr. Mallone."

"And how's my patient?" He grabbed a stool and pulled it closer to her. "Are you feeling better today?"

She nodded. She had to admit that she could rest more here than she would be at home, even with the intermittent interruptions. Luckily they had medicines that were helping her to relax. At this point, she wasn't disappointed that she was missing work. They would survive until she could be back on her feet and ready to assist the patients. Her patients needed her to be rested and healthy anyway.

"Good to hear. So, I just wanted to warn you about something so you didn't feel like we were leaving you in the dark."

Maddie frowned. "Is something wrong? Did you find something on my tests? You can be straight with me. I'm a big girl."

He reached out and touched her arm. "Whoa, calm down. Nothing as drastic as that. It's just that the truth is the medication can only help you for so long. There's more than you'll need, but you also have to be open to it. We can't pressure you into anything, but I can make a strong suggestion." Maddie frowned. Whatever it was, it didn't sound great. He was preparing her for a grave situation. She could feel it. She looked down at her clenched hands. Maddie exhaled and nodded, prepared to hear whatever Dr. Mallone needed to tell her. "I have ordered a Psych evaluation for you for tomorrow."

"What?" Maddie squealed. "A psych evaluation? Dr. Mallone, I'm fine. Sure, I get anxious sometimes, but it's nothing I can't handle. I mean, yes, I've been more than a little stressed lately, but you said it yourself, I need some rest. I don't want to waste psych's time. I know we're slammed around here.."

"Now, Maddie. You're not being reasonable. The fact remains that you had a panic attack yesterday morning. It's not normal, and if you don't get down to the root cause, then all the medication in the world won't help you. It's a routine evaluation. It won't hurt. If anything, millions of people with anxiety have found that their lives have greatly improved once they introduced medication."

Maddie shook her head. She wasn't one of those patients. This all seemed inappropriate and unnecessary. "I appreciate your concern, but it's not needed."

He stood up. "With all due respect, you're being stubborn."

"Dr. Mallone, we need you in the ER. Five car pile up, and they're short on hands."

"I'm coming." He looked back at her. "Just consider it. Please. I understand you're concerned about how you'll be perceived. But I can promise you that none of that will matter if you find yourself back in the hospital. I have to go, but I'll wait for your answer."

He turned around and left the room. Maddie didn't want to be stubborn about the matter but was already getting medicine. Why couldn't that be the answer? She would seek out friends and her dad to get her help if she needed something else. That's what would be most beneficial to her.

There was a knock on her door. She looked up and saw Millicent, one of the morning nurses. "Good morning, my dear." Millicent was in her early sixties but still moving like she had forty years left. She had a bounce that reminded Maddie that age was merely a number. This morning she had flowers in her hand and placed them on the bedside table.

"For me?"

"Yep. Someone just dropped them off. There's even a card." She handed the card over to Maddie. "Do you need anything before I give you your space to enjoy the beautiful bouquet?"

"No. I'm good. Thank you!" Maddie waited until Millicent left the room, and she opened the envelope, revealing a card with flowers the same color as her bouquet.

The simple writing on the front read, *Thinking of you.* Inside, the inscription read: *Just wanted to drop you a line, Maddie, and tell you how much you have been in my thoughts over the past twenty-four hours. I hope that you get some much-needed rest. I care about you greatly and hate to see you in pain. With love, Lourdes.* Maddie read through the card three times, tears stinging the back of her eyes. If Lourdes cared enough to give her this beautiful bouquet and card, then maybe it was time for Maddie to follow through with her supposed lifestyle changes. She figured it wouldn't kill her to look into the meditation app. Maddie missed taking time to cook for herself. She used to make so many elaborate meals. Cooking used to be fun. For the past couple of months, she'd treated her body like an afterthought. It was time for her to take herself seriously.

Maddie flicked the tears from her eyes and hit the call button. It wasn't even a minute before Millicent rushed into the room. "You need something?"

"Will you please let Dr. Mallone know I'll consent to the psych evaluation?"

"Gladly, Maddie. Need anything else?"

"Maybe some more water."

"My pleasure." Millicent left, and Maddie read the card three times. It was just the right push she needed to ensure she would get better. For the past two months, almost everyone told her she needed to get better. But with Lourdes, it was different. She had never felt such genuine love before in her life, and she wanted to be worthy of that love. She wanted to be the best possible partner for Lourdes. But she also wanted to be the best nurse for her patients, to give them the care they deserved without whittling herself away into a husk of who she once was. She wanted to get better, not just because Lourdes loved her, but because she loved herself, too.

CHAPTER THIRTY-EIGHT

DOCTOR'S ORDERS

To say it was a relief to be home was an understatement. But two days later, when Maddie could rest in her own bed, she realized then how much she had taken for granted. Her dad had pleaded with her to allow him to stay at her place, especially when she was adamant that she was staying in her own bed. However, Maddie had to be forceful. She didn't need someone to take care of her. Maddie had gotten three peaceful nights of sleep and was thrilled to be in her own room. Despite her car being at the hospital, she allowed him to take her home, but he assured her he would get someone to help him drive her back to the apartment. She was satisfied when it meant being out of the hospital.

Cheddar meowed, and she scratched the back of his ears. He clearly didn't understand why she wasn't there to feed him.

Her Dad periodically checked on him and filled his bowls, but Cheddar and Maddie were in a much better place.

"Maddie? Are you still there? You zoned out."

Maddie laughed and looked at her screen, "Sorry, Eric. It's been an exhausting day."

"I know, and I won't keep you much longer, but you were just about to tell me about the psych eval."

"Honestly, it wasn't as bad as I feared it would be. I'll admit that I felt much more at ease when it was done. I went into it, dreading it like I was about to get a tooth pulled. It was significantly less excruciating."

Eric laughed. "You still are full of drama, aren't you?" He winked, then pressed on.

"I just had some testing. I saw Peter Walters."

"Oh yeah? I've heard great things about him."

Eric grinned. "And I heard he's cute and single."

"Down, boy," Maddie teased. "You're cute, too, but you aren't single."

"Hey, a man can dream. I have never cautioned James about dreaming outside of our relationship. If anything, it keeps the love alive. Trust me." He clapped his hands together. "But now, what did Mcdreamy have to tell you?"

Maddie snickered. "He diagnosed me with Generalized Anxiety Disorder. He said it's not uncommon. Apparently, managing stress is key. He said I most likely had an acute anxiety episode, but it should all improve as I learn to manage my stress. He prescribed me a low dose of Ativan and said I only needed to take it if I feel another episode coming on. And a low dose of Zoloft for daily anxiety management. After the evaluation, I already felt much better."

"That sounds amazing, Maddie. I'm so happy that you took the steps. But what are the next steps to this healthier you?"

"Well, I have to do a follow-up with Dr. Mallone tomorrow afternoon. It's just to see how my first night back at the apartment treated me. And I have to pick up my prescription" She sighed and leaned back in bed.

"Uh oh. I know that sigh. What aren't you telling me?"

"Dr. Walters ordered me to stay off work for two weeks and no social media either! Two weeks, can you imagine?" She huffed and shook her head. She had already been off three days. That was torture enough. She wanted to be back to helping her patients out. What harm would that do if she had the assistance to improve?

"You do realize that staying off work for two weeks is only so your body can heal, right? You'll be back before you know it. It would be best if you had this time to rest. You might not think so, but your body knows so."

Maddie rolled her eyes. Deep down, she knew he was right, but it felt like a stab to her heart that she would have to steer clear of the patients she loved.

"I know, but it's still rough. Dr. Walters wants me to do outpatient therapy, as well. It's hard to imagine that working with patients has brought me anxiety."

"Well, it's not just working with patients. Maddie. You know, as well as I do, that your breakup was also a stressor."

"That was the reason we broke up. My stress was getting in the way of our relationship."

"True," he replied. "But that only added to the stress. You are such a kindhearted person that once the hospital started changing, you couldn't imagine letting the patients suffer. So you pushed yourself harder. You worked more. You dug so deep that it would cause strain on anyone in that position."

While he was right, Maddie's thoughts returned to Lourdes and the breakup. If she hadn't been so caught up in attempting to change the world, they might have still been a couple, and she might not have wound up in the hospital. She looked over at the flowers and smiled. She wanted to believe that as she evolved and grew, Lourdes would return to her side. "There you are again, in that zone." He laughed, tearing her eyes away from the flowers.

Maddie blushed and scanned the phone over to look at the flowers. "See those flowers?"

"They're gorgeous. Who are they from?"

Maddie turned the phone back towards her, "Lourdes."

His jaw dropped, and Maddie snickered. "Along with a card that said she was thinking of me and praying for me, and she hopes I feel better. ."

"Wow! That's certainly a step. I wonder why she reached out. Then again, she's probably just worried because she sees you as a patient. I'm sure that's it."

Maddie rolled her eyes, which elicited a laugh from Eric. "You know, joke all you want. I know it's a sweet gesture." She dropped her gaze back to the flowers. She wished she hadn't taken this long to see that she needed help.

"You guys belong together, Maddie. Just give it time. You'll be back in good graces before you know it. I would say this was just a start in the right direction." Maddie nodded. They could work their way back to each other, but he was right. They were slow in that process. "I best be going, but take care of yourself."

"I'll try. Talk later. Bye, Eric."

"Bye, Girlie."

She disconnected the call and smiled as she leaned back in her bed. Cheddar rested his chin on her leg. Maddie rubbed behind his ears, and he purred loudly. She was on the right track. That was the most important thing.

CHAPTER THIRTY-NINE

DECISIONS TO UNPACK

Maddie arrived at her appointment with Dr. Mallone thirty minutes early. If she was being honest, she was mostly hoping to catch a glimpse of Lourdes. Maddie could thank her for the flowers if they accidentally bumped into one another. She sent a short thank you text once she received them, but the only response she received was you're welcome. Even though it shouldn't have given her a lot to consider, her mind was racing with possibilities of what Lourdes truly meant by those words.

No matter how hard Maddie attempted to seek out Lourdes' meaning, she came up empty-handed. Instead, Maddie paced around the waiting room for thirty minutes. She kept checking her watch nervously. She didn't know why she was so frantic to get the appointment over. It was simply a checkup they could have managed over the phone. Yet, he was worried that, for some reason, she would be shoved back into a hospital bed, ready to submit to more tests. She rechecked her watch. Now, five minutes late. The lobby didn't seem very busy. She tapped her foot, growing impatient as the minutes ticked by.

"Maddie?" She jumped up, startled.

The receptionist tilted her head and gave Maddie a funny look. "Yes?"

"Dr. Mallone wanted me to tell you there's been an emergency that's kept him. If you don't mind waiting, he will be ready for you in another twenty minutes."

Maddie nodded her head. She had been there long enough. What difference would twenty minutes make? She sat down and waited. The longer she waited, the more nervous she became. She looked over to the hallway linking the waiting room to another department, and her heart skipped a beat. There stood Lourdes in her white lab coat and gorgeous smile. She was talking to another doctor, unaware that Maddie had her eyes off in her direction.

When Lourdes was through talking and turned her way, that's when their eyes connected. Lourdes nodded and started in her direction. Was she really coming to say hi? Maddie swallowed the lump that had formed.

"Maddie? Dr. Mallone is ready for you."

Maddie felt a wave of air rush through her body. The receptionist directed her to Dr. Mallone's office at the worst possible time. Lourdes stopped walking. Maddie could feel Lourdes' gaze on her back as she walked into the ward. Maddie wanted to scream; this wasn't how her romance novel was supposed to play out.

"Have a seat, and the doctor will be with you."

Maddie took a seat on the bed and waited, left to her own devices and nerves. Luckily, she was only there a few minutes before he popped into the room. "Good afternoon, Maddie. I'm sorry to have kept you waiting. How are you doing today?" Maddie nodded, but her heart was aching because her other half was wandering those same halls.

"This should be relatively painless."

He wasn't wrong. For ten minutes, they sat there and talked. Mostly about the weather and whether Maddie felt the psych evaluation was helpful. Maddie was quite honest with her thoughts on the matter. Dr. Mallone nodded and smiled as he listened.

"I'm glad I took the opportunity you gave me. I don't think we wasted a session," she admitted.

"I am happy to hear that. Keep up with your meds, and I am certain that in no time, you will be an even better version of yourself."

As Maddie left the room, she practically rushed around the corner, hoping that Lourdes would be waiting. She looked around and sighed. Lourdes had more important things to do than wait for her.

Before Maddie left the hospital, she went to human resources. She had to get the paperwork signed to start her FMLA leave. Her trip to HR ended up being far more discouraging than her visit with Dr. Mallone.

"I don't understand. What do you mean I have to attend a meeting?"

Clarissa, who covered the HR front office most days, didn't blink.

"It's protocol, Maddie. When someone has to take an FMLA leave for their mental health, the hospital wants to ensure that nothing like this will happen again. As your chart states, you are having trouble with anxiety and stress. These meetings are here as a mental health resource for our staff. Her phone rang, and she held up her hand. "Excuse me."

Maddie looked down at the paperwork in front of her. She was only on one signature and had a slew of others to read. Maddie skipped a few pages and continued to read. Much of it was legal jargon, which she didn't quite comprehend, but none sounded too bad. The only thing that made her nervous was the prospect of the meeting. It was bad enough that the whole hospital knew what had transpired in that elevator, but now she had to be humiliated again in front of the entire HR department. "Sorry about that. Now, where were we? Ah yes. The meetings. It's really an individual meeting, something you can set up on your own time. It just has to be completed before you return. There is one other option. But I'm not sure how you'd feel about it."

"Another option? What is it? Anything."

"Well, before attending a meeting, you can agree to switch career fields. Maybe nursing is too stressful for you after all. That's totally fine. There's no harm in that. If you choose to do so, you can change fields, and we'll call it an even switch. No worries at all."

She thrust a brochure in front of Maddie. "There are hundreds of options. You must scan the QR code in your spare time and choose the one that best suits you."

Maddie looked through the brochure and rolled her eyes. "I

literally just came in here to sign the paperwork and leave. Is this necessary to make the decision now?"

"Of course not!" Clarissa opened the paperwork to the back page and pointed to the line. "Sign here, and you can choose your options later. I advise you to do it quickly so you don't get caught last minute."

"Understood." Maddie quickly signed. "Is that it?"

"One more thing. You have some mail." Clarissa reached under the counter and drew out a pile. She handed it over, and Maddie glanced at the top item. It was a card that read, "We'll miss you!"

"What's this?"

"You know how word gets around in CAPMED. Some of your co-workers wanted to express their wishes for improving your health." Her phone rang again. "I'll be looking forward to hearing from you. Take care." She grabbed the phone as Maddie ciphered through the cards. She felt like she wanted to cry. She dashed out of the hospital so no one would catch the tears in the corners of her eyes. It meant the world if people really wanted to wish her well.

There was a moment of hesitation where Maddie wanted to go to the Cardio floor and see Lourdes, but she dismissed that thought and left through the front doors.

Once outside, she scanned the QR code and pulled up the list of career choices. She skimmed down through them, mentally checking them off as not good enough. Then she stopped at one that caught her attention, *nursing informatics*. She read through the description and was mildly intrigued. For starters, she'd still be helping patients without being their direct caregiver. She considered that quietly. That might be something that would help her anxiety and relieve her daily stress.

She closed the browser window and hurried to her car. She could at least do some research. It would be a bonus if some of her classes transferred from the university. She felt rejuvenated for the first time since stepping into the HR office. She was ready for new possibilities.

CHAPTER FORTY

HER FATHER'S FLAME

Maddie didn't know why she was so nervous, but her palms hadn't stopped sweating since she left the apartment. She looked over to the small car parked behind her father's. Maddie wanted to meet Lydia and was relieved that her father had found a woman he enjoyed spending time with. However, she felt like a little girl again, ready to meet someone that could ultimately be her mommy. Maddie laughed at the possibility. She wasn't a child, and as long as her dad was happy, so was she.

The door flung open, and her dad pulled her into the house. "I'm so glad you could make it." He hugged her tightly, then kissed the top of her forehead. "Just seeing you now makes me confident that you will be alright.

Maddie nodded. "I'm going to be great, Dad." She squeezed

him tighter, then spotted the woman standing behind him. She was around 5'7, with kind blue eyes and faint smile lines around her mouth. Her bleach-blonde hair was combed and coiffed. She wore a blue knee-length sundress and open-toed wedge heels. She smoothed her hands over the fabric of her dress, clearly nervous. Maddie pulled back and held out her hand. "And you must be Lydia."

The woman nodded, then stepped in closer. "I'm a hugger, do you mind?" Maddie shook her head. Lydia clutched Maddie to her, and Maddie's nostrils filled with the scent of a powdery, cloying perfume. "I've heard so much about you, Maddie. Your dad is very, very proud," Lydia gushed.

When Maddie pulled away and forced a smile onto her face, she swallowed, glancing between her father and the woman she was meeting for the first time. For some reason, she felt like she was about to burst into tears. "I've heard a lot about you, as well."

This was true, but her dad only started bringing Lydia up in conversation three weeks ago. How long had this relationship been going on? She was sure she would gather all the news throughout their meal. She took in a whiff.

"Dinner smells amazing."

"It's Lydia's signature dish," her father spoke, "Grilled Chicken and Rice. Along with steamed vegetables. I wanted to add Teriyaki sauce to the menu, but the warden refused." He winked at Lydia and reached for her hand.

Maddie couldn't believe how easy they were with one another. Yet, they were teasing one another like they were life-long partners. It was refreshing.

Maddie glanced at Lydia. "And for that, I'm relieved. My

dad needs someone to remind him to make healthy choices when I'm not around. ."

Her dad huffed, then chuckled. "Honey, go on in the dining room. We'll grab the food and meet you in a few minutes."

As Maddie went to the dining room, she stopped and looked at the same pictures they had on the walls from when she was younger and lived in the house. Most had stayed the same from when Maddie moved. She felt instantly at ease when she walked through the door, knowing she didn't have to question whether things would be different in her old home.

She sat down in the same seat that she always sat in. She could fully relax and look forward to a home-cooked meal that she didn't have to cook. It didn't take long for her dad and Lydia to have the food ready on the dining room table.

"Dig in. I hope you enjoy it," Lydia exclaimed. She was all smiles, almost giddy. It brought a smile to Maddie, as she looked just as happy to be there as her father looked to have her there.

After they each had their plates filled, Lydia didn't hesitate. "Do you mind if I give the blessing? It's been a long time since I've been around a table filled with food, and I always enjoyed these moments."

"Be our guest," Maddie's dad beamed with pride as Maddie lowered her head.

"Heavenly Father. We thank you for this meal this evening. Please look over my David and his daughter, Maddie. They will be great blessings in my life. Guide us in knowing what the future will bring us and how bright you can make it. In Jesus' name, we pray. Amen."

"Amen!" her dad declared. Maddie looked up and found

him grinning from ear to ear. Maddie cleared her throat and looked down at the food. "It looks amazing, Lydia."

She took a bite and nodded with enthusiasm. "It tastes even better." She grabbed her napkin and dabbed her mouth.

"Thank you, Maddie," Lydia looked angelic as she grinned and continued to eat.

"So, do you come from a large family?" Maddie wondered.

"Ten brothers and sisters," she said.

"Growing up, we had two bathrooms. The girls and the boys." She laughed.

"When I went off to college, it was hard to believe I only had to share with my roommates."

"Wow! I can't imagine. It was hard enough with just my father and me." Maddie laughed, and her dad opened his mouth.

"Just kidding, Dad," She winked and took a sip of her water.

"But that's impressive."

"We managed. I wouldn't have had it any other way." Lydia's smile had never once left her face.

Lydia's seemingly endless optimism floored Maddie. She could only hope that she would one day be able to think about the future with the same level of excitement rather than the panic that usually settled in her gut when Maddie contemplated what she wanted to do next. "

So, tell me how you two met," Maddie was genuinely curious. Her dad wasn't suave.

Her father and Lydia gave each other a knowing glance, and then Lydia laughed slightly. "You tell it, David ."

Maddie smirked. The only time she'd ever heard anyone call him David was when he was stuck in line at the DMV. She didn't interrupt as her dad cleared his throat to continue their story.

"Frozen chicken," he began. Maddie tilted her head, and he laughed.

"You heard me right. We were both in the frozen chicken aisle at the grocery store. I was trying to decide between brands. Just as I reached for one, this hand came out behind me and snatched up the last bag." He laughed loudly.

"I was so astonished that I looked to see where the hand had come from. There she was, looking absolutely radiant in the middle of the grocery store, fluorescent lights and all Needless to say, we got to talking."

"I confessed that I didn't even want the bag. I noticed this handsome guy reaching for it and figured I would take the chance." Maddie's jaw dropped, and Lydia grinned.

"Next thing I knew, we had a dinner date. I was so nervous. I swore David was going to ditch me at the restaurant."

"I would have been a fool," he commented.

"That was the best chicken I ever bought." He winked, and Maddie thought she would melt in her seat. She couldn't remember seeing her father gushing like a lovestruck teenager, but it was sweet.

"That is so sweet," Maddie said.

"Do you have any children? Ever been married? Do you like kids?"

"Slow down, Maddie." Her dad laughed, shaking his head.

"Save the third degree for dessert." He winked at Maddie.

"Come on, Dad. You can't blame me for being curious. I've never seen him so excited about someone before," Maddie explained to Lydia.

Lydia reached out and took his hand. "I don't mind. I'm happy to share. I was married, briefly. We weren't right for one another and knew after about a year we needed to go our separate ways. We parted on okay terms, but it was meant to be. I never had children, but I have several nieces and nephews and love them each tremendously. So, yes, a big fan of kids. Both young and old." She looked over to Maddie's father and grinned.

"And I must confess I've never been this happy, either. Your father brings out the best in me."

Maddie felt an instant wave of relief wash over her. Those were the best words Lydia could have spoken. Truthfully, she was glad her dad had someone else looking out for him that wasn't her. While he would never tell her outright, Maddie figured that her dad had to be at least a little lonely. It was wonderful to see him smiling. Lydia seemed equally enamored. The last thing Maddie wanted was for her dad to be left pining for someone who didn't love him back. But watching Lydia and her dad interact throughout the night put any worries that Maddie had about Lydia and her intentions to rest. She wouldn't be calling her mom anytime soon, but she was genuinely excited for her dad.

TALKING TO LYDIA WAS LIKE TALKING TO A BEST FRIEND. SHE was thirty years older than Maddie, but Maddie didn't feel the sense that Lydia was there to be the motherly type. After all, Maddie had gone all these years with just her father. Lydia seemed to respect that. Honestly, it was refreshing to see that she cared for her dad and respected the existing relationship between Maddie and her father. She made a mental note to cross 'evil step-mom' off her list of worries.

"Can I get you both something to drink?" Her father stood up and grabbed the dishes.

Maddie arched her brow. "Dad, you're clearing the table? What have you done with my father? Let me do that." Maddie jumped up to reach for the plates, but he quickly pulled his arm back and shook his head.

"You two go ahead and get to know each other some more. I know you have more questions. I've got this." He offered Maddie a wink, which caused her to smile. Before shaking her head, she waited until he had left the dining room.

"The last time my father cleared the table, I was probably ten. You must be a good influence on him."

Lydia beamed. "I'm thinking it might be the other way around."

Lydia's eyes dimmed before she looked away at Maddie's contact. "I haven't been completely honest with you this evening, Maddie."

Maddie frowned. Here it was. The moment that Lydia dropped the ball. She didn't even want to swallow to break into the mood. She stared at Lydia, wide-eyed and nervous about what Lydia might share. Any harmful details involving her father would surely be the demise of Lydia and her father's relationship. Maddie would be sure of that. She took a deep breath and waited for Lydia to shatter her dad's hopes and dreams.

"It makes me nervous to talk about this."

"You can tell me anything," Maddie started. Still, she braced herself for whatever devastating news Lydia had to share.

"After my divorce, I dated only one other guy. I suppose it was a whirlwind romance. I was trying to get back on that horse, hopeful that anyone would be able to get my failed marriage out of my mind. I started a new job and went full force into it as if that job would be the only thing keeping me alive. It was there that I met Trevor. He was younger than me. But more importantly, he was my new boss. He promised me the world, and I was working hard, so I felt I deserved it. I didn't realize I was getting ahead solely because I was with Trevor."

Maddie's dad came in, and Lydia paused the story. He grabbed a few more dishes and then was gone. Maddie turned back to her, and she continued.

"As my stress levels rose, my relationship status with Trevor increased. Maybe God planned on me divorcing, only to get remarried a year later. I thought that Trevor and I were soulmates. But then, after a year, things started to falter. I was so stressed that my hair was falling out in the shower. Then, Trevor started to get abusive. He hit me to the point where I thought maybe I deserved it. The abuse made me question my life, but it made me believe that I had to keep working hard because I thought my job was the only thing that made me worthwhile. Clearly, I wasn't a good wife. Otherwise, Trevor wouldn't hit me, right? That's how messed up my thinking was. I justified his abuse by telling myself that I was the problem."

Again, Maddie's father returned to the room, and Maddie waited with her mouth agape, not wanting to disregard the story. He left as if he didn't see them, and Lydia released a breath.

"It took me an entire year and a hospital stay to realize I

deserved better. I quit my job, and I went and stayed with one of my sisters and her family down south. I vowed that I wouldn't want to be in another relationship as long as I lived because the only happiness that mattered was my own. Fast forward two years, and I came back here, fully rested, ready for my life to continue. That's when I met your father. Now, I must admit; I'm telling you this because your dad told me about your incident in the hospital. I know that's a terrifying place to be when you feel like you can't trust your own mind or your own body. But I want to take this time to promise it will get better. It might not get better in a week or even a month, but it does. You have to trust that you deserve good things because you do. You deserve to be happy and healthy and have a job that doesn't make you want to panic every time you walk through the door. And I also know that making that change is really scary, too, so I'm here if you ever want to talk, okay? I'll have your dad text you my number, and you can call or text, whatever you're most comfortable with."

Maddie opened her mouth when she saw her dad pop back around the corner. "There, the dishes are in the dishwasher, and now we don't have to worry about them. How are my two favorite gals?" He walked over and placed a kiss on the top of Maddie's head before planting a sweet kiss on Lydia's lips.

"Will you excuse me?" Maddie got up and left the dining room, both pairs of eyes on her as she felt them when she rounded the corner. She entered the bathroom and closed the door, falling back against the door, Lydia's story still heavy on her heart. Maddie retrieved her phone from her pocket and pulled up the internet browser. Her search for careers was still readily available. She pulled up the description for Nursing

Informatics and read the post over again. Maddie hit the speed dial to the hospital and waited for the prompts when she dialed in the HR voicemail.

"You've reached HR. Leave a message after the beep, and I'll return the call as soon as possible. Thank you, and have a great day."

"Hey, Clarissa. It's Maddie Anderson. Please call me back when you get this message. I have an inquiry to make about one of the other positions. I look forward to hearing back from you."

Maddie replaced her phone, then checked herself in the mirror. She wasn't crying. That was a good sign. She left the bathroom and returned to the dining room, where her dad sat alone.

She frowned. "Where's Lydia?"

He looked up. "She went outside to make a call. Her niece has a project due in school, and she thought you and I could use some alone time. Everything alright?"

Maddie nodded and moved into the seat next to him. "I really like her, Dad."

He grinned. "I was hoping you'd say that." He reached out and squeezed Maddie's hand.

"And before you ask, I knew about her situation with Trevor. We tell each other everything."

"So, she knows about my issues?"

"They're not issues. Lydia wanted to let you know that you're not alone. We all have problems to overcome. Some are bigger than others, but none of them are trivial. And she wants you to know she's here for you if you ever need someone to talk to."

After she got over the initial irritation that her dad had told

Lydia about her problems, Maddie realized that it might not be so bad to have someone to talk to, especially someone who knew what she was going through. Lydia was right; these kinds of changes were scary. She squeezed her father's hand and leaned into him. "I love you, Dad."

"Love you, too, sweetheart." They embraced, and this was the first time Maddie felt that weight slowly lifting off her chest.

CHAPTER FORTY-ONE

NEW JOURNEY

As Maddie began her new career, pulling out of nursing and right into informatics, she realized it was an easier transition than expected. Informatics combined both healthcare and IT. Luckily, all of her classes had transferred. Nursing informatics still focuses on patient care. The only significant step she had to take to change careers was the paid training and a course the hospital offered. With the money she had in her savings, the lack of pay didn't even strain her. She also had her father's and Lydia's support, which made things all the easier.

It only took her two months to get everything finalized before she was prepared to start her course at the hospital. The three-month-long class covered the job and trained her to enter the field. Even better, they promised to offer all enrollees a position should they desire to extend their career with CAPMED. Another bonus of informatics was that Nursing Informatics specialists acted as the liaison between the IT specialists developing new healthcare software and the nurses on the floor, which meant that Maddie could still see her friends. For Maddie, she kept her options open to whatever her heart would choose. She wouldn't close any doors but felt hopeful about her new career.

Twenty people started the course aged anywhere from their late teens, right out of high school, up to Maddie's age. With one exception, a woman was returning to the workforce after having her three kids. Eva was fifty-four with blonde hair and green eyes. She was the most excited of Maddie's new classmates. Maddie smiled every time Eva asked a question. She felt inspired and moved by Eva's choice to change. If Eva could leap into a brand new career at 54, then Maddie could do so at 25. They became fast friends. Three weeks into the course, though, only five students remained. Maddie couldn't quite comprehend why so many people dropped out. She saw nursing informatics as a position to help people thrive. Yet, as the instructor stated, *It's just not for everyone.*

Eva remained, which was a relief to Maddie. She anticipated that both of them would be able to continue their Nursing Informatics career with CAPMED.

Their latest assignment was to analyze a real-life situation where they could evaluate the situation and decide the steps to take to process a patient's data. Maddie loved the course because it allowed them to throw themselves into real-life situations before starting the actual job. There were times when Maddie worried that she would fail the class altogether. But Maddie didn't let her stress get the best of her. Instead, she used some breathing exercises that her therapist taught her and started a 2-person study group with Eva. Soon, she was thriving in the class, which was fascinating in and of itself. "You can each email me the link to your online project, and I'll review it and have feedback for you next week. Have a great weekend!"

The five packed up their laptops and headed outside the room. Maddie waited for Eva to join her.

"How do you think you did?" Maddie asked.

Eva gave a weak smile, "Remember, it's been a long time since I was used to doing homework. And I'm still getting used to it." She laughed.

"But, all in all, I would say that I did the best I could. Isn't that what it's all about? You can only do your best, right?"

Maddie nodded, reveling in those words. Eva's positive outlook on life only gave Maddie room to think. They got on the elevator, and the doors closed behind them.

"How can you always be so positive?" Maddie asked. "You have a smile on your face 24/7. You never seem to let anything break your spirit."

Eva laughed, "Oh, Maddie. If my husband and kids heard you say that, they would certainly raise some eyebrows. We all have our moments. But then I take a step back and think and realize that my life could be so much worse. People struggle for a roof over their heads or food on their tables. People are struggling because their loved ones are sick, and they can't afford treatment. I decided I wanted to be in a position where I could eventually help them. I know I'm ancient, but I figured this would be the best way for me to help people in need. Plus, you never know until you try.

Suddenly the doors opened, and Maddie turned. Her jaw dropped. "Lourdes!"

Lourdes turned from the woman that stood beside her. Her smile faded almost immediately. But as they stood there, the smile started to return only slightly. "Maddie!"

Maddie swallowed the lump and then glanced at the woman beside Lourdes. The woman smiled, looked at Lourdes, and looked back at Maddie. Maddie's stomach dropped. The stranger standing awfully close to Lourdes also happened to be gorgeous. She was 5'10 with a blunt jet-black bob and large, green eyes. She had the same olive skin tone as Lourdes, with no blemishes in sight. She was dressed impeccably in a chic denim jumpsuit, a sharp contrast to Maddie's messy bun, day-old scrubs, and stress acne. "How've you been?" Maddie asked, stepping off the elevator and spotting Eva stepping next to her.

"Good. Great. No complaints." Lourdes glanced at her friend and then looked at Maddie. "This is Giselle. Giselle, this is Maddie."

"Nice to meet you," Maddie mumbled.

"Likewise," Giselle replied.

"I've heard so much about you."

With that, Lourdes nudged Giselle in the side and then turned to Maddie. "Um, so yeah, you're here, CAPMED."

She frowned. "Everything okay?"

"Everything is fine. Great." Maddie longed to ask why Lourdes had moved on so quickly. She looked at Eva. "This is Eva. A few weeks ago, we started a course in Nursing Informatics."

Lourdes' eyes widened. "That's great! I'm certain you're going to thrive in that."

Maddie's smile weakened. "Yeah. Well, it was good seeing you, Lourdes. Nice to meet you, Giselle, but we best get going. Tell everyone I said hi." She grabbed Eva's arm, and they hurried towards the front door.

"Friend of yours?" Eva asked.

Maddie didn't stop until they were outside. She turned to look back into the hospital but couldn't see either Lourdes or Giselle.

"Someone I used to know," Maddie muttered.

She sighed, "She looked happy, didn't she?"

Eva shrugged. "I mean, before seeing you, she looked pretty happy. I don't know her, so I can't really judge that."

Maddie huffed. "That's what I thought, though." She turned and started heading towards the parking lot, Eva close behind. "Lourdes and I used to be a thing until work stress got in our way. Well, it got in my way. We broke up a few months ago.."

Maddie stopped at her car and turned to Eva. "There hasn't been a day since I haven't thought of her or wondered what she was doing. I considered reaching out to her and telling her about my big change. But I always stopped myself. Lourdes wanted to move on, so I needed to respect that. And just like that, it looks like she has."

"Maddie, Dear. You can't tell that she's moved on. That could be a friend. Heck, you were with a friend." Eva laughed.

"Very possible it was something similar. Or a co-worker. You don't know."

Maddie tilted her head. "I've seen that look before. She's given me that look before. It's not a friend." She reached for her door. "I have to go. I'll see you next week!"

"Are you sure you want to be alone? We could go grab a drink or something."

Maddie shrugged. "That's really sweet of you, Eva, but I don't think I'd be the best company right now. I'll call you later." She got in her car and started it, a weight still holding her down.

As she got further away from the hospital, she cringed at her first meeting with Lourdes.

"Call Eric." She had worked so hard to make a difference, but seeing that Lourdes had moved on was enough to break her all over again. She reached up and flicked the tear away. Of course, this happened when she hoped she could fully get over Lourdes.

"Hey, girl."

"Can you talk?" Maddie sucked in a deep breath.

"For you? Always."

It finally happened. I ran into Lourdes at the hospital," Maddie started.

Eric sighed but said nothing.

Maddie continued, "I know that we said it was a possibility. After all, Lourdes still worked there, and the hospital was only so big, but I did not prepare myself for seeing her. What's even worse? I ran into her and her girlfriend."

"Girlfriend?"

They might have just started dating if Eric didn't know about it, but Maddie saw what she saw. "They were looking all chummy as I got off the elevator. It must be new if you sound so surprised."

"Well, Lourdes and I aren't best friends in any sense of the word, but we still work closely together. I would think I would have suspected if she had taken a lover. Are you sure?"

Maddie couldn't even giggle at Eric's use of the word lover, "I saw what I saw," Maddie huffed.

"I mean, it's been a long enough time. I don't know why I'm so surprised. Just because I haven't moved on doesn't mean Lourdes wouldn't. She deserves to be happy, and I am happy for her if she's happy."

"Whoa, slow down, Maddie. Let me do some investigating. I'm pretty good at that, you know." He snickered. "I'll see what I can find out. Don't go jumping to any conclusions. You're spiraling. I can feel the all-encompassing doom coming through the phone."

"Doom isn't exactly how I'd describe it. Heartbroken, maybe. It's the first time I'm seeing her in so long, and we loved each other." Maddie turned into the parking lot behind her building and sighed. "I guess I always envisioned we'd one day find our way back to each other, and since I got the help I needed and made the necessary change. I know I'm a better version of myself. I was looking forward to the day I could show up at her door and say,' This is the woman you fell in love with."

"And it could still happen."

While Maddie longed to believe that, her heart shattered from seeing the beautiful woman smiling before her and knowing she wasn't smiling because of her. Getting over a heartache like that would take longer than a few months, but Maddie had to trust that she would eventually get there.

CHAPTER FORTY-TWO

HEALING

No matter how hard I try, Maddie, I can't find any sign that Lourdes has a girlfriend. Eric had done his best, no doubt. She couldn't bicker with him over that, but as the days went on from that latest bump-in, Maddie knew that Giselle and Lourdes were bound to be the hottest item since Maddie and Lourdes broke up.

A month passed, and she threw herself into her coursework and did her best to just put Lourdes out of her mind. Thinking too long about their failed relationship was an obstacle she had to overcome. Otherwise, it would be the demise of her recovery.

Even though Maddie was busy with the course and studying when she wasn't at the hospital, she had to ensure she kept her eye on the real prize; staying healthy and leading a better life.

She maintained her weekly therapy sessions and tossed herself into maintaining her health. Maddie resumed regular jogs. She only consumed the occasional burger. Her health had greatly improved over time.

Maddie took a long swig of water as she stepped out of her car and looked out over the park. She opened up her Instagram and smiled, taking a selfie at the start of the trail. *Hello, Friends. It's a gorgeous Saturday morning, and the birds are chirping! I'm about to head out to train for my next 5k for the American Heart Foundation this June. If you'd like to register to run or donate, the link is in my bio! Drop a comment below if you'll be there, and make sure to say hi if you see me! I love all of you, and I'll see you soon!* Maddie pressed "post," turned on her music, and started jogging. Tegan and Sara came on through her earbuds, and Maddie grinned. She didn't stop once throughout her run. She was happy to be back. The park was busy, but the kids and dogs didn't once interrupt her mood. Maddie closed her eyes and continued to jog, enjoying the fresh air and the soothing atmosphere. She could run like this for hours and never wanted to stop. Maddie no longer needed espresso shots to get her through a jog. She wasn't running to prove something to herself. She was running because it made her happy.

As Maddie rounded the trail, at least an hour of running already in, she spotted her. Lourdes was leaning up against a tree, her eyes closed. As Maddie drew nearer, she internally fought with two options, run right on by or stop and say hi. Lourdes was alone, and Maddie couldn't tear her eyes away. She still had the most beautiful and pristine complexion Maddie had ever seen. Maddie inhaled, and just like that, Lourdes opened her eyes. Their eyes met, and Lourdes offered a small wave. Was that Maddie's invention, or Lourdes wanting Maddie to wave and move on? Maddie's desire remained, and she slowed her jog.

"Hey!"

Lourdes gave a gracious grin as she nodded. "Hey!"

Maddie looked around, looking for Giselle, but Lourdes was alone. She saw the basket next to Lourdes and smiled. "Came out for a picnic, I presume?"

Lourdes shrugged. "Something like that. I saw this tree, and it seems like a great spot for a picnic. You know how that goes."

Maddie nodded. "I do." She glanced around, then turned to Lourdes. "I don't want to interrupt you and your alone time. Or, perhaps, you're waiting for someone. I…" She stepped back away from Lourdes. "I should leave you to it."

"Maddie, wait!"

Maddie paused. She would probably never want to leave if she stayed, but Lourdes deserved better than that. She deserved Giselle, who obviously made her very happy.

"I have more than enough. You could stay and join me."

Maddie turned around and looked down at the blanket and basket. "Are you sure? You're not waiting for anyone?"

Lourdes shook her head, "Unless you don't think your girl-friend would like you fraternizing with the enemy." Lourdes gave a nervous giggle.

Maddie frowned. "Girlfriend?"

"Yeah, that woman I saw you with last month. I figured that was a girlfriend."

Maddie's jaw dropped, and then she started laughing. She

felt her chest caving in. Laughter bubbled up out of her mouth. She hadn't laughed this hard in a long time.

"You thought that was my girlfriend? Eva is old enough to be my mother." She continued to laugh, shaking her head.

"We're in class together. We're just friends, that's all."

She covered her face again, shaking her head. "I can't even imagine what you would have thought or why you expected she was, but believe me. She's not."

Lourdes beamed. "I guess I just assumed. And I know you like older women." She cupped her hand over her mouth.

"I shouldn't have gone there."

Maddie giggled.

"Well, older, maybe, but even Eva is out of the question. Besides, she's married with kids. She's just my friend." Maddie laughed, then rocked back on her heels. And yet, that wasn't the real issue there.

"I was more concerned that your girlfriend wouldn't want me sharing a picnic with you."

Lourdes snickered. "If I had a girlfriend, that'd be news to me."

Maddie arched an eyebrow. "Oh? You broke up?"

Lourdes frowned. "What are you talking about?"

"Giselle!"

Lourdes' eyes narrowed in, and then she started to laugh. Her eyes began watering, and she flicked the tears away. She hunched over, and Maddie watched her, but she couldn't stop joining the laughter. It felt good to laugh at the moment and not even know why they were laughing.

"Maddie, Giselle is my cousin. She came in from Texas, and

I was giving her a tour of the hospital. You thought she was my...." She hunched over again and started laughing. "Wait until she hears that one."

Maddie fell back against the same tree Lourdes had once been leaning against. Could she have gotten it that wrong? When the laughter finally died, Lourdes shook her head and fell back against the tree.

"Maddie, we both got the wrong idea. Now that that's situated, will you please join me for a picnic?"

Maddie smiled and settled down onto the blanket next to Lourdes.

Maddie and Lourdes made the slow walk back to the parking lot. Maddie carried the blanket as Lourdes carried the basket.

"It sounds like you've made some great improvement Maddie. I'm so happy to hear."

"Honestly, when we broke up, it felt like the world was ending. But you were right. I needed to learn how to take care of myself. You didn't break up with me out of spite. You were trying to push me to actually take charge of my life. At first, I ignored you. I ignored everyone around me. I ignored literally every gut feeling that I had that something was wrong. I ignored myself so hard that I got an ulcer. The last thing I needed was to be in a relationship. So, thank you. Thank you for looking out for me when I couldn't look out for myself and pushing me in the right direction."

"I was happy to be that push," Lourdes commented. Things turned quiet, and Maddie felt the air brush against her skin. The morning turned out far better than she expected. As she sat with Lourdes, Maddie's anxieties slowly disappeared. They didn't dive into drama or the past. They just talked about life and what they had been up to since they last were together. They were both there just enjoying one another's company, and Maddie didn't want to waste a single minute. Lourdes released a breath beside her, and Maddie caught her, glancing at her from the corner of her eye. "May I be honest with you?"

"I wish that you would," Maddie softly answered.

"Well, the truth is, after we saw each other, I couldn't stop thinking about you. I was so happy to hear that you were doing well, but I was heartbroken to think that you had moved on and found someone that could make you happier than I could."

No one ever could. Maddie remained quiet and just processed the words as they came through. Maddie waited on Lourdes' to continue with bated breath.

"I wanted to be happy for you, but it hurt inside that you had moved on."

Maddie bit her lower lip, grateful to hear the exact words from Lourdes that she had also considered.

"I thought about reaching out to you but wasn't sure if you would even want to hear from me, so I just dropped it and told myself that you were happy, and that was all I needed to know. But I didn't like that we had completely fallen out of one another's lives."

"Neither did I," Maddie admitted. She stopped at her car and turned to Lourdes. "I wanted to reach out to you, as well. But I wasn't sure you wanted to hear from me."

Lourdes smirked. "It seems we both were mistaken." She took a deep breath, and her eyes darted to the ground. She looked nervous and unsure. "When I saw your Insta post, I decided to give fate a little push."

Maddie opened her mouth, snapped it shut, and allowed Lourdes to continue.

"If we couldn't connect long enough to have a picnic together, I would know it was time for me to move on. If I saw that you were happy with your girlfriend," She smirked and looked back up again, meeting Maddie's gaze. "Then that would be my sign to walk away and leave you to your happiness."

"So, you stalked me?" Maddie smirked, and Lourdes nodded.

"Sometimes you have to do what you have to do. I don't know what the future will hold. None of us do, but I know there's no hope for a future if we're not talking. And I wanted to see if there was any hope left. Are you mad?"

Maddie shook her head. "How could I be mad? I think today needed to happen. I also think we both needed a little push."

Lourdes sighed, a wave of relief washing over her face. "So, I'll see you around??"

Maddie nodded. If they could see where things could go, she was relieved beyond words that Lourdes had taken it upon herself. And part of her even questioned if putting it out to social media where she was, wasn't an open invitation to the woman that still had a piece of her heart. They'd already wasted so much time.

As Lourdes got in her car, Maddie pulled out her phone and found her post. She posted an update with a selfie grinning from ear to ear. *I can't express how much I needed this run and how much I'm now looking forward to what the future could hold. Love to all.* Before she got in her car, a notification sounded, and it was a like from Lourdes. Maddie grinned and slid into her driver's seat. The future was hers for the taking.

CHAPTER FORTY-THREE

BREATHING AGAIN

Maddie reached up way over her head, stretching to the ceiling and then leaning over and touching the floor. She exhaled as she made the movement and stayed in that position until she spotted Cheddar from the corner of her eye. She laughed and pulled Cheddar onto her lap.

"We've made great strides, haven't we?" She snuggled closer to him, pulled out her phone, and took a selfie. She went into her Instagram and added the caption: *just me and my stretching buddy. Have a great day, everyone!*

Her followers followed her on the journey from improving her health to her new career path. They had all been so supportive. It was only fitting that they would follow along as she started her new career. Maddie was in the middle of paid training in the medical records department. Both Eva and Maddie accepted that as their next step in nursing informatics.

Maddie's ulcer had healed entirely; it was the best time for her to take on the next challenge, and she was looking forward to it. A notification sounded, and she smiled when she spotted Lourdes' name. They were in a much better place. Maddie remained optimistic about where things could go.

Her phone rang, and she spotted an incoming FaceTime call from Eric.

She eagerly answered, "Hello, my friend."

"You're in a good mood today." Eric laughed, and she leaned back against the couch, scratching Cheddar's head and feeling at peace.

"And why not? Life is grand, isn't it?"

He smirked. "Did you and Lourdes finally reconcile in the bedroom?"

Maddie rolled her eyes. "Is it all about sex for you?" She laughed when she saw the appalled look on his face.

"I'm kidding. No. We're still taking things slow, but we're friends again, which is the most important thing. I can't express how grateful I am for that."

"You sound like a Hallmark card." Eric winked at her, then laughed. Maddie rolled her eyes as Cheddar jumped off her lap and went over to his bed.

"I'm glad that you're being so optimistic, though. I mean, I still think you two belong together. And it's great to know that you quit the stubborn act and are actually doing something about it."

Maddie crossed her legs and stretched out on the floor. They both knew that Lourdes had taken that first step. Semantics aside, Maddie was happy that someone other than her had taken the initiative. Someone knocked on her door, and Maddie jumped up from the floor.

"Just a sec, Eric. Someone's at the door."

Maddie padded to the front door barefoot and peeped through the peephole to find her father and Lydia.

"Do you know who it is?" Eric asked.

"You can never be too careful."

Maddie rolled her eyes. "It's my father and his girlfriend. I'll call you back."

"Talk soon!"

She disconnected the call. "This is a pleasant surprise." Maddie hugged her father, then leaned over and hugged Lydia. Over the past few months, her father's relationship continued to grow. Maddie had now come to view Lydia as a vital part of her life.

"Well, we just thought we'd pop in and see how you're doing!" Her father snaked his arm around Lydia's waist. Lydia hadn't once lost that sparkle in her eyes. Maddie glanced between her father and Lydia and then back again.

"Is that all?" Maddie inquired.

Lydia was the first to break her silence with a laugh. "I told you, David, that she wouldn't buy that. We're engaged!" She held out her hand and thrust her finger in front of Maddie.

Maddie grabbed hold of her hand and stared at the sparkling diamond. "Oh my goodness, I'm so happy for you both." She threw her arms around their shoulders, and they all embraced. Tears sprung to Maddie's eyes, but for once, they were happy tears.

Lourdes: Good luck today. I know you are going to do great!

The simple text from Lourdes left Maddie beaming as she entered the medical records department and looked around for a familiar face. Immediately, she spotted Eva, who hurried over to her.

"Oh my goodness, Maddie. I'm as nervous as a baby going in for their first shot."

"Don't be silly," Maddie replied. "Babies don't know they're getting a shot."

Eva smiled, and at that moment, she seemed to calm down. "I haven't had a medical job for ten years."

"You've got this, Eva. Besides, we're going to be doing it together. No need to worry. Got it?" Maddie exclaimed.

Eva nodded and sighed. "I don't know what I'd do if you weren't here with me."

All Maddie and Eva needed were those five minutes to relax. Eva wasn't the only one afraid. Maddie had taken on this challenge and was determined to do her best. A woman with dark hair and green eyes exited the back room and greeted them at the desk. "Hello, I'm Hadley. And you must be Eva and Maddie?"

"I'm Maddie, and this is Eva." Maddie pointed to her friend. "We're both excited to be here."

Hadley smiled, "Let me show you both around." They took a tour that lasted just under an hour. What Maddie didn't anticipate was how big the hospital's medical records department was. It wasn't just on the tenth floor, but a whole basement of records housing all the archived files. Every time they entered a different room, they were in awe of how many files they would have to learn. Soon, both women were feeling o

Hadley introduced them to four other employees through the tour, each seeming busy but not filled with the nameless all-encompassing dread. The fact that no one seemed to be having a panic attack reassured Maddie. She could do this. Learning the ropes would take some time, but she would figure it out. Once they had wrapped back around the main floor, Hadley turned to them. "I do know it can be quite overwhelming but know that we do our best to keep our department adequately staffed. Eva, you can work with Beth. Maddie, follow me. I'm going to have you sit with Kristine."

Maddie looked over her shoulder as Eva looked like she had lost her best friend. She hoped Eva wouldn't let her insecurities get the best of her. Kristine got Maddie signed up on the computer system and then began going over how the system worked.

"Do you feel comfortable on the computer?"

"Absolutely!" Maddie was anxious to learn about doing an excellent job in medical records. When she met up with Eva, she felt like she was brimming with knowledge.

"I'm overwhelmed," Eva said, falling into the seat across from her. "Aren't you?"

"I am, but I think in the end, we'll figure it out. We both are smart. We both excelled in the course. So, I'm not going to let my anxiety get the best of me. I'm excited about what we'll learn. We can only go up from here."

"Ugh, Maddie. I wish I had the confidence you have."

Maddie was proud to hear the older woman state that.

Maybe she had come along farther than she even knew herself. Her phone dinged, and she reached into her pocket and withdrew it to find the message.

Lourdes: How are things going? You can respond later, but would you be up for getting together later? We could go to the diner or something. Just let me know.

"Good news?" Eva asked.

"Huh?"

"You're grinning like a woman that has a secret. Or like..." Her eyes widened. "A woman in love."

Maddie blushed, looking away from Eva, confident she would see the truth written on her face. "It's not like that," she lied. "It's just a text. Nothing more. Nothing less." Her cheeks burned as she looked down at her phone, feeling Eva's eyes still lingering on her.

Maddie: I'm learning a ton. It's super informative. I get done here at five. I'll be free anytime after that.

Lourdes: I'll meet you at the diner at five-thirty.

"You may think I don't know what I'm talking about, but I have a teenage daughter, if you'll remember, and you have the same expression that she does."

Maddie laughed. "Is that so?" She slid her phone back into her pocket, appreciative of Eva's teasing. Maybe she looked like a teenage girl filled with love and hope. Maddie didn't want to ruin anything this time. She was ready to experience love once more.

CHAPTER FORTY-FOUR

RENEWED HOPE

When Maddie entered the diner, Lourdes already had the corner booth. She looked up, on instinct, as Maddie entered, and they greeted one another with a smile. Lourdes stood as Maddie reached the table.

"I'm glad you could come."

Lourdes didn't realize this, but Maddie had been waiting for this moment for months. Not only was she going to meet Lourdes, but she was also going to meet Lourdes as a happier and healthier version of herself, the version of herself that Lourdes knew she could be. "Thank you for inviting me."

Maddie and Lourdes sat down, and Maddie feared that the awkwardness would overwhelm her. What if they wouldn't be able to get past what they had gone through? They had a wonderful morning at the park, but that was an impromptu experience, where this felt more like a date. Maddie didn't want to pinch herself because if she did, she knew it would all be over. Yet, she was scared even to breathe. What if they couldn't fully overcome what caused them to break up? Already, she could feel her mind starting to spiral out of control. She walked herself through some deep breathing exercises that her therapist taught her.

Maddie and Lourdes ordered veggie burgers and fries, and Maddie felt herself relax. Once the waitress was gone, they fell into an easy conversation. It was as if no time had passed. There was no lingering awkwardness or feelings of regret. Instead, Lourdes was excited to hear about Maddie's new job.

Lourdes leaned forward, the booth squeaking under her, "How was your day?"

"I have some great co-workers," Maddie began, "Kristen is training me."

"Kristen Bridgeway?"

"You know her?" Maddie asked. Maddie was always stunned by the sheer amount of people who knew and loved Lourdes.

"She worked at the front desk in the ER when I started at the hospital. I'd heard she went to Medical records. She's a sweet girl."

"Yeah, I like her teaching style. And my boss, Hadley, I adore her. Oh, and my friend, Eva, is in the same department. So, I already know someone. But I think it's going to be a perfect fit. And once I'm done with training, I'll be put on the fast track to a nursing informatics specialist program. They are developing it for the hospital, and Eva and I are helping to develop it. I'm not sure that Eva is looking to go that far, so I could fly solo there. If I decide it's what I want to do. But the possibilities are truly endless."

"And you're literally glowing." Lourdes stared at her for so long that Maddie felt her cheeks burning again. She looked down at her glass of water, hoping Lourdes couldn't sense her embarrassment. She drank her water, trying to flush out her red cheeks.

"I gave up espresso -- no more double or triple-shots. I'll drink a cup of coffee every once and awhile. Other than that, I'm officially a tea girl. I feel better for it."

She took another sip of her water and then bit down on her lip. "But how have you been? How's work? The patients?"

"Work's been pretty good. I know some of the patients still miss you. If I'm being honest, I've missed you." Lourdes gave a slight smirk.

"But everyone is doing well. The department has hired a few part-time employees to take some of the stress off the rest of the staff. But, most importantly, I'm glad you're doing so well, Maddie. That really makes me happy."

"I…" Her words trailed off when the waitress returned and left them their food. She waited until they were alone again before continuing, "I know I have you to thank for much of this. You cared enough to show me that I needed to get help. For that, I'm indebted to you."

"Maddie, you don't need to thank me. I was happy to do it. Even if it meant taking the backseat for you to get what you deserved." Lourdes took a bite of her burger, and Maddie popped a french fry into her mouth. Even though so much time had gone between them, it was as if none of that empty time mattered.

They ate much of it in silence, yet when either of them talked, some genuine conversation kept the evening going.

"By the way," Maddie began. "Turns out you were right about memories. They tend to sneak up on you." Maddie sipped on her water, and Lourdes leaned in, her eyes wide. "I've started to remember a couple of things about my mom. She left when I was so young, but I recall good times, going to the store with her, singing songs in the car, and so forth. It helps me reflect on the fact that she wasn't always the leaving type."

"That's great, Maddie. I know sometimes memories don't always help in a good way. So, I'm happy to hear that you had some healthy memories coming to you."

Maddie smiled, and the table turned silent. Except for a few glances shared across the table, they remained present. They had been there for two hours, and Maddie appreciated every minute of their time in the diner.

"Maddie," Lourdes began. "There's been something eating at me, which I really want to discuss with you. I don't want you to think I'm drudging up the past or unsympathetic to everything you've been through. It's just something I've been thinking about a lot."

Maddie took a long sip of her water and slowly lowered her glass, unsure about the direction of the conversation. She nodded, waiting, anticipating every word Lourdes wanted to say.

"The patient that passed away all those years ago. The one that ultimately made me realize I needed to change my ways. There's more to that story. You see, she wasn't just a patient. We had started a romantic relationship. They always say you shouldn't get involved with your patients. Unfortunately, it hit me out of the blue, and there wasn't any turning back. The relationship nearly cost me my job. And when she passed away, it nearly cost me my life. I guess I thought I couldn't let things between us continue, especially while I knew you were in a tough spot. I didn't want to see you spiral into this abyss. So, I backed away. It wasn't just because you needed it. It was because I did, too. I needed space to process her death for real, no escape, no trips. At the same time, I feared I would lose you if you didn't get the help, and I didn't want to go through that again."

Maddie looked down at her empty glass of water and longed for another drink. She swallowed, hoping that would suffice.

She looked up and gave a heartfelt smile. "Do you wanna take a walk?"

Lourdes sighed and nodded. Maddie reached into her purse, grabbed some money, and tossed it to the table.

"You shouldn't do that," Lourdes argued. "I invited you."

"I want to," Maddie replied.

"Let's go." They left the diner, and Maddie laced her fingers through Lourdes' hand on their way out the door. They walked out into the crisp night air. Summer was just about to start. The sky was a luscious dusky blue. Maddie felt the weight of Lourdes' calloused palm against her own. She felt the tension release between her shoulder blades. Maddie was quiet, stunned at how someone else's presence could feel like relief embodied.

As they walked, the silence calmed Maddie's anxious thoughts. They made it one block, then two. Lourdes never let go of her hand. "Do you know it's been three years since I've had a serious partner?"

"I didn't realize," Lourdes quietly stated. She swung their arms together in an easy rhythm. "I guess I didn't know when or how to let you know, but yeah, three years. I had a couple of little flings. But my last serious relationship ended in not a great place. We were tight, best friends. I was in college. She was working at a radio station. I thought we would get married. But I was young and naïve, and eventually, I realized that we wanted different things. But I thought we could work through our differences since we were in love. I threw my whole life into that relationship. I worked just as hard as I worked as a nurse. You could say I worked twice as hard to try and convince Raven to marry me."

"Wow, was it worth the effort?"

Maddie laughed. "Not even a little bit. While I was working hard to make our relationship work. She was working even harder to break things off. I just couldn't see it. I was blinded by what I thought was love. I nearly broke myself trying to be the perfect partner or at least the idea of what I thought Raven wanted. But, you see, I was Raven's first girlfriend. Ultimately she decided that it wasn't quite what she wanted. She wanted to be with a guy.

Meanwhile, I was dreaming up our wedding registry, but she had already decided that I wasn't the person she would marry. You can see how that would mess someone up. It made it really hard to get close to people. Even when I tried to move on, something stopped me from being able to be vulnerable. The minute I got close to someone, I remembered that pain. I threw myself into my job and told myself it wasn't worth the hurt."

"I'm sorry, Maddie. You don't deserve that."

"I didn't see it that way." Maddie stopped walking as they reached Millennium Park. The city was alive with the prospect of summer. The sunlight shimmered off of the metallic exterior of the Bean. Tourists snapped Selfies next to it, smiling at how the sculpture distorted their faces into cartoonish caricatures. Children played in the fountains, their bare feet slapping against the damp pavement. They splashed each other and screamed. Everyone in the park seemed giddy and full of life. Businessmen sat on the grass, loosening their ties and relishing the feeling of the earth beneath them. Families of tourists gawked at the collages of faces displayed on the massive LED screen behind the fountain, a rotating cast of Chicagoans.

Maddie and Lourdes found an open bench and sat down. She turned to Lourdes, who hung on Maddie's every word.

Maddie continued, "Every time I got close to someone, I heard Raven's voice in my head. Why wasn't I good enough? I was powerless to my tendency to self-sabotage. Whenever I would try to get close to someone, I would do something to push them away. I didn't want to get hurt like Raven had hurt me. It all felt doomed from the start.."

"Maddie, your relationship wasn't your fault. Raven should have been honest with you and not had you jumping through hoops to be with her. She wasn't committed to you. That's on her, not you. As for pushing people away, it makes sense. Anyone would react the same way."

Maddie turned and looked off into the sunset. She brushed a loose strand of her hair behind her ear. Lourdes continued to hold her hand in the loving and caring way Maddie always longed for and desired.

"When you broke it off, I felt abandoned. But I see now that I need to work on myself for our relationship to thrive. So, I tried to start working on myself a bit, but then I was thrust into a new department out of nowhere, and suddenly I was right back where I started, working myself to the bone. So even though I thought I was getting better, I wasn't. I was stuffing my feelings down and telling myself that counted as progress. But then…"

She turned back to face Lourdes. "I learned that you were the one that helped me out of the elevator. You got me to the ER, which showed you would never abandon me. You were always there for me. I just didn't want to see it. I was too headstrong to see it. So now, I've been working on myself for real this time. Not for anyone, just for me. But I would like it if you were there to see me thrive, y'know? I feel like I owe it to you to let you see me when I'm healthy."

"Maddie," Lourdes reached up and touched the side of Maddie's face. Maddie closed her eyes. She had dreamt a million times of this very moment. Lourdes would look her in the eyes, say they had worked so hard to get to this moment. She waited for Lourdes to finally tell her that she wanted to pick up where they had left off.

Lourdes looked at her with nothing but love. "I never wanted to abandon you. It killed me that we couldn't be together.."

"I've missed you, Lourdes."

"And I've missed you."

Lourdes moved in closer to her, slinging her arm around the back of the bench and pulling Maddie close. "I want us to try again. We can be better than we ever were. But what do you want?"

Maddie grinned. She couldn't help but stare at Lourdes' luscious lips. She took a deep breath, "Well, my dad is getting married next weekend."

Lourdes' eyes widened.

Maddie shrugged, "It's a long story, but she's a great woman. Would you be my date?"

MT CASSEN BOOKS

Available In Paperback, Ebook, And Audio Formats. Click Here:
https://mybook.to/MELODYINHERHEART

Available In Paperback, Ebook, And Audio Formats. Click Here:
https://mybook.to/FIGHTINGHERTOUCH

Available In Paperback, Ebook, And Audio Formats. Click Here:
https://mybook.to/PROTECTINGHERHEART

Available In Paperback, Ebook, And Audio Formats. Click Here:
https://mybook.to/TOOLITTLETOOLATE

YOU CAN HELP OTHERS!

A big thank you for trusting my book with your time, attention, and support. Here are three points to remember about reader comments (aka book reviews):

1. I read all reader comments so I can fix any errors and make my next book even better. "**Get busy polishing or get busy rusting**," is my motto as a writer.
2. Aren't reviews a boon for readers? I never buy books without checking out the reviews. What about You?
3. Now, you're all ready to drop a comment, but analysis paralysis gets the better of you. You might think: *What would I even write about? Who's going to read my review, anyway?*

Please snap out of your analysis paralysis. I have added here some questions on which other readers would want your opinions: a) How much of Maddie's refusal to take good advice comes from her temperament and how much from her youth? b) What kind of impression did Lourdes make on you? c) What would you like to communicate to other readers who may be interested in this book? Think of these questions as kick-starters for your review.

Please drop your honest opinions here:

https://www.amazon.com/review/create-review?ASIN= B0C7ZRVQG6

or click on the QR Code below:

That would make my day! Thank you!

Please subscribe to my newsletter and grab a free full-length romance novel from:

https://BookHip.com/LJDAWWT

Or click or scan the QR code below:

Happy Reading,

Morgan

P.S: Thanks, www.kindlepreneur.com, for the QR code generator, and www.booklinker.com for the universal links.

ABOUT THE AUTHOR

Morgan Cassen

WITH ROXIE

Morgan Cassen writes Lesbian Romance. Her mission is to make the world safer for the telling of sapphic stories. Yes, she knows that there are millions of romance writers and billions of romance novels. Why would she even think of adding to the pile? Well, Morgan has seen enough to know that the truly interesting stories are not what happens between human beings. That gig can seem mechanical and unemotional — and better shelved in the action and thriller category, at least compared to its older, tempestuous sister. Let's bring out Ms. Inner Conflict, the queen of all drama in the human world -- the ruler of the emotional map. This is the conflict between everything you've worked for and everything your heart desires. You never imagined that all that hard work you put in over the years would put you increasingly far from everything your heart really wanted. Also, how about the conflict between the past and the future? Being true to the past would require you to push the future so far away from the present. But how long can you postpone the future? What if your whole framing of the past can't stand the scrutiny of thoughtful analysis today even as you resolutely keep the future out of your mental horizon? Huh, what do you do with that kind of conflict? The conflict between human beings can look so . . . what's the word? Tame? Yes, tame compared to the real thing: conflict between you and *you*. You are the hero and villain at the same time, but the nub of the problem is that the villain thinks she is the hero, while the hero is all caught up in doubt and indecision. Which you will you choose when nobody else will make that choice for you? You get to make that choice, and your comforting, trusty friend — procrastination — has indicated that help is running late. The time has finally come for you to choose. See, inner conflict is where it's at. Inner conflict in regular people living ordinary lives is what Morgan writes about in her books. Well, that's only half the story, so here's a more accurate sentence: Morgan writes about ordinary people living ordinary lives and finding life-changing love that will help them grow as humans. Fair warning: there are no perfect people in Morgan's books. These are lovable, kind, generous people with strong moral purpose. However, all these wonderful qualities sometimes (ok, often) come with quite a lot of maddening qualities as well, like being thick-headed and thin-skinned, clear in purpose but clueless in strategy, ready to fight the world for a cause, and unwilling to draw boundaries. Also, there are no billionaires here to rescue damsels from predicaments, nor are there any vampires to connect us to other words. Perhaps the only thing extraordinary is that ordinary people can relate to these characters. And that is all the motivation Morgan needs to keep on writing.

Please join her as she writes the stories of breakup and love that tug at heartstrings.

Stalk the author using the link below:

www.mtcassen.com

ABOUT PETER PALMIERI
(MEDICAL ADVISOR)

Peter Palmieri, M.D., M.B.A. is a licensed physician with over 20 years of practice experience in Chicago, Dallas, Houston, and the Rio Grande Valley in Texas. He received his B.A. from the University of California San Diego, with a double major in Animal Physiology and Psychology. He earned his medical degree from Loyola  University Stritch School of Medicine and a Healthcare M.B.A. from The George Washington University. He is a regular contributor of original articles to a variety of health and wellness blogs.

ABOUT KAREN STOCKDALE
(MEDICAL ADVISOR)

Karen Stockdale, MBA, BSN, RN is an experienced nurse in the fields of cardiology and medical/surgical nursing. She has also worked as a nurse manager, hospital quality and safety administrator, and quality consultant. She obtained her ASN-RN in 2003 and her BSN in 2012 from Southwest Baptist University. Karen completed an MBA in Healthcare Management in 2017. She currently writes for several healthcare and tech blogs and whitepapers, as well as developing continuing education courses for nurses.

Karen's websites are:
https://www.linkedin.com/in/karen-stockdale-5aab2584/
and
http://writemedical.net/

ABOUT ROSIE ACCOLA
(COPYEDITOR)

Rosie Accola is a queer poet, editor, and zine-maker who lives in Michigan. Their writing explores how reality t.v. functions as autofiction and the intersection between pop culture and poetics. They graduated with their MFA in Creative Writing from Naropa  University in 2022. In 2019, they published their first full-length poetry collection, "Referential Body," with Ghost City Press. You can find them on Substack, where they publish the RoZone, a monthly newsletter about the craft of writing and arts and crafts.